I MARRIED A MINOTAUR

Prime Mating Agency

REGINE ABEL

COVER DESIGN BY
Regine Abel

Copyright © 2022

CONTENTS

I MARRIED A MINOTAUR

Tiny, sassy, but oh so fierce

Rihanna is condemned to a twenty-year sentence on the most savage prison planet in the sector for a crime she didn't commit. On the day of her transfer, she's offered a deal to commute her sentence: an arranged marriage with a grumpy orc-minotaur who has muscles for days, devilish red eyes, and an insufferably smart mouth. Despite his species' reputation for being violent brutes, Rihanna soon finds herself drawn to the gentle giant that lurks beneath his terrifying appearance.

Fearsome, savage, and yet so fluffy

When the agency informs Zatruk he's been matched, the last thing he expects is for his mate to be such a tiny human. With his people rapidly entering blood rage, and the looming threat of war, he needs a queen to stand by his side as he strives to save his people, not a delicate flower. But he soon discovers that behind her fragile appearance, his little female hides a fierce and dauntless soul, with a sassy attitude that stirs him in unexpected ways.

With time running out, will Rihanna be the blessing he needs to achieve the peace his people desperately desire, or will they self-destruct?

DEDICATION

To those who fight to tame their inner beast, no matter how hard and challenging the journey.

Only when we all work together and ensure everyone has what they need to thrive, prosper, and be happy, will we achieve harmony. As long as we're divided, as long as we try to enrich ourselves at the detriment of others, we'll remain stuck in this endless cycle.

To anyone who strives for peace.

CHAPTER 1

RIHANNA

Sitting in my cell, I stared at the gray walls without seeing them. Twenty years... Twenty fucking years I would be spending in jail because my no-good associate had made me the fall guy. Sure, as a smuggler and bounty hunter, I'd always traipsed on the shadier side of the law. But I'd never done the hardcore stuff. I had standards. Sadly for my sorry butt, Gabe got greedy, lied to me, then bounced when things got hairy.

It had been a simple deal for some black-market replacement parts and electronics. Even if we'd gotten caught, they would have let us off with a slap on the wrist, maybe a fine depending on how stuck-up the enforcers were and, worst case scenario, the interdiction to land on Grubrya for a few months. Instead of spare parts, we got busted for illegal arms trade on the planet with the strictest anti-armament laws in the Obos sector.

Twenty years... Only seven years less than my entire life so far. Saying I was screwed would be the understatement of the century. Judge Wuras had gone all out on my ass, too. Of all the places he could have sent me to serve my sentence, he chose the prison planet Molvi—the most brutal and depraved penitentiary of Obos. Assuming I even survived to see the end of my sentence, I'd be a shadow of myself.

My heart leapt at the sound of the thick metal door of my cell unlocking. I silenced my instinctive urge to plead for mercy and ask for an appeal. None would be granted. I rose from the uncomfortable cot I'd been sitting on, the only thing beside a toilet and a sink in the tiny holding space. Lifting my arms before me, I let the guard cuff me. His face was completely emotionless. I was but another convict getting shipped out of his detention facility.

I felt faint as he led me out of my cell. I might as well have been a dead woman walking, on my way to a lethal injection. Frankly, that might have been more merciful than the long ride aboard the prison transport ship that would take me to the hell-hole I'd call home for the next two decades.

To my shock, instead of taking the left turn at the junction towards the ship hangar, the guard took a right towards the inter-rogation rooms. Why the heck would they take me there? Had they caught Gabe? Had my name been linked to some random other crime they wanted to grill me over before I left? Did…?

My brain froze when the door of the room opened, and instead of the brutish face of some Obosian inspector, a wise and noble-looking Temern rose from his seat to greet me.

"The shackles are not necessary," the Temern said to the guard. "Miss Makeba is not a threat."

My jaw dropped while the guard frowned. As empaths, Temerns were infallible in assessing people's emotions. Some people even speculated that they were able to read minds. However, my understanding was that they merely mastered their power so much that they could interpret people's emotions and reactions with such accuracy as to give the impression they read minds.

"Please," the Temern insisted when the guard hesitated.

Making a face as if he'd bitten into something foul, the guard gave the Temern a stiff nod. He ordered me to sit in the chair across the table from the Temern, then unshackled me.

"See that you behave, little human, or I will make you regret it sorely," the guard growled in a menacing tone.

I fought the instinctive urge to roll my eyes at that pathetic need to flaunt his power, and merely nodded. Despite the stiffness of his beak, I didn't miss how the Temern tried to repress an amused smile. That made me instantly like him. But then, it was extremely hard to dislike a Temern.

"I'll be right outside if you need anything," the guard told the Temern.

"Thank you. But we should be fine," he replied politely before casting a meaningful glance at the door.

The guard begrudgingly left the room, although I could sense his curiosity was as great as mine. As soon as the door closed, the Temern shifted his wings before taking a seat and smiling at me. His bird-like, bipedal species came in a variety of colors. In his case, he reminded me of a bird of paradise with golden feathers, maroon wings, a long fluffy white tail, and the most mesmerizing silver eyes. I couldn't quite tell his age, but he had to be in his mid to late fifties.

"Alone at last, Miss Makeba. Please, let me introduce myself. My name is Kayog Voln, Principal Agent of the Prime Mating Agency."

My brain tilted, and his smile broadened at my reaction.

"Prime Mating Agency? Did you get lost? I mean, no disrespect, Master Voln, but I thought you were a prosecutor or lawyer, maybe here to offer me a last-minute deal if I cooperated on something," I said, completely baffled.

"I am not lost, Miss Makeba," he said in an amused tone. "I am very much where I intended to be. And while I am not a prosecutor, I am here to offer you a last-minute deal to spare you from that twenty-year sentence. But please, call me Kayog. I am rather informal."

"A deal? For real?" I asked, my heart filling with an impossible hope.

He nodded. "Mmhmm."

"Wow, okay. I'm all ears! And yeah, sure, I can call you Kayog. Feel free to call me Rihanna."

"Excellent. Well, Rihanna, one of my people who worked on your case alerted me to your situation," the Temern continued. "While you have led a rather *interesting* life, your sentence was overly harsh, especially since you are innocent of the specific crime you've been condemned for."

"So, Torgal *knew* I told the truth! Why didn't he get me exonerated?!"

Kayog gave me a sympathetic look. "Because he can't. The law relies on facts that can be proven. Our empathic assessments are not tangible proof. I could lie because I like you. Most judges will take our evaluation into account, but condemnation or exoneration cannot be solely based on our word."

"Right, I can see that, but it still blows," I mumbled.

"Torgal tried to get you a significantly reduced sentence, but the judge wouldn't budge. He could sense some personal vendetta. May I ask how you alienated Judge Wuras?"

I rolled my eyes and scrunched my face in anger. "*I* never did anything to that judge. But I have a way of getting involved with the wrong people. A couple of years ago, I dated a man who conned Judge Wuras. He got off on a technicality. I broke up with him right after the trial ended because I didn't like what it had revealed about him. But ever since, the judge has been after everyone from his inner circle at the time."

"That's unfortunate."

"Tell me about it. So, what does Torgal think you can do for me?"

"Well, he gave me his detailed assessment of your personality in the hopes I could find a match for you," Kayog said.

I blinked, wondering if he'd eaten some funky mushrooms.

"A match? I'm not trying to find a boyfriend or get married. My ass is being shipped to the foulest prison planet on this side of the galaxy. A long-distance romance with some random guy is the last thing I need!"

Kayog chuckled. "Please, bear with me, Rihanna. All will be clear in a moment."

"Right, sorry," I said, giving him a sheepish expression. "As you can guess, I'm a little stressed out right now."

"Understandable," he said with a gentle, almost paternal smile. "How familiar are you with the Prime Mating Agency?"

I shrugged. "I know the common stuff. You guys find life partners for primitive aliens. The couple has a six-month—I think—trial period. But it usually ends with a happily ever after."

"That's a good summation," he said in an amused voice. "But as we work closely with the United Planets Organization—which largely finances our activities—it grants us certain powers, such as commuting a prison sentence, if a match could be made that would benefit the interests of the UPO."

My eyes widened, and I straightened in my chair. "Okay, you've got my full attention."

He chuckled. "Based on Torgal's evaluation, I lined up a series of potential mates for you. I had hoped that, once I met you in person and evaluated your personality, one of them would emerge as a great match. The deal would be that, if you consented to one of the matches, you would go to that partner's planet and be expected to genuinely try to make the union work for the duration of the trial period. If the union succeeded, you would simply remain with your husband. But if it failed, you would be free to leave and do what you please with your life."

"Prison sentence annulled?" I asked, my voice bubbling with excitement.

"Prison sentence and entire case expunged," Kayog confirmed.

"Badass! So? Am I a match for one of them?" I asked, my eyes flicking between his.

My heart sank when he appeared to hesitate.

"There are a couple of acceptable pairings. Not wonderful, but you could have an agreeable life together," Kayog said, cautiously.

"I'll take it! If it will keep my sorry butt from landing on Molvi, I'll take it," I said eagerly.

Worst case, I'll divorce in six months. Big whoop! Beats twenty years of hell!

Kayog gave me an indulgent smile. "However, now that I have met you, I have a better sense of who you are. I never would have even considered that male as a candidate. And yet, there is no question in my mind that you are his perfect match."

"Okay. And who is he?" I asked, unsure how I felt about that.

"Zatruk Abbas, the Yurus Chieftain from Cibbos."

"A Yurus?" I asked, frowning. "The name sounds familiar, but I can't quite picture the species."

"To a human, you would likely compare them to a mix between a minotaur and an orc."

I gaped at him, wondering if I had heard him correctly. His silver eyes sparked with mirth, and his stiff mouth stretched in amusement at my visible shock. He placed a small holocard on the table in front of us. He then tapped a few instructions on his datapad. Seconds later, the 3D hologram of a ghost-white, furry mountain of muscles, with the horns, ears, tail and feet of a bull, stared at me with a somewhat orcish face, mouth tusks included.

I didn't know how long I stared at the male before looking up at Kayog in disbelief.

"The Yurus live on Cibbos," Kayog continued, totally unfazed by my reaction. "There is another native species on that planet, the Zelconians, bird folks and distant kin of the Temerns. And more recently, the human colony of Kastan settled there. Seven months ago, the Yurus initiated a war against the humans.

Without the assistance of the Zelconians, the colony would have been wiped out. Although the Yurus' new leader, Zatruk, has maintained a fragile peace, his people are naturally violent and belligerent. The UPO would like to bring them into the fold to keep the peace on Cibbos."

I blinked, wondering once again what kind of drugs that birdman was on. "Let me get this straight. You want me to hook up with an orc-minotaur, whose people are violent warmongers, and who got their butts kicked in the war *they* initiated. And all that because the UPO wants them to chill? How the hell is me marrying bulging muscles over there going to fix that? How the heck am I a *perfect match* for him?!"

I shook my head, trying to see the logic but failing miserably.

"I mean, I'm a smuggler and bounty hunter. I know people. Greed or lust for power usually motivates them. The UPO is not a charitable organization. If they would allow you to save my ass from twenty years in jail by marrying that Yurus, there's way more in it for them than peace. What's the real deal? What do the Yurus have that the UPO wants?"

"Very astute, Rihanna. But the answer is nothing. The Yurus have nothing the UPO wants. But the Zelconians do. They produce the most powerful crystals in the galaxy, better even than the sidinium our spaceships use for their power cores."

My eyes suddenly widened in understanding. "The Zelcon crystals!"

"Yes, named as such in the rest of the galaxy after the Zelco-nians," Kayog concurred. "The UPO doesn't want another war with the Yurus, as it could jeopardize their negotiations with the Zelconians. Zatruk, the new leader of the Yurus, is far more reasonable. But he faces an uphill battle. A marriage through the PMA between him and a human will avail his people with unique new opportunities."

"Okay, but why me? How could I possibly be the perfect

match for that guy and that species?" I asked, still completely baffled.

"The Yurus respect strength. Although you have dabbled in a lot of shady business, you've always remained on the more ethical side and been honorable in all of your dealings. You have a good understanding of people, and especially of people with his type of culture. You are strong, smart, not easily intimidated, an accomplished hunter and fighter, and street smart. You can be a great adviser to him as he redefines the future of his people."

I breathed out loudly. Although flattered by that string of compliments, I felt overwhelmed. "What about the other candidates on your list?"

The Temern's face closed off, all warmth fading from his features as he took on a stern expression. "I will not make you an offer for those other males, not when I have found your perfect match. It would be unfair to them, and to you."

I glared at him, annoyed beyond words, even though I'd expected that answer. "So, it's either six months with that Yurus, or twenty years on Molvi?"

"Actually, in this specific instance, it will be a one-year trial period."

"What?" I exclaimed, lifting my palms questioningly. "You said it was six-months!"

"*I* didn't actually say it, *you* did," Kayog said gently, but firmly. "And yes, usually it is but, under the circumstances, I need a greater commitment from you. It still beats twenty years on Molvi, don't you agree? Although, I already know you will *not* want to leave after that year is up."

I didn't respond. However, there was no doubt my face made no mystery that I expected to haul ass out of Cibbos as soon as my time was up.

"Also, let me reiterate that you *must* make a genuine effort to make the union a success throughout the trial period," Kayog warned. "For this union to be valid, you must marry him

8

according to human laws, and then according to Yurus customs on the day of your arrival on Cibbos. The marriage must then be consummated on your wedding night. Failure to meet any of these conditions will result in the annulment of this agreement, and you will be sent to Molvi."

My shoulders slumped as I stared at the Temern in disbelief. "Sheesh, you guys sure aren't making this easy. Why not give the couple a chance to get to know each other before they have to bang?"

"Because it is a psychological hurdle," Kayog explained in a sympathetic voice. "It creates unnecessary tension and stress the longer it drags on. We've been running this agency for many decades now. And we have found that piercing that abscess right at the beginning is highly beneficial. Yes, it is stressful at first, but then it is done, and the couple realizes it really was no big deal. In fact, in the vast majority of cases, it brings the couple a lot closer right from the start."

"But a violence-prone furry beast?" I said in a pathetically whiny tone that made even me embarrassed.

Kayog chuckled. "I promise that you will love that furry beast. I have yet to make a single pairing that didn't end in a happy marriage. And I have no intention of breaking that streak now... or ever."

I pursed my lips, wanting to argue but not really having any argument to do so. The Temerns' reputation in general was stellar, and the success rate of that agency was indeed legendary.

"If I accept, what happens then?"

"You will leave right away for Cibbos," Kayog said.

"Wait, but what about him? You said you just realized he was my perfect match. Shouldn't he know about me and give his consent?"

Kayog shook his head. "Zatruk has already stated that he would accept any mate I judged adequate for him. He trusts me to choose right. So, what will it be, Rihanna?"

I glared at him. "One year married to a stranger versus twenty in hell. What do you think? You already knew what my answer would be."

He grinned. "I suspected you would make the smart choice. But take heart, my dear. You will soon realize it was the best decision of your life."

CHAPTER 2
RIHANNA

Once I agreed to that insane—and yet blessed—offer from the Temern, I spent three days getting jabbed and prodded in quarantine to make sure I'd received all the necessary vaccines before I could settle on Cibbos. While the prison's personnel were less-than-gentle with me, the transport ship Kayog appointed to take me to my new home turned out to be the most luxurious experience of my life. Too bad the trip took less than two days.

After reaching the orbital space station of Cibbos, a shuttle took me down to the spaceport on the surface. If nothing else, I couldn't complain about the stunning and savage beauty of Cibbos. In the distance, I could see the majestic silhouette of the mountains of Synsara. From what little I'd read about the planet, the Zelconians had built their main city within it.

At first glance, Cibbos looked deceptively like Earth with its blue sky, single sun, and the greenery of its untamed land. However, the shapes and sizes of the trees, their leaves, and the mesmerizing plants gave away the fact this was definitely another world. Some of them were so unique they resembled an elaborate abstract sculpture. While I'd never been the type of girl to visit museums and art galleries, I appreciated nature's beauty and raw artistry. I looked forward to taking a stroll through the woods to experience it firsthand.

As the shuttle approached and then landed at the spaceport, my wandering thoughts gave way to my rapidly growing nervousness. I'd made my peace with what I had committed to. One year to regain my freedom was nothing, in the greater scheme of things. Sure, that Yurus was freaking me out a little, but in all fairness, he looked reasonably attractive in that holo-gram. As long as we could tolerate each other, all would be well. I just needed to make it through one year.

Still, I needed to bang that mountain of muscle and fur tonight. While not too thrilled at that prospect, I took solace in the fact that, as a woman, I could simply lie down and think happy thoughts while he got the deed done so we could tick off that box of the contract.

Just like the space station, the spaceport looked both recent and quite small. As a primitive planet that had been under the Prime Directive until a few decades ago, it wasn't too surprising. The security check was nearly non-existent before I ended up in the main hall, my bag of essentials clutched in my hand.

The place was a ghost town, making it easy to spot Kayog standing alone, a few meters from the arrival gate. He greeted me warmly, and we exchanged the usual pleasantries. He offered to carry my bag for me, but I gently declined. It wasn't heavy.

"Your mate is already here in the small meeting room where we will perform the ceremony," Kayog said enthusiastically.

"Here?! We're getting married in the spaceport?" I exclaimed, my nerves acting up again.

"Yes. It is an expedited version of the ceremony. A pure formality for legal purposes," he explained, while gesturing for me to follow him as he began walking towards that room. "Allan

Stuart, the Spiritual Counselor of the Kastan colony, has kindly agreed to preside over the ceremony as a favor to me. As I previously mentioned to you, under the leadership of Chieftain Vyrax, the Yurus had initiated a war against the human colony. He died in that battle. Your mate became the new leader and agreed to peace. But there is still tension between them. Do not be surprised if Counselor Allan seems a little cool."

"That should be fun," I said sarcastically.

"Indeed," Kayog said, sounding amused.

The place was rather depressing with its white walls and grayish floors. The only thing of interest were the large windows along the walkway on the right that looked out onto the peaceful scenery outside. It took us no time to reach the meeting room door, quite literally located a hundred meters from the arrival gate, and only twenty meters from the departure one. A red light over the door frame indicated the room was currently occupied.

Just like the rest of the spaceport, the meeting room desperately needed the loving hand of an interior decorator. More white walls and gray floors, a sturdy, rectangular, wooden table big enough to seat ten people, matching cushioned chairs, and a giant screen hanging on the wall constituted the entirety of the furnishings of the place.

And standing at opposite ends of the table, the Counselor and my future husband.

I barely spared a glance at the skinny older man with a hawkish nose and dressed all in black who was clearly Counselor Allan. I was too busy gaping at the ridiculously tall and large beast that I had come here to marry.

By the hologram alone, I'd guessed he was tall, but this was absurd. Even standing five meters away from him, I nearly had to break my neck to look up at him. That guy had to be at least seven feet tall, and easily weighed close to three hundred pounds of pure muscle. Considering my measly height of 5'1 and my weight of one hundred and twelve pounds, he would probably think me scrawny.

Thanks to his albinism, he looked like an ancient northern god sculpted in marble with his massive biceps covered in a shiny fur, chiseled abs, long, silver-white hair with a single braid on each side of his fearsome face, massive bull horns, and hooved feet. The fact that he was completely naked, but for a rather fancy, embroidered loincloth, underlined even more each of his traits.

He, too, was staring at me, his red eyes almost appearing to glow in their intensity. I closed my gaping mouth audibly, realizing how rude I must have looked to him. But his face was impossible to read.

"Well, we're all here," Kayog said in a joyful tone, as if he were oblivious to my shock and the tension filling the room. He was no doubt brushing it off to avoid making matters worse. "Counselor Allan, Zatruk, please meet the bride, Rihanna Makeba. Rihanna, this is Counselor Allan and, as you can guess, this is your betrothed, Zatruk Abbas."

"Pleasure to meet you, Counselor Allan," I mumbled, to which he responded with a polite bow of his head. I turned to look at Zatruk who was still staring at me with that unreadable expression. "And you, Zatruk."

He grunted in response, looking utterly unimpressed, before turning his red eyes towards Kayog. "She is a legal adult, correct?"

I gasped loudly in disbelief, my eyes all but popping out of my head. "Yes, I am an adult, and I can answer for myself," I replied in outrage before Kayog could respond. "I just happen to be short. Do I really look like a kid to you?"

"You have the height of one," he said matter-of-factly.

"But not the curves of one, do I?" I snapped back, putting my hands defiantly on my hips.

Even as the words left my mouth, I kicked myself. I *was*

petite. For someone so massive, it made sense for him to wonder if I had reached maturity. My mouth could be my worst enemy. Alienating the guy who could keep my butt out of jail because I was being over-sensitive about my height was the epitome of stupid.

The Counselor gasped, his prudish sensibilities apparently offended by my comment. That Zatruk's gaze slowly roamed over me in an assessing fashion suddenly made me want to squirm and cross my arms over my chest to partially hide. Naturally, I forced myself to remain still, but I now regretted not taking greater care of my appearance before coming here. Compared to his simple but elegant attire, I looked a little unkempt with my simple black leather pants and matching sleeveless leather top.

His plump lips quivered with what I assumed to be a sliver of amusement. "In that, you are correct. Your curves are definitely not childish. But I'm afraid you have shocked the human Counselor," he added, casting a mocking sideways glance at Counselor Allan.

The older man pinched his naturally thin lips, making them all but disappear in a thin line.

"I'm sure he'll get over it," I mumbled under my breath.

I doubted the Counselor had heard me, but Zatruk's expression made no mystery he had.

The Counselor cleared his throat. "Now that the introductions have been made, are we ready to proceed with the ceremony?"

"Sure," I said, feeling guilty for my once again rude behavior.

None of this was like me. But that Yurus was keeping me from thinking straight. I'd have to apologize to the Counselor. Sadly, prudish and stuck-up people always had a way of getting under my skin. It was the haughtiness they always displayed, like they were better, superior, when in reality they were just self-righteous assholes whose treatment of others often belied the so-called virtuous principles by which they claimed to live.

"Yes," Zatruk replied.

He had a deep, booming voice that perfectly suited his imposing stature.

As Kayog and I were still standing by the door, which gave on the middle of the room, the Temern gestured for me to go join Zatruk on the right side of the table, which had the most empty space. He followed in my wake and, as he would look stupid shouting at us from across the room, the Counselor came to join us.

Allan and Kayog both stood by the head of the table, while Zatruk and I stood a couple of meters in front of them, closer to the wall.

"Please face each other and hold both of each other's hands," the Counselor instructed.

Zatruk and I complied, which forced me to come closer still to my future husband. His height was absolutely ridiculous. If I looked straight ahead, I found myself staring at the most insanely muscular chest in the universe, his perky nipples all but tauntingly winking at me. My hands disappeared in his massive ones. They were strong, warm, and properly calloused for having been well-used. But above all, they were gentle despite their firm grip.

"Rihanna Makeba, do you freely take this Yurus male, Zatruk Abbas, as your lawfully wedded husband?" he asked.

"I do," I replied.

"Zatruk Abbas, do you freely take this human female, Rihanna Makeba, as your lawfully wedded wife?" Counselor Allan then asked him.

"I do," Zatruk replied, his voice so deep I could have sworn the floor trembled beneath me.

"Kayog Voln, do you bear witness that this female, Rihanna Makeba, and this male, Zatruk Abbas, freely commit and desire to be legally married to each other in accordance with both human and galactic laws?"

Kayog nodded. "Yes, I confirm it."

"By the power vested in me by the Clerical College of Earth and the United Planets Organization, I declare you husband and wife," the Counselor said, a subtle note of disgust and disapproval seeping into his voice. "Zatruk Abbas, you may kiss your bride."

I was pissed off at the Counselor. Judging by the sideways glance Zatruk gave him, my new husband was likely itching to bash his skull in. My stomach fluttered when Zatruk returned his attention to me. Even though I had to break my neck to look at him, up close, that Yurus was turning out to be rather attractive. More importantly, he had a very nice pair of lips and his tusks were of a reasonable size, not the mammoth ones that gave Orcs fucked up mouths. His tusks also looked pristine, not dirty and messy as I had feared. That would have been quite the turn off.

Pulse racing, I lifted my head to receive his kiss while hoisting myself to my tippy toes. To my shock, rather than bending down the—relatively long—distance to kiss me, Zatruk released my hands, placed his on my hips and picked me up.

I yelped, my hands immediately resting on his broad shoulders and my legs instinctively wrapping around his waist.

"Whoa! You didn't have to pick me up!"

He shrugged. "You're tiny." He spoke those words as if they were an obvious justification for his action. "It's easier to pick you up than to break my back bending to reach your lips."

I scrunched my face, unsure if I wanted to laugh or be offended. "Are you so old that your back is already busted?" I deadpanned.

His lips quivered again. This time, I didn't doubt it was with repressed amusement. "Hardly. I just like my comfort."

"You shouldn't tease me for being short. I don't point out that you're ridiculously tall and big," I countered.

He shrugged again. "You gape instead."

I exhaled loudly while narrowing my eyes at him. I *had* gaped rather rudely when I first saw him. But jeez, that male was a freaking mountain.

"I think you're just trying to show off how strong you are."

"I *am* strong. I'm glad you noticed."

The factual way in which he said it as if it was obvious made it all more obnoxiously smug. As much as I wanted to smack him for being a smart ass, I couldn't deny how much I enjoyed someone having a quick repartee.

"You're going to be a handful, aren't you?" I said at last.

Careful not to stab me in the face with his massive horns, Zatruk looked down at my left hand, still holding on to his shoulder. As soon as he turned his red gaze back towards me, I knew he was going to utter something outrageous to get a rise out of me.

"Considering the size of your proportionally tiny hands, I doubt both of yours will suffice to handle me."

My jaw dropped at the same time as Counselor Allan emitted another outraged gasp, reminding me we had an audience. A sideways glance at Allan and Kayog nearly had me bursting in laughter. Kayog was holding the tip of his beak in his fist, a typical gesture with bird folks to either express their contrition or hide their amusement. I had no doubt the latter applied here. But it was the Counselor that nearly cracked me up. The way he'd pressed his palm to his chest, I had no doubt he'd be clutching his pearls if he had any.

I turned back to Zatruk. "Someone's boasting. And you've shocked the Counselor."

He smiled smugly at me. "I never boast. You'll find out soon enough." He then cast a disdainful glance at the Counselor before looking back at me. "The Counselor will get over it."

I couldn't help snorting—which I quickly repressed—to have

him thus echoing my words. Zatruk was officially a bit of an ass… and I was digging it.

Kayog clearing his throat reminded me we'd indeed been stalling the proceeding with our banter.

"Right, well, you still haven't kissed the bride, as was asked of you," I said, trying to sound nonchalant about it.

This time, a triumphant yet predatory smile stretched his lips.

"Someone is quite eager. I can't blame you."

The nerve!! I was opening my mouth to respond, but his lips crushing mine silenced me. Holy cow! I didn't know what I had expected, but certainly not for my toes to instantly curl. All of a sudden, the world faded around us. I became acutely aware of every single chiseled curve of his muscular body pressing against mine, the softness of the fur lining his shoulders under my palms, the searing heat of his hands on the back of my thighs, the silkiness of his long hair brushing against my cheeks, and the plump warmth of his mouth on mine.

I couldn't tell how long the kiss lasted. My brain had stopped functioning the moment our lips touched. It could have been a second or a minute. All I knew was that the instant he broke the kiss, I felt utterly bereft. Our eyes locked, and once more, time appeared to stand still.

Kayog and Counselor Allan clapping their hands snapped us out of it. Looking partly embarrassed and partly reluctant, Zatruk put me back on my feet. They felt oddly wobbly. One look at Kayog annoyed the hell out of me. The Temern had that "I told you" air about him as he stared at me. Obviously, he'd felt my physical response to being kissed by Zatruk… which was frankly rather embarrassing.

Okay, getting kissed by a massive beast with an attitude had turned me on. That didn't mean I was ready to fall head over heels in love with him.

Clearly eager to be done, Counselor Allan had both Zatruk

and I press our thumbs in the signature box of the marriage certificate.

"Well, this completes this procedure," Kayog said. "Do not forget to hold the Yurus wedding ritual as soon as you reach your city, Mutarak. You also know what other duties must be observed for this union to be legal."

"We will get it done," I said firmly. "I really appreciate everything you've done for me, Master Voln."

"It is my pleasure, my dear Rihanna," Kayog said in that sweet paternal voice of his. "You will be pleased to know that I managed to recover all of your weapons, tools, and personal items from the impound. They should be delivered here to you within the next forty-eight hours along with my wedding present for you two."

"Are you kidding?! Oh, my God! You're the freaking best!" I exclaimed.

In my joy, I impulsively hugged the older male. He stiffened in shock, and I cringed inwardly. But before I could pull away and pathetically apologize, he relaxed, returned my embrace and, to my shock, also wrapped his wings around me. It was my first time getting a winged hug. It felt so gentle, paternal, and protective, I almost teared up.

Kayog released me with a gentle smile.

"Sorry," I said sheepishly. "I don't usually hug people like that. But some of my stuff really means a lot to me. I thought I had lost them for good."

"It's okay. No harm done. However, you should know that, in the Yurus culture, a female only hugs an adult male like this to express that she desires to lay with him," Kayog said with an amused expression.

My eyes nearly popped out of my head. "Whoa, what?! No!" My head jerked towards Zatruk who was observing us with an unreadable expression. "I wasn't coming on to him!"

"He's aware," Kayog said with a chuckle. "You think I'd still be calmly standing here otherwise? Being an empath helps tremendously with self-preservation."

I snorted and shook my head at the Temern. I would miss him. "Anything else I should know about the Yurus?"

"You have plenty of time before you to have fun discovering it all, my dear."

With that, we exchanged our last goodbyes with the Temern and the human counselor before going our separate ways.

CHAPTER 3
ZATRUK

I didn't know what to think of the female the Temern had deemed my perfect mate. How could an adult be so tiny? And yet, as she had quite accurately pointed out, the luscious curves of her body made it indubitably clear that she had reached full maturity.

Still, she was so small and fragile-looking... While it fired up my protective instincts, it would also set my clanmates' tongues wagging with dumb and provocative comments. I could foresee a lot of skull-bashing in my near future. Thankfully, Rihanna was proving to be no meek and timid creature. I had no use for that. I loved the fire in her eyes, the impertinent way she talked back to me. I would take great pleasure in mentally sparring with her.

Based solely on her height and size, and from her initial shock when she first saw me, I had expected her to cower at my first frown. Had that been the case, perfect mate or not, I would have sent her right back from whence she came.

When Kayog had first approached me about taking a mate through the Prime Mating Agency, I'd assumed he would find me a match similar to Luana Torres—the daughter of the human colony leader. She had been the first and only human female to have piqued my interest. She was pleasant enough to the eye and held an undeniable strength behind her gentle façade. The way she'd boldly expressed her disapproval and contempt at me executing Vyrax had been quite fascinating. Had she not already married the Zelconian hybrid, I might have considered wooing her.

But now, I was finding myself far more intrigued by my little Rihanna. Although she obviously lacked the Yurus traits I usually enjoyed in our females, my mate was an attractive human woman. Her small stature didn't affect in any way her perfect proportions. The way she flawlessly fit in my arms when I held her earlier still lingered. And that beautiful brown skin, dark and creamy, had contrasted in the most delightful way with my white skin and fur. Her large, doe eyes with incredibly long lashes were mesmerizing, especially when they sparked with mischief or aggravation. I could see myself annoying her just for the sake of her eyes lighting that way again.

And those lips…

I had not imagined such a response from Rihanna to my kissing her. My mate had been aroused… a nice surprise. By Yurus standards, I was deemed a handsome male. I had no clue how humans perceive us and our aesthetic. Rihanna had chosen me out of desperation, not out of attraction. For that reason, I had expected her becoming drawn to me would be an uphill battle. But that kiss gave me hope our first night wouldn't be too unpleasant.

Assuming she can handle me…

But I badly needed to educate her on our ways. Had she embraced another male the way she did Kayog, I would have had to bash his skull in. I had no qualms doing it either. In fact, I'd take great pleasure in it. However, I was working on reining in the more violent side of our people. My mate giving me excuses to indulge in my primal urges would impede that journey.

I repressed a smile as she stole yet another furtive glance at me as we silently exited the spaceport. Ahead of us, the human counselor was hurrying to his flying mount. I gestured at him with my chin.

"The Counselor will ride a zeebis to return to Kastan," I explained. "I initially considered fetching you riding one of those, but I didn't know if you were afraid of heights, so I came with my krogi instead."

"I'm not afraid of heights. I've done a lot of skydiving and hand gliding for fun," she said, stretching her neck to get a better view. "Oh wow! Is that a…? That looks like a winged ibex ram!"

"I don't know what an ibex is, but it is indeed akin to a ram," I replied, pleased to find out she didn't fear a bit of danger. "The human colony of Kastan breeds and trades them. We do not often make use of the zeebises, but we have our own, caught and tamed from the wild."

"Well, I'm certainly looking forward to flying a zeebis in the not-too-distant future."

"That will be arranged," I said, pleased by the enthusiastic glimmer in her pitch-black eyes. "This is Okous, my krogi," I said, pointing at my massive mount leashed by the entrance.

"Whoa! Now *that's* badass," Rihanna whispered as if to herself, her eyes lighting up as she hurried ahead of me towards the parking area where Okous waited.

My chest swelled with pride and delight for both the awed expression on her face, and the absence of a skittish reaction in front of what some females considered a fearsome beast. Although Okous wouldn't have attacked her, I nodded in approval when my female stopped at a non-threatening distance from the creature, not wanting to unduly provoke it.

Thanks to his double set of vicious horns and his tusks, Okous could eviscerate a target with a single swipe of his head. His clawed feet could shred an enemy to pieces, and his scale-covered tail could smash bones and stones.

"You may approach," I said, catching up to her, and pushing her forward with a gentle pressure on her lower back.

Okous observed us with his usual stoicism, his red eyes—the same color as mine—lingering on my mate.

"He looks so cool, like if a dragon and a bull had a baby together," Rihanna said with amusement. "I'm guessing he can hunt and battle?"

"Yes. But if you're hunting prey for food, only use the krogi as a mount to intercept. They are fearless, no matter how impressive the beast. If you dismount and tell it to attack, the krogi will tear them to pieces. They can be quite messy."

"I believe it," Rihanna said with excitement, her hand gently caressing the mane that protruded between the spiked scales covering Okous's nape.

Her gaze then shifted to my double ax secured on the side of my krogi. Pride filled me once more at her open admiration.

"Badass weapon," she said.

"Thank you," I replied.

Once again, my mate's reaction pleased me. When he'd messaged me to inform me that I'd been matched, Kayog had mentioned that Rihanna was a hunter among other things. I still had trouble picturing such a delicate female chasing down a wild beast, but her current behavior certainly seemed to confirm it.

"Let's get you on the saddle," I said, putting down her bag.

By the way she looked up and down the sides of the krogi, I guessed she was searching for some sort of stirrups. Silly female... She yelped when I picked her up by the hips and lifted her onto the back of the creature. Although startled, once she realized what I was doing, Rihanna went along, passing her left leg on the other side of the beast before settling comfortably on the saddle.

I took a second to admire how regal my female looked on top of Okous. Her delighted grin only made her more stunning. I extended her bag back to her. Rihanna thanked me as she settled it in front of her. I detached Okous's reins from the post and gave it to my mate. She took it without question and scooted forward to make room for me.

How adorable...

I hoisted myself behind Rihanna in one swift movement, and took the reins from her. I then wrapped my arm around her waist and dragged her backward until her back snuggly rested against my chest. She inhaled sharply. It was subtle, and I didn't know how to interpret it. My female turned her head to look at me over her shoulder. We locked eyes, and I held her gaze unwaveringly, keeping a neutral expression on my face, but silently daring her to protest my embrace.

Her face, too, was unreadable. After a beat, Rihanna's gaze lowered to my beard. "Nice braid," she said before turning back to look ahead.

I snorted, but then barely repressed a purr when Rihanna leaned back, her head resting against me. I ever so slightly tightened my hold around her slender waist. She pulled her bag closer, holding the handle with one hand, and rested her other palm on my forearm embracing her.

Yes, my little female had been created to fit perfectly against me.

"Let's get you home, my mate," I said. "Speak up if you feel any pain or discomfort."

"You better believe I will. I'm not shy when it comes to comfort... or lack thereof," Rihanna replied teasingly.

I snorted and spurred Okous to get moving. "I'm glad to hear it."

In no time, the krogi was running at a fast but comfortable pace through the woods. I felt almost sorry that this would be a mere thirty-minute ride. I wasn't particularly eager to release my Rihanna. Her soft warmth against me would likely become an addiction.

"Where did you get that weapon?" Rihanna asked. "The

craftsmanship is amazing, and it looks made of deutenium. That metal is nearly impossible to get a hold of."

"I did not *get* it, I *made* it."

Rihanna jerked her head left to look at me over her shoulder with an air of pure shock. "*You* crafted that ax?"

I frowned, unsure whether to be flattered or offended by the disbelief in her voice. "Yes, I did. I craft all of my own weapons. Any worthy Yurus learns how to craft his own weapons from childhood."

"Oh wow, you're really good! That's a beautiful ax."

"Thank you, my mate."

Although my female's genuine compliment deeply touched me, I maintained a neutral expression while thanking her. This wasn't the type of emotions an alpha male displayed.

"But how did you get your hands on the deutenium? I mean, it *is* deutenium, right?"

I nodded. "It is indeed deutenium. We mine it. We have endless reserves of it."

Rihanna's jaw dropped. "Jeez! Then why aren't you guys selling more of it? Are you deliberately restricting the quantities on offer to create scarcity and hike the prices?"

I shook my head. "I'm afraid you are mistaken, my mate. There is no demand for deutenium. First, as my people have not yet developed interstellar travel capacity, we cannot really contact other worlds to offer our goods. The mercenaries who visited us showed some interest in our weapons, but eventually deemed them unsuitable. We did trade some deutenium with them. However, they turned down any additional offers."

Rihanna frowned, confusion descending over her delicate features. "That's weird. The few deutenium weapons I've seen were selling for crazy amounts. And most people who owned one weren't too keen on parting with them. I think your mercs were clueless."

I shrugged. "It is possible. In truth, they were mostly interested in the Zelconians' crystals. But that's a story for another time."

"Well, whatever their reasons, I hope you know I'll be hounding you to make me a couple of deutenium blades."

I burst out laughing. Our females didn't fight. But the image that popped up in my head of my tiny female with a pair of massive blades in her hands was just too hilarious. I doubted she'd even be able to lift a single one.

Rihanna frowned again, a displeased look on her face as she weakly elbowed me. "It's not funny. I'm serious."

"You want blades, huh? But whatever for?" I asked, genuinely curious. "Kayog mentioned you were a criminal."

"I'm not a criminal! I'm a hunter and a smuggler!" my mate retorted before turning to face ahead and slumping against me.

"The Temern took you out of jail before you were sent to a prison planet to serve your twenty-year sentence," I countered.

Her shady past didn't bother me. We'd all done questionable things at one point or another. That Kayog vouched for her character had merely been further reassurance. But I couldn't picture Rihanna taking part in such activities. She looked too... adorable.

"Because my associate smuggled some illegal weapons in our cargo hold without informing me. The minute he found out the authorities were on to him, he ran and let me take the fall," she replied, anger seeping into her voice. "If I ever get my hands on that asshole—"

"I will bash his head in for wronging my mate," I said, interrupting her.

Right on cue, Rihanna turned to look at me over her shoulder with an outraged expression. I repressed a smile, loving that feisty fire in her eyes.

"I can fight my own battles, thank you very much. As a bounty hunter, I've dealt with far more lethal targets than that pathetic jerk," Rihanna said with a haughty tone.

I didn't even try to resist the urge of needling her some more. "And what exactly qualifies as a *lethal* target for you? A lost pet? A runaway juvenile?"

"You're really trying to provoke me, aren't you?" Rihanna asked, scrunching her face at me. "You like riling me up, don't you?"

Of course, I do. How can I not?

There was something exciting in the way she glared at me, about that delightful annoyance devoid of any real anger. Then, out of nowhere, the image of us coupling while she was furious with me had my blood rushing to my groin. I immediately chased it away. I didn't want to distress my mate with an untimely arousal, especially since my loincloth would do little to hide it.

I took on an innocent expression. "Whatever would make you say that? I'm merely curious about your past activities."

"I bet you are," she mumbled, totally on to me, which made me chuckle. "But no, not pets. I hunt the real criminals: thieves, space pirates, and murderers."

"Your tiny self hunts down hardened criminals?" I asked dubiously. I didn't actually doubt her, but I utterly failed to picture it.

Rihanna lifted her chin defiantly, a smug smile tugging at her lips. "For your information, a blaster doesn't care about the size of the finger that pulls the trigger. A well-aimed shot or a perfectly tossed dagger will always find its mark. And I happen to be a total badass with both."

"*You* can throw blades?"

"I sure can! And with deadly precision at that!" she boasted with a delightfully confident smile that once more made me want to kiss her.

I stopped Okous in the middle of the forest and dismounted. Rihanna stared at me with wide eyes, confusion etched on her face. I lifted her off the krogi's back. Instead of putting her down on her feet, I held her against my side with a single arm around her thighs. She instinctively passed her right arm around my neck for support, the side of her breast pressing against my shoulder.

"What are you doing?" Rihanna asked, baffled. "And you can put me down. I can walk, you know?"

I looked at her with my typical expression that she would soon learn meant 'don't-argue-with-me' as I yanked out one of my blades from the weapons strap incorporated in Okous's saddle.

When I didn't answer, Rihanna raised the palm of her free hand in a questioning fashion while staring at me in disbelief. Instead, still carrying her, I started walking towards a tall tree.

"Is this a Yurus thing, or just you, being you?" my mate asked.

"What thing?" I asked.

"You picking me up all the time."

"What if it was?" I asked, tilting my head to the side.

"What if it was what? A Yurus thing?"

I nodded. "Yes."

"Then that would be weird as hell!"

And it would indeed be. We didn't carry our females like that. I just *really* liked holding her. I could see myself carrying my mate around all day, especially since she basically weighed nothing. It would drive her insane... which, in itself, would be an added bonus.

"There are many things you will likely find weird in the Yurus culture," I said, neither denying nor confirming, knowing she would assume the latter. I pointed at a tree. "For now, I would like to put your boast to the test. Throw this blade into the center of this tree's knot."

"While you're carrying me around?" she asked, sounding unimpressed.

I chuckled and let my gaze roam over her pretty face. "I think I like you, Rihanna Makeba."

She shrugged, trying to act uncaring, and failing to hide that my comment pleased her. "Everyone does, even the people that screw me over. I'm adorable like that."

I snorted, moved a few more meters away from the tree and reluctantly set my mate down. All begrudging playfulness immediately faded from my female's face as she stared at the tree while extending an open palm towards me. In that instant, I saw a first glimpse of the focused hunter in my female. *Jaafan!* That was sexy.

As soon as I placed the blade in her hand, Rihanna's eyes widened in shock, her arm dropping from the weight of the weapon. She stared at it with disbelief before looking at me with an outraged expression.

"The fuck is that?! This shit weighs a ton! That's not a throwing blade!"

I frowned. "It is a proper Yurus blade."

"You mean it's a I'm-a-giant-with-enough-freaking-muscles-for-ten blade! No normal person can fight with that, let alone throw it. We'd break our wrists!"

"That's because you're tiny," I countered, bewildered she would challenge the quality of my weapon.

"And you're fluffy! That doesn't change the fact that your blade is wrong," she retorted, examining it with both hands.

"I'm not fluffy!" I said, offended.

She gave me a 'seriously?' type of look. "That silky fur on your chest and arms says otherwise. I've been leaning against it for the past fifteen to twenty minutes, and I can assure you that you're definitely fluffy. But that's beside the point. For this length, by galactic standards, this blade should weigh between two hundred and two-hundred-and-fifty grams. While some stronger species like theirs a little heavier, a blade used as a throwing knife should never exceed four hundred grams. This is, at the very least, six hundred grams."

I frowned, annoyed to have been unaware of such standards. "This blade is seven-hundred-and-fifty grams."

Rihanna rolled her eyes. "No freaking wonder!"

"It is the standard weight for the Yurus," I said, aggravated by my own defensive tone.

"If the rest of your people are as massive as you are, sure, I can see that. But if that's what you guys tried to sell to those mercs, no wonder they passed. I'm not going to break my wrist trying to throw this," Rihanna continued in a taunting tone. "When my stuff arrives, I'll show you how it's done. It will rock your socks. Well... your hooves."

That expression made no sense whatsoever, but I could still guess at what she inferred.

"For what it's worth, it's a gorgeous blade and the craftsmanship is once more flawless. The blade is perfect, but the handle is too big for a comfortable grip. Considering how massive your hand is, the current handle makes sense, but you've got to scale it to your potential customers' size and strength. Which means, I'm still expecting you to craft me a set."

She handed me back the blade and smiled with amusement at my disgruntled face. Although disappointed she didn't toss it at the tree, the way she had handled the weapon impressed me.

"We shall see once you've proven your so-called deadly precision," I grumbled.

"See, we shall," she replied with a shameless grin.

Determined not to give her the last word, I picked her up again, holding her against my side as I made my way back to Okous. Her taunting smile faded, and she frowned at me.

"Seriously?" she asked, even as she passed her arm around my shoulders.

I liked my mate.

Smiling smugly, still holding her with one arm, I took my

sweet time placing my blade back in its sheath while Rihanna stared at me. I would have given anything to know what thoughts were currently crossing her mind. If I didn't know better—which I actually didn't—I'd presume she was plotting and scheming about some way to get even. That thought thrilled me.

I sat my mate on the krogi. Once again, she scooted forward to make room for me. However, as soon as I mounted behind her, Rihanna didn't give me a chance to draw her to me. She moved back on her own, then leaned against me with a familiarity that took me aback.

No doubt sensing I was staring at her, she looked at me over her shoulder and shrugged. "You're fluffy, which makes you comfy."

She turned back ahead, but not so fast I missed the satisfied smile on her lips. She grabbed my right hand, pulling it in order to wrap my arm around her waist, then dragged her bag closer to her.

Fluffy! I was the *jaafing* Great Chieftain of all the Yurus clans of Cibbos. I was bloodthirsty, lethal, merciless, and terrifying. Not *jaafing* fluffy! I muttered something under my breath and immediately felt Rihanna's shoulders bouncing from her silent laugh.

Wretched female... She's perfect.

"This is a beautiful and peaceful forest," Rihanna said pensively as Okous resumed galloping.

"Do not be deceived, my mate," I cautioned. "I have taken the safe path home, but many dangers lurk in other areas of this forest. Cibbos is dangerous. I will show you the safe places for you to go, but you must never venture alone deeper into the forest. The flora can be as lethal as the fauna."

"Understood," she said with a nod.

It pleased me tremendously that she should take my warning seriously, and not make a scene about me attempting to control her. Cibbos was not to be underestimated.

"So, what should I expect in your village? And especially, what happens in a Yurus wedding?"

"We don't really have formal marriages."

"What? But we need to marry according to your culture for this to be valid!" Rihanna exclaimed, worry seeping into her voice.

"Do not fear, my mate. We will hold what serves as the equivalent of a human wedding. When a Yurus male wishes to take a specific female as his mate, he publicly stakes his claim," I explained. "If the female consents, they will be deemed mated, unless another challenges that claim."

"Challenges the claim, even if the female consented?" Rihanna asked, stunned.

"Yes, if the other male wants the female for himself, or merely wishes to spite his rival, he will issue a challenge."

"Can the first male refuse?"

I snorted. "No. Well, technically yes. But that would equal to forfeiting his claim on the female, as he would be deemed defeated by default."

"Well, that's messed up. So, they fight. It's not a battle to the death, I hope?"

I chuckled and shook my head. "No. They fight until one of the two is knocked out, trapped in a submission hold, or concedes defeat."

"Okay, and then what? The female goes to the winner?"

"No," I said, my voice hardening. "The female must *always* consent. If she doesn't want the winner, he will leave empty-handed, aside from the satisfaction of the loser not getting her."

"But what if the female wants the loser," Rihanna objected.

I huffed, casting a sideways amused glance at her. "No female will take a loser."

"Sheesh… Does that happen often? Males challenging the groom just to spite him?"

"*'Often'* is a relative word. But yes, it happens. Yurus males like to fight. Everything is an excuse to start a brawl, even a fight they know they can't win."

"Sounds charming," Rihanna said, her voice dripping with so much sarcasm I couldn't help but chuckle. "Does that mean someone will challenge you for me?"

"Doubtful, but possible."

This time, Rihanna turned to look at me with worry in her eyes. "Seriously? What if someone does?"

I shrugged. "I'll crack their skull," I replied as if it was obvious... since it was.

"Right, but what if you lose? Our contract demands we marry twice, the second time *today*. What then?"

That stung my pride. I frowned at my female, offended she would even consider that a remote possibility.

"I *never* lose, my mate. The day I do, I will no longer be the Great Chieftain."

CHAPTER 4

RIHANNA

The forest gave way to a large valley. I stared in awe at the massive fortress erected smack in the middle as Okous raced towards it. The Yurus village of Mutarak reminded me of an ancient fortified city that had been updated with recent technologies. Huge stone and deutenium walls encircled the sprawling settlement.

At a glance, I could spot a number of traps and defenses along the perimeter. Some could have been better dissimulated, but I had a trained eye to detect such pesky things. With the open plain surrounding, no would-be invader could make a stealth approach without using extremely advanced technology. The countless turrets, murder holes, and embrasures along the walls made me wonder how often they got raided to warrant such borderline paranoid defenses.

My stomach fluttered with nerves and trepidation as the reinforced doors of the cities parted to allow us through. To my pleasant surprise, the city looked clean, well-maintained, and far more modern than I expected for a so-called primitive species. It reminded me of a modern medieval city with its abundance of stone and wood, its streets covered in some sort of pavement, and very little greenery anywhere.

Stunned at first by the mostly empty streets, that feeling shifted to shock when we turned around a massive stone building to reveal the large square ahead. The loud cheering sounds rising from the crowd gathered there wasn't prompted by the return of their leader and his new bride, but by what seemed to be a brawl between six males.

I stared in awe at the brutality of the blows being exchanged. I hissed with sympathy when one of the pugilists kicked his opponent square in the chest with the flat of his hoof. The poor male flew back, landing hard on the stone pavement, and smacking the back of his head against the ground. He made as if to get back up, then collapsed back down, stunned or knocked out.

A roar rose from the crowd, some rejoicing, others visibly pissed. Two bystanders jumped in to drag out the unconscious fighter. It took me seconds to realize some kind of currency was being exchanged between the gawkers, no doubt betting on the fighters. A couple of the brawlers drew my attention. One with a dark brown fur, almost black, looked particularly vicious. Although his speed didn't break records, his blows were calculated, accurate, and savage. The other one that held my attention had hazelnut fur. Big and brawny, I would have expected him to dominate the field. But it only took me seconds to see why he was getting spanked instead.

As a second fighter was knocked out, angry shouts erupted from the crowd. Two of the observers launched into a heated argument. I could only speculate one of them had lost and was refusing to pay up. They'd barely exchanged a few loud words than the people surrounding them tossed them into the brawl with the others.

"Whoa! Is that a common occurrence here?" I asked, a little bewildered.

"Yes," Zatruk replied with resignation. "Multiple times a day."

"Sheesh. Well, that poor light-brown-furred male is getting trounced," I said, feeling a bit of pity for him.

Zatruk snorted and shook his head with disdain. "Wonjin is an idiot. He received too many blows to the head over the years. But he's also addicted to receiving punishments. He can never pass up a chance to brawl and always gets spanked."

As he spoke those words, people in the crowd started noticing our approach. They gradually stopped shouting, shifting their gazes from the fight to observe us... or more specifically me. Even the brawlers eventually stood still.

I resisted the urge to squirm, hating being the center of attention. However, the females' assessing gazes made me the most uncomfortable. What thoughts were crossing their minds? How much did they find me lacking? Then an even more unpleasant thought popped in my head. Was one of them an ex-mistress, concubine, or girlfriend Zatruk had cast aside the minute Kayog had found me for him? Did one of them harbor some kind of jealousy? Were the females as violence-prone as their males?

Like the males, the females had a pair of horns, cute bull ears, small tusks framing their mouths, a bull tail, unguligrade legs with hooves, and some light fur along their shoulders, arms and thighs. They also came in various shades of skin and fur color, which pretty much matched the spectrum of human hair colors. However, the females appeared generally smaller and definitely more lithe and slender than the males. Size-wise, they were comparable to a tall human female. They also wore beautifully ornate loincloths and matching sashes to cover their breasts.

Zatruk stopped Okous by the square as people parted to make way for us. He dismounted, helped me down, and set me on my feet. For the first time, I almost wished he would carry me like he'd taken to do, just so that I wouldn't look and feel so miniscule next to him.

"Mutarak Clan, I present to you the human bounty hunter, Rihanna Makeba. My mate..."

I cringed inwardly when the crowd gave in to the expected chuckles, disbelieving and amused looks, and mocking snorts. It stung more than I wanted to admit. I should be used to it by now for facing it every single time I met with a potential new client or with the quarry I'd been hired to bring in. However, coming from those meant to be my new people—at least for the next year—it was an even more bitter pill to swallow.

Wonjin, who had regained consciousness after his previous spanking, burst out laughing while ogling me with his dark eyes. "Your mate or adopted youngling?" he shouted tauntingly at Zatruk, eliciting a few chuckles from the crowd. "Looks like our Great Chieftain has decided to become a nanny!"

My blood boiled with each of his words. "I'm not a child! I'm a fully mature woman," I shouted back before Zatruk could respond... assuming he had even intended to. His totally impassive expression was impossible to read.

"A woman? In that outfit? What is that, anyway? Long diapers?" Wonjin asked mockingly, making more of the crowd—especially the males—erupt in further laughter.

"Yes, a woman who can put you on your back in less than ten seconds, Furry Ass," I hissed.

"Rihanna!" Zatruk said in a harsh tone, his brow creasing in a frown while the crowd gasped in shock and outrage. "Do not issue challenges you can't win. Once you lose, he'll own you."

I shrugged dismissively. "I won't lose. I've seen him fight. He's predictable," I whispered.

Wonjin burst out laughing. "I'm not going to fight a little girl. But if you want a spanking, that can be arranged. A bit of discipline is always good to remind juveniles to stay in their place."

Zatruk made as if to take a step towards Wonjin, having clearly taken offense at his clanmate hinting at touching his woman. But I grabbed his forearm, making him stop to look at me questioningly. However, my gaze remained locked on Wonjin. This was my fight to win.

"Ooh, so your big, bad, furry ass is too scared to accept my challenge?" I asked, my voice dripping with disdain. "What happened? Did you also lose your balls when you got your furry ass handed to you in the last brawl? You seem quite adept at getting spanked."

"Rihanna!" Zatruk hissed, his voice filled with anger this time, while the crowd Oohed in shock.

"Don't worry. I've got this," I said reassuringly, gently tapping his forearm in an appeasing gesture.

Pissed off, his outrage further fueled by the crowd taunting him and calling him Furry Ass, Wonjin stepped forward on the open area of the town square that had served as a makeshift arena.

"I will win you and teach you proper respect, female!"

Zatruk cursed under his breath in Yurusian, his red eyes appearing to glow with fury when he leveled them on me. "And when he does, I'll win you back, and then we'll have a serious talk."

"Oh, ye of little faith," I said, teasingly. "You wound me. But I'm not going to lose."

Zatruk's aggravated growl almost made me laugh. I advanced towards my opponent, stopping a short way from the center of the plaza. Raising both hands before me, I gestured for him to come at me.

He quite literally charged like a bull, but on two legs.

I stood still, entering that battle focus mental zone, perfectly timing the moment to burst into action. Seconds before he would reach for me, I dodged, moving sideways while slamming my fist in the spot that would match a human's right kidney, before getting behind him. As expected, and as I had noticed on a couple of occasions during his previous brawl, he flinched, bending sideways in pain. However, instead of retaliating with his usual back swipe, he tried to grab me. Although relieved he hadn't tried to strike me, I felt a little bad for the unfair advantage his reluctance to hurt a female was giving me.

I'd prepared for the back swipe, but ended up dodging the grab attempt instead. I ducked, kicked the back of his knee before he could regain his balance, and spun around to slam my elbow on his chest, making him fall onto his back.

The crowd erupted in a deafening roar interspersed with incredulous *jaafans*, which I presumed to be their curse words generally meaning fuck.

I took a couple of steps back and smugly put my hands on my hips, putting as much sass as I could muster in both my stance and my voice. "Sheesh. That was barely six seconds!"

Wonjin jumped back to his hooves, anger, disbelief, and outrage fighting for dominance on his orcish features. "I am not defeated! Fight!" he shouted, slamming both of his fists on his chest.

I shook my head with my most obnoxious expression. "Tut, tut, tut! Not so fast, Furry Ass. I said I'd put you on your back in less than ten seconds." I spread my arms wide, looking around at the crowd to take them as witness. "And I did!"

"*Jaafan!* She did!" shouted a reddish-furred male. "She did!"

Part of the crowd repeated 'she did' in some kind of a chant, while others shouted 'on his back' in a loop. Unable to resist, I winked at Wonjin, who roared in rage.

"Remove yourself, Furry Ass," Zatruk shouted above the chanting of the crowd as he approached me.

He placed a possessive hand around my waist, drawing me to him. The vicious pride on his face almost made me want to thump my chest.

Wonjin quietly moved to the edge of the square with the rest of the crowd, a few of whom seized the opportunity to mock him for getting bested by a 'little girl.'

Zatruk raised a hand to quiet down the crowd. "I claim this female as my mate," he shouted to them before turning to look at me. "Do you accept my claim, Rihanna Makeba?"

I smiled and nodded. "Yes, Zatruk Abbas. I accept your claim."

His lips stretched into a triumphant smile, which gave him a predatory air that I found quite sexy. He then turned to once more address the crowd. "Does anyone dare challenge that she is mine?"

To my shock, gone was the initial mockery. Instead, quite a few males were now casting covetous glances my way. Some even eyed Zatruk, looking as if they were sizing him up to assess their chances of taking him down. In the end, all of them appeared to think better of it and none took on the challenge. Relief and an intense sense of pride in my man flooded through me. Zatruk looked badass, but that none of these battle-hardened males dared to challenge him clearly stated they didn't believe they could win.

"Wise decision," Zatruk shouted mockingly. "I will have a feast for my mate. Set it up," he ordered before turning his red eyes towards a dejected Wonjin. "Furry Ass, go stable Okous, and then bring my mate's bag to our dwelling."

I flinched inwardly, feeling horrible for Wonjin as the people around him mocked him, a couple smacking him in the back of the head or shoving him. Sure, I had just humiliated him, but that had been necessary to ensure more bearable living conditions here for me. Had I allowed his mocking me as a child to stand, or let Zatruk fight that battle for me, I'd constantly get bullied and harassed whenever he wasn't around to keep the idiots in check. There was no way I would have spent the next year playing tattle tale to my husband every time someone was acting mean to me.

Growing up, it had always been my go-to tactic, initially in school and later in my bounty hunter business. First, identify the bullies. Analyze their strengths and weaknesses. Figure out which ones I could exploit, and publicly spank one of them as a warning to the others that I wasn't to be messed with. And I always did all of this *before* they could turn me into their local punching bag.

With his arm now around my shoulders, Zatruk led me towards the most imposing building a short distance from the square. That my husband didn't pick me up as he had done previously only confirmed my suspicion that Yurus males carrying their females around had been bullshit. I couldn't quite say why Zatruk had done it at the spaceport and in the forest—not that I had really minded. To be honest, I had rather enjoyed it, even though he'd been obnoxious about it. However, that would be a discussion for a different time.

Once we were far enough from indiscreet ears, I raised the topic bothering me.

"I don't think you should call him Furry Ass," I said carefully. "You, being their leader, signals to everyone to keep doing so."

He frowned and looked at me with a stunned expression. "No, my mate. What I call him has no bearing on what others do. *You* named him. We are following *your* lead. If you wish him to be called differently, simply rename him publicly."

"Me?!" I exclaimed, baffled. "Why are you all following my lead?"

"Because he's your slave now. For as long as you remain his mistress, you decide how he is to be addressed, among other things," Zatruk said matter-of-factly.

I stopped dead in my tracks, mouth gaping and eyes all but popping out of my head as I stared at him in disbelief. "My slave? What the fuck do you mean by that?"

He looked at me as if I was asking a self-evident question—which it probably was. "He lost a challenge to you. You won him. He's your property to do with as you please for as long as you own him, until you either choose to release him or lose a challenge to someone who seeks to free him. However, no one will challenge you for him, and a slave may not challenge his master."

I continued to stare at him, speechless for a few more seconds. "Are you saying that if I had lost, I would have become his slave?"

Zatruk's expression darkened, his previous displeasure with me resurfacing. "Yes. You would have been his. And I would have had to stomp him into the ground to win you back. As I told you back at the spaceport, you must learn our ways before you act. Do not issue challenges without fully understanding the implications of a loss."

I nodded, properly chastised. "You're right, I'm sorry. I'm not trying to be difficult, but just so you know, I only issued that challenge because I knew for sure that I would win. I may be a little impulsive at times, but I promise that I'm not stupid."

Far from appeasing him, my answer only seemed to annoy him further. "Have you ever fought a Yurus before that you could be so certain of your victory?"

"No, of course not. However, the goal was never to defeat him," I countered. "The challenge I issued was only being able to put him on his back. I *knew* I could do that easily because Wonjin is predictable. But I'm not dumb enough to think I could defeat a Yurus male in a fist fight. Without weapons, I wouldn't stand a chance to beat Wonjin or any other males out there. I'm well aware of my limitations. As I'm a sore loser, I never make a bet I can't win."

"I am pleased to hear it," he said, his voice and face still stern.

Pressing his palm on the small of my back, Zatruk nudged me forward, and we resumed walking towards his house.

"So... what does a slave entail?" I asked, shuddering at the thought of what could have happened.

Zatruk gave me a sideways glance and smirked. "Everything

except what you are likely thinking." He chuckled at my surprised expression. "We are a brutal and savage people among males, but we are protective towards our females. Had you lost the challenge, you would have been the first female slave in memory. That said, as with a male, you would have essentially become his grunt, servant, and if he wished to humiliate you, a source of entertainment."

"So, it *does* include what I thought!" I exclaimed.

"No, silly female," Zatruk said, opening the imposing, ornate metal doors of his dwelling. "No sexual favors can be demanded of slaves. Couplings must always be consensual between all partners involved. But when it comes to entertainment, if he was kind, your master would simply make you sing and dance for him. If he was cruel, he would make you walk around on all fours like an animal, or cover your skin in krogi feces for his amusement. The clan would likely take bets on how long you would last before you started retching."

I looked at him in horror. "Why are you making it sound like something that actually happened?"

Zatruk chuckled. "Because it did," he said as if it was self-evident. "And those were some of the lesser abuses inflicted to losers, including Wonjin, when they got enslaved."

"Gee whiz! I'm really starting to feel sorry for that poor guy," I said, horrified.

But all thoughts of Wonjin and krogi feces vanished as I stepped inside Zatruk's house. I didn't quite know what I had expected, but not this beautiful blend of rustic, medieval, and modern. The same light brown and beige stones covered some of the walls, the floor being adorned in larger, darker stones. Wooden beams and arches formed the high, vaulted ceiling, while glow stones embedded as ornaments in the walls or encased in exquisitely sculpted lamps—free standing or wall-mounted—illuminated the spacious entrance hall.

Zatruk's gaze weighed heavily on me as he studied my reaction to what was now my new home. I didn't have to speak for him to know I was blown away.

Between the giant skulls on the back wall of creatures I couldn't even begin to guess their species, hung a beautifully embroidered, three-meter-long banner. On each side wall, a large stone archway led on the left to some kind of gathering room, and on the right to what could serve both as a banquet room or meeting hall. The latter was beautiful with its humongous wood and metal table, long enough to seat twenty people. So were the giant Yurus stone statues carved in the left and right corners of the rectangular room, appearing to hold the ceiling while gazing out the tall gothic windows looking out onto the plaza. However, it was the gathering room that held my interest.

First, I fell in love with the massive stone fireplace and its intricately sculpted mantle. Then with the countless seats, from stone and wooden chairs to couches and cushions, many of which were covered with thick furs. A few stunning weapons and more impressive skulls decorated some sections of the walls, but in a tasteful, uncluttered way. The same huge gothic windows framed the fireplace, also looking out onto the plaza.

To my shock, Zatruk activated a remote, and the image of the giant painting of a pair of krogis clashing their double set of horns in battle above the fireplace turned into a vidscreen.

I could totally see myself sprawling all over the various couches and cushions in the room to read, relax, or enjoy whatever weird programs the Yurus had playing here. Judging by the almost throne-like seat in the middle of the back wall, facing the fireplace, I suspected it to be Zatruk's place, and one he used often.

"Your home is beautiful," I said in all sincerity.

"*Our* home, my mate," Zatruk rectified in a gentle tone. "Come, let me show you the rest."

A discreet door at the back of the gathering room, which appeared to serve as a living area, led to the most impressive gourmet kitchen I had ever seen. It had at least two islands, cupboards galore, a massive cooling unit, a huge cooking plate next to a grill, long and large enough to cook a two-meter-long rack of ribs.

"Holy cow! Do you cook here?" I asked, flabbergasted.

"Sometimes. Usually, one of the females does my cooking and cleaning," Zatruk said nonchalantly before luring me out through another door.

We ended up in a large hallway with multiple doors located on the right side of the house. One of them opened on his office. The amount of technology within clashed with the rest of the house. It was a spacious room with a surprisingly clean and uncluttered desk, and a pair of holographic screens. A large work table with seating for ten occupied another corner of the room. At the back, 3D maquettes, both holographic and physical, sat atop a long counter lining the length of the wall. The constructions, vaguely reminiscent of a colosseum, made me wonder what kind of project my husband was working on.

The next room took my breath away. It was a huge forge with state-of-the-art equipment. Appended to it, the most amazing armory I'd ever laid eyes upon. Naturally, every sword, staff, dagger, and throwing blades were scaled for the powerful giant he was. But I fully intended to twist his fluffy arms into making Rihanna-scaled versions of these beauties. My mind was already racing with some of the nanotech enhancements that could be added to my set.

"I can't wait to see you working on a weapon. This is really impressive."

Although he tried to keep a nonchalant expression, Zatruk stood a little taller under the praise. "I'll be glad to show you. Just be aware it gets pretty hot."

"I can handle the heat," I said smugly.

He led me through the rest of the house—or should I say castle?—with five bedrooms, three hygiene rooms, and the humongous master bedroom with its own en suite. I didn't even know how to describe the size of the master bed, it was so massive. If you dropped me in the middle of the mattress, I'd need an eyeglass to see the edge on the horizon.

Zatruk walked to a paneled section of the wall, revealing a hidden door that opened onto my dream walk-in closet. Hanging racks galore, a huge central island with drawers for accessories, shoe racks next to a plush circular bench covered in a brown and beige fur. Naturally, a floor to ceiling mirror would allow me to admire the final results. On a tiny section on the left wall, Zatruk's loincloths were neatly stacked in the upper section of a series of shelves, leaving the lower ones—at an accessible height for me—available.

"I have added these slots for your footwear as I understand human females have a great variety of them. If you need more poles added to hang your clothes, I will take care of it. I only use these two drawers from this island. The rest is all yours."

"Remember you said that," I teased. "If you guys have some nice clothes shops, expect this walk-in to become packed."

He snorted. "Then I guess it's a good thing we don't. But the seamstresses will be happy to make for you whatever you wish. For now, however, I will go fetch your bag. Wonjin just brought it in."

My eyes widened. "How do you know?"

"I heard him," he said smugly, flicking his long, floppy ears before heading out.

I watched his muscular back as he left the room, my gaze dropping to the long tail with its fluffy tip, pausing for a second to admire the round, grabbable behind that his loincloth failed to hide. As he vanished from view, I shook my head at the realization that I was seriously starting to find my furry orc-minotaur husband sexy. And tonight, I'd be sharing this massive bed with him.

CHAPTER 5

ZATRUK

As we settled down outside on the plaza for the feast, I couldn't help but puff out my chest with pride for the envious gazes other males were casting on my female. I still couldn't believe Rihanna had challenged Wonjin and won. Our females, taller, bigger, and stronger even than an average human male, didn't fight. Then here was my tiny female, a seductively compact little bundle of fierceness. Kayog did say she would be my perfect Queen... my little sylphin.

I both wanted to spank her for her recklessness and kiss her for how watching her had turned me on. But more importantly, she had earned the respect and admiration of the clan—an important achievement under the circumstances. With all the challenges I currently juggled, not having to worry about constantly beating up idiots for disrespecting my mate was a major relief.

However, now wasn't the time to dwell on the problems of my people and the slimy mountain of feces Vyrax and his stupidity had dropped on my lap. I should have killed him sooner before he launched that nonsensical war against the humans. He should have backed down the minute he saw the Zelconians had allied with the colony. But no, his stupid pride and bloodlust made him blind, and he paid the ultimate price while setting the rest of us back.

I grunted in annoyance, silently berating myself for further letting my thoughts wander down that slippery slope. Tonight was my wedding night. It was a time to drink, eat, and rejoice. And later, I would claim my female. A fire stirred low in my loins at the thought of my sylphin beneath me.

I cast a sideways glance at Rihanna only to find her staring at me inquisitively. I realized she had likely heard my grunt.

"All is well, Rihanna. For now, prepare to savor the meal our females have prepared for us with the *lamaii* I captured for you this morning."

"For me?" she asked, watching four of my clanmates carrying the large beast still on the spit to place it in the middle of the square.

"Of course. I wouldn't have someone else feed my mate and our guests on our wedding feast," I said, as if it was self-evident.

"That's really sweet," she said, with a smile.

I frowned at her offensive words. "I'm not sweet," I whispered sternly.

Rihanna's smile broadened, and her obsidian eyes sparkled. She leaned forward to whisper to me. "Yes, I think you're very sweet, on top of being fluffy, and having the cutest ears."

I glared at her, annoyed beyond words. Even though I knew she was deliberately trying to provoke me, I was also convinced she actually believed those words. I should be pleased that my mate thought positively of me and my appearance—at least by human standards—but calling a Yurus male, an apex alpha at that, sweet, fluffy, and cute were fighting words. The fact that she'd whispered them only confirmed she knew it or suspected as much.

Wonjin coming to pour some mead in my mate's cup, and then in mine, kept me from answering. Rihanna's troubled expression, noticing Wonjin was the only male serving, reminded me I had much to teach her about our ways. In spite of her bluster—and indeed skills—my mate still hid within the typically soft and tender heart of a female.

Relven, our head cook, quickly carved the meat, filling large plates for the other females to bring to the tables laid out in rows in front of the head table occupied solely by Rihanna and me. Wonjin held the first plate she filled. He brought it to our table, placed two choice pieces in Rihanna's plate, then a few more in my own plate, settling the rest in front of us. My mate whispered a thank you, her look of unease increasing.

That displeased me tremendously.

Wonjin came back a few more times, bringing us generous portions of the various side dishes. Once done, he went to sit on the ground by the two large tables framing the spit, and on which sat the extra portions of side dishes in temperature-controlled containers.

With the females being done and seated to join in the feast, I rose to my feet to give the go ahead to start eating. For once, everyone had behaved and waited.

"In honor of my mate, feast, drink, and be merry!"

My clan all raised their mugs of mead and shouted in unison. *"Kyadju vojee! Holje! Shuntawi!"*

"What was that?" Rihanna asked when I sat back down.

"They shouted 'Long life, happiness, and fertility.' It is the common blessing to newly mated couples," I explained. "Now eat and let me know what you think of our cuisine."

Rihanna smiled before looking at the generous amount of food Wonjin had filled her plate with. However, her smile faded as she looked up to see her slave still sitting on the floor by the spit.

"Why is he sitting there?" Rihanna asked with a frown. "Isn't he going to eat?"

"You have not given him permission to eat," I replied calmly.

"Are you serious?! Does he also need my permission to pee?" she asked, anger seeping into her voice.

"As a matter of fact, yes. He's not allowed to sleep, shower, or relieve himself without your permission. If he can no longer hold it, he will have no other choice than to soil himself, for which you will be entitled to punish him."

"This is ridiculous," my female hissed through her teeth, anger now obvious on her features. She looked at Wonjin who was staring at the ground. "Wonjin!"

His head jerked up upon hearing her calling out his name. He pinched his lips, rose to his hooves, and approached obediently when my mate gestured for him to do so. The happy chatter around the tables died down as everyone eyed the scene with curiosity. By the malicious glimmer in some of their eyes, they were clearly anticipating for my mate to chastise him for some slight, real or perceived.

"How can I serve?" he said in a grumbling tone, stopping in front of our table.

"By not serving anymore," Rihanna said, projecting her voice loudly enough for all to hear. "I release you from my service. You are free. Now, please go enjoy the feast with everyone else."

The stunned silence that welcomed her words reflected the shock on Wonjin's face. He blinked, looking as if he wasn't sure if he had heard her correctly. His gaze flicked to me before returning to my female, his confusion and disbelief plain to see.

"You have heard my mate, Wonjin. You are free. Now go eat," I snarled at him.

My words snapped him out of his shocked daze. Still visibly confused as to why he'd been released so easily when the standard was to keep a challenge loser enslaved for two weeks, he bowed his head at Rihanna before going for a free spot at a table to our right.

She turned to look at me, her gaze daring me to question her decision.

I smiled, amused by the situation. "You are soft," I said, teasingly.

To my surprise, Rihanna didn't reply with her usual sarcasm. She held my gaze with an unreadable expression on her face.

"No, this is not me being soft. It's me being human. If that makes me soft in the eyes of the Yurus, then I'll proudly take the title. A punishment should reflect the offense. This is excessive. Frankly, I cannot think of any offense that could justify this."

Without another word, Rihanna turned to her plate, picked up her utensils, visibly too big and too heavy, and started cutting her meat.

Her words and reaction to Wonjin's situation troubled me. Was it truly excessive? Granted, the rights afforded to the master could go fairly far. However, no one truly went to such extremes. Sure, making someone wet themselves, collapse from lack of sleep, or cover themselves in feces verged on the crueler side, but these usually only happened once in a purple sky, and normally as a prank between long-time rivals. For the first time, I genuinely wondered just how barbaric and primitive the humans and Zelconians perceived my people to be.

To my relief, the tension this incident had initially triggered between us quickly faded, and my mate and I resumed having an amiable conversation while she appeared to enjoy the food.

She glanced around us at the clan with a baffled expression. "Why are half the women sitting on a male to eat, but not the others? There is plenty of room around the tables for them to sit in their own chair."

"Those females are sitting on their mates. The others are not yet paired, widowed, juvenile, or angry with their partner," I replied with a grin.

"What does that mean? That if you're married—and not

angry with your husband—you're supposed to sit on his lap to eat?"

I nodded.

She frowned. "I'm not sitting on your lap. Is that a real thing or are you pulling my leg again like with the 'Yurus carrying their women around' bull crap you fed me earlier?"

"I am not responsible for what you assumed, my mate," I said, without the slightest hint of remorse. "Just like I cannot be at fault if you decide to deny the truth of what you see before your very eyes."

Rihanna scrunched her face, looking like she wanted to throw something at me. She then glanced back at the many mated pairs where the female sat on her male's lap, examining them with uncertainty.

As the meal ended, the males carried off the heavy tables and the spit, freeing the central space so that our females could perform some of our traditional dances while both our males and females sang, and played on percussion instruments.

It pleased me how peaceful the evening had turned out, one of the longest stretches of time my people had gone without some fight or brawl erupting. It was largely thanks to the praxilla leaf powder I now had the cooks occasionally sneak into the meals and drinks to help control our males' genetic tendencies towards violence.

It was ethically and morally wrong to do this without their consent. But our bloodlust was a weakness holding my people back from the potential of a greater future and destroying us from within. I was slowly but surely converting them to a new way of life. We would rise from this stagnation and self-destruction... even if I had to beat it into them.

Although my mate seemed to enjoy the show, she didn't balk when I finally rose from my chair and extended a hand towards her, taking it before leading her to our home. The hour was growing late. Despite it being still early for me, Rihanna had to deal with the different time on our planet. Furthermore, we had one last part to fulfill in our contract—one that I was greatly looking forward to, but that I also wanted done properly. A poor performance on my part this night could negatively impact the rest of our relationship.

Rihanna had come here with the intention of leaving as soon as our first year was up. I planned on changing her mind on that front. Kayog had deemed her my perfect mate, and based on my interactions with her so far, I believed time would prove him right.

As we made our way to our bedroom, Rihanna began exhibiting the first real signs of nervousness in my presence. Aside from her initial shock at seeing my height and size when we first met, my mate had impressed me with how she'd taken things in stride. I'd expected a rather angry female, begrudgingly consenting to this arrangement out of desperation and almost resenting me for my indirect part in this alternate version of her prison sentence.

But not my little sylphin.

It had been refreshing to see how she had played along, not fighting the terms she had freely agreed to. However, coupling understandably represented the most challenging clause of the agreement to fulfill. Although the Yurus culture was very laid back when it came to sexuality, our females usually required some sort of emotional connection before they granted their favors. Despite the undeniable connection I felt with my mate, was this too early for her?

Rihanna was attracted to me, but I wanted her to crave my touch, not fear it, and not yield to me merely out of duty. I wanted her hands and her mouth on me, eager and willing. I wanted her to writhe beneath me, begging for more.

What if her nervousness is due to our size difference?

That gave me pause. If that was the issue, we would easily overcome it together with patience and care. Her small size *did* concern me. I would need to be careful not to damage her in the throes of passion.

But first, I needed her to relax.

As soon as we entered the room, Rihanna went to stand at the foot of the bed and clasped her hands before her. She looked at me wide eyed, failing miserably at her attempt to appear neutral.

"I will go shower before I come to you," I said in a gentle voice. "I will leave the en suite to you, so that you may prepare for bed."

She seemed surprised at first, then her lips quirked up in a relieved and grateful smile. "Okay, thank you."

"Take however much time as you need, my mate. There is no rush and no pressure. Do you understand?"

This time, she slowly nodded, the serious tone of my voice and expression making my underlying meaning clear. "I understand, Zatruk. I appreciate it."

I smiled then left the room. I made my way to one of the guestrooms' hygiene rooms and made quick work of showering. I didn't want to smell like a krogi once I mated with her. In truth, I was a bit obsessed with cleanliness, as my mate would no doubt soon discover. It wasn't a very common trait among my peers.

Yurus males could be real slobs. Most didn't bother with utensils and just ate with their hands, spilled half of their mead on their beards and chests, and wiped the drips with the back of their hands or arms. I believed that my albinism had played a large part in this obsession. While my brethren's sloppy habits didn't really show too much on their darker furs, the slightest mess loudly screamed its presence on my alabaster skin and fur. It quickly looked quite repulsive.

My clanmates thought me vain that I constantly appeared to be grooming and preening. As I didn't care about their opinions, I never bothered to set them straight. But that albino skin also meant I needed to regularly drink large quantities of jerresh juice to allow me to traipse about safely under the burning sun of Cibbos.

Once done, I dried, combed my hair and beard, and brushed my fur to prevent it from clotting or getting tangled. I stared at myself in the mirror, an annoyed smile settling on my face as I remembered how Rihanna had taunted me about being fluffy and having cute ears. Right now, freshly washed, my fur certainly looked quite fluffy. I couldn't wait for her to slip her fingers through it. I almost braided my hair and beard again, but decided against it. I wanted Rihanna to be able to play with them, too, unimpeded.

I debated whether or not to put my loincloth back on or wrap a towel around me. In the end, I chose against it. I slept naked anyway. Whatever did or didn't happen tonight, this was something she would need to get used to. Yurus didn't wear undergarments.

I entered the bedroom to find it empty. My ears twitched as I strained them to listen for my mate in the hygiene room. The discreet hum of the dryer reached me. I went inside the walk-in to place my bracer inside a drawer of the island, and tossed my loincloth into the laundry basket, only to see Rihanna's clothes already sitting at the bottom. An odd warmth spread through my chest at the simple domestic feel of it all.

I'd wanted a mate for a long time, but none of our females had stirred me enough for that. As the Great Chieftain of our people, I had visited all the clans. Yet, I'd failed to find a single female that had given me the urge to settle down. However, since my ascension, many had expressed their interest in the role. As I'd known it had been more about being mated to the Great Chieftain than actually out of deep affection for me, I'd happily shot down any advances.

Now, I couldn't be happier I had waited.

I returned inside the bedroom at the same time Rihanna exited the hygiene room. She seemed startled by my presence, apparently not having heard my return. Surprise gave way to shock as she took in my nudity, quickly averting her eyes when they reached my groin.

She looked stunning in a sheer blue dress that hid nothing of her naked body underneath it. Flimsy strings held the dress on her shoulders. The very low cleavage showed part of the creamy brown curves of her breasts, the light fabric giving me a glimpse of her darker nipples. Despite the ripples and folds of the skirt preventing a clear view of her nether region, I noted the absence of any underwear.

The way Rihanna's hands twitched on each side of her body, I suspected she was fighting the urge to clasp them in front of her again, if only to partially hide what her sensual outfit was exposing to my greedy eyes.

"You look beautiful, my mate," I said in a gentle voice.

Her grateful but timid smile turned to confusion when I headed towards the bed instead of going to her. I sat down at the edge and extended my hand. She swallowed hard, took in a deep breath, and came to me with resolute steps that only made my admiration for her grow another notch. She placed her hand in mine and slightly recoiled when I drew her onto my lap.

Rihanna didn't resist or balk. She merely clasped her hands on her lap, pressed her right arm to her side to limit its contact with my exposed shaft, and looked at me nervously.

"As per the human vows we exchanged, we are married, for better or for worse," I said in a soft voice. "As your mate, and as a Yurus male, it is my duty to try and always ensure things are for the better for you and what offspring we might one day be blessed with. Cibbos is a harsh world with many dangers and just as many beauties. But the one thing you will never have to fear here, is me."

She smiled, some tension bleeding from her shoulders. "I believe it," she said with a nervous laugh. "I may not know you yet, but I trust you."

I smiled back and gently caressed her hair. Like me, she had undone her braids. Her hair was incredibly soft and a little bouncy under my touch. I had never seen or felt such a wondrous texture before. The very tight curls made it look much shorter than when it had been braided.

"I can see and feel your worry and nervousness because of what is supposed to happen now," I continued in a cautious tone. "I do not want to ever be the cause of such discomfort for you. I will also never force myself on a female who doesn't want me, least of all my mate."

She shook her head, emphatically. "No! No, it's not that. You... I mean... You're well made. You've got a really nice body and a nice face, too. What I'm trying to say is that I do find you attractive. You're just crazy massive and like you said, I'm kind of tiny," she added sheepishly.

I chuckled. "Indeed, we are. However, I am patient, and you stretch. I am not worried about that, nor should you be," I continued, becoming serious again. "When that time comes, I *will* take good care of you. But I want you to come to me willingly, because you want to be mine, not because a contract demands you surrender to me."

Rihanna frowned, her back stiffening again. "We *have* to do it tonight. We agreed to the contract."

"*Jaafan* that!" I said with a dismissive gesture. "Nobody will force you or me to couple against our will. It's not like they have cameras here or will give us a medical exam tomorrow to verify."

Rihanna's frown deepened, and she shifted uneasily on my lap. "Right, but Kayog trusted us to act in good faith. He held his end of the deal, we should hold ours. Anything less would be dishonorable."

"And we will, when you are ready," I countered.

She tilted her head to the side and gave me a strange look. "I asked Kayog why rush it to the first night instead of waiting. He had an interesting answer for it, and I tend to agree with him," Rihanna said pensively. "Why delay the inevitable while extending the time we'll stress over it? You're huge. That's not going to change. Whether tonight or in three weeks, you're not going to shrink. But with each passing day, I'll just picture it worse, and worse, and even worse."

"True," I conceded, "but by then you will have grown fond enough of me that you won't even care about the initial discomfort because you will *want* to be with me."

"You're presuming I will grow to like you," she retorted, regaining some of that sass I liked so much. "Chances are that, in three weeks, I won't be able to stand you. So, waiting until then to get that clause out of the way will become a *real* chore, not to say torture!"

I snorted then chuckled. "You might also be correct in that."

She smiled, her face softening as she studied my features. Her smile faded as she raised a hand to gently caress my brow with her fingertips. They traced a path down my cheek before combing through my beard. Her eyes had followed the movement of her hand before flicking back up to lock with mine.

"I want us to do it," Rihanna said in a soft voice. "Because of the contract, yes, and also because I want to. Yes, I'm nervous, but I trust you to take care of me."

"Are you sure, my mate?" I insisted, my eyes flicking between hers to assess her sincerity.

She nodded, holding my gaze unwaveringly. "I am."

"Very well. But if you get scared or change your mind at any time, just speak up, and I will stop. You are the one in control, and you will always be safe with me. Do you understand?"

Rihanna nodded again, a happy smile settling on her lips as she wrapped her arms around my neck. Drawing her closer to me, I claimed her mouth in a gentle kiss. She pressed herself against me, the sheer fabric of her dress making her almost feel naked. Almost... As I deepened the kiss, Rihanna slipped her fingers through my hair, eliciting an approving purr from me.

She gasped when I lifted her up, turned her, then set her back down so that she would sit facing me on my lap, her legs on each side of my thighs. Rihanna's pupils dilated, and a shiver coursed through her when I slid both my hands under the hem of her dress, gliding them up her back in a gentle caress while lifting her garment. My mate raised her arms to allow me to get rid of the dress. She placed her hands back on my shoulders, hanging on to me while yet another shiver ran down her spine.

I wrapped my arms around her, holding her tightly as I reclaimed her mouth. A growl of pleasure rumbled through my throat at the feel of her bare skin against me. She was so soft and warm. Blood rushed to my groin in response to the proximity of my mate's core brushing against it. I could remain forever like this with her delicate body in my embrace, but the urge to explore was too strong.

Fisting one hand in her hair, I gently tugged her head back, breaking the kiss to brush my lips over her face and neck. Her skin erupted in tiny little bumps as she shivered once more. I bent her lower, my spare hand supporting her back. Rihanna submitted willingly, trusting that I wouldn't let her fall. I rubbed my face on her silky skin, kissing her clavicles before pursuing my journey down towards the hardening buds of her nipples, a much darker brown than her skin. I traced the edges of her areolas with my tongue, circling closer to her nipple before sucking it into my mouth.

Rihanna's voluptuous moan resonated directly in my loins. I turned my attention to her other breast while releasing her hair to settle one hand beneath the round and firm globe of her behind. Lifting my mate slightly, I lowered my hardening shaft so that it would be under her instead of between us. My female stiffened in surprise when I drew her closer to press our pelvises tightly together, and she finally felt my swelling *vylus* against her clitoris. As soon as I activated it, a throaty moan rose from Rihanna's throat.

The short appendage became engorged with a Yurus male's arousal, lengthening and thickening it. Simply with our will, we could set it in motion, flicking from side to side to stimulate our female's erogenous area, just above her slit. Contrary to the human woman's single clitoris, Yurus females had a *vyltia* made of between four and six small, highly sensitive, nipple-shaped bumps above their opening that served a similar purpose. They rarely climaxed from penetration, but quickly fell apart from proper stimulation of their *vyltia*.

And my *vylus* already had my female nearing the edge. I straightened her to reclaim her mouth, the taste of her moans against my lips fanning the flame of desire. While our tongues mingled, I slipped my hand around her behind, my fingers reaching out for her opening. A triumphant growl escaped me at finding her slick with arousal for me. I gently probed her slit, my arm around her tightening as she began to tremble with her impending climax. I pushed one finger inside of her and then a second, working them in and out, first slowly and then increasingly faster.

Rihanna's body suddenly seized, and she threw her head back with a sharp cry as ecstasy swept her away. She was so beautiful, lips parted, her lids tightly closed in an almost painful —yet blissful—expression, as she trembled in my arms. I feasted my eyes on her without slowing my ministrations until she started to come back to reality.

Holding my female with one arm, I stood up only so that I could lay her down on the bed before climbing next to her. For the next eternity, I explored her body with my hands and my mouth, reveling in her delicate scent and the slightly salty taste of her skin, and discovering her sensitive spots. At the same time, I stretched her, using two, then three fingers, scissoring in and out as I prepared her to receive me. To my pleasant surprise, my fingers inadvertently stumbled on a particularly responsive bundle of nerves inside her. Between that and my mouth on Rihanna's clitoris, I soon had my mate riding another orgasm.

Lying down on my back, I pulled Rihanna on top of me, kissing and caressing her, until her climax waned. I gently rubbed my erection against her, trying to silence the inferno raging in my loins, I so ached with need for her.

"It is better you set the pace," I whispered, my voice gravelly with unfulfilled desire. "Take as much or as little of me as you can handle."

She smiled at me, her lips swollen from my kisses, her eyes sensuously hooded, and her skin flushed from the pleasure I'd given her. Propping herself on her knees, spread on each side of me, Rihanna slipped a hand between us and wrapped it around my length. I hissed with pleasure at her touch as she aligned my cock with her opening. Despite my previous effort, my female was still very tight as she began to lower herself onto me with shallow movements.

Grinding my teeth to silence the excruciating urge to grab her hips and impale her on my cock while I rammed myself upwards into her, I forced myself instead to caress her silky skin, fondle her breasts, and massage her clit while whispering words of encouragement. I couldn't tell how long it lasted as we made slow progress. It could have been two minutes or ten, but felt like an eternity to me.

When I was halfway sheathed, Rihanna's body suddenly yielded, and I found myself buried to the hilt. My mate gasped, her face tensing with what had likely been a sharp, burning pain. My grunt of pleasure-pain overlapped it. My abdominal muscles contracted spasmodically as I reined myself in, remaining still for my female to adjust to my girth. I made her lie down on top of me, one hand caressing her back in a soothing motion while the other held her behind firmly pressed down to increase our pelvic contact as I reactivated my *vylus*.

Her moans in my ears set my blood on fire. I continued to hold off until Rihanna started caressing my chest and kissing my neck. As it was easier for me to thrust up into her than her trying to ride me in that position, I began moving slowly. She was so *jaafing* tight, each stroke was blissfully excruciating, setting my skin ablaze and my loins on fire.

As Rihanna started moving in counterpoint of my movements, meeting me thrust for thrust, I picked up the pace. Soon, my female had straightened as she straddled me, her nails digging into my chest, her head thrown back as she gyrated over me. Yielding to my burning passion, I gripped her behind with both hands, a savage growl rising from my throat as I pounded upwards into my female.

My mate emitted a strangled moan, the nails of her right hand digging further into my flesh with the most exquisite sting, while she began fondling one of her breasts with the other. She was magnificent, bouncing over me, her curly hair disheveled, lips parted to release an endless flow of moans, and her face dissolved in an expression of pure ecstasy.

She cried out my name and would have fallen backwards if not for me holding her up when a violent orgasm slammed into her. Her inner walls clamping down on my cock, gripping it in the most delicious vise, nearly made me come undone. But I wasn't ready to fill her with my seed.

Flipping us around, I slipped my arms behind her knees, spreading her wide open for me. Once more, I barely resisted ramming myself in, but proved far less gentle as I took my female again. She didn't seem to mind, even begging me for more as I began taking her deeper, faster, harder, until her head was rolling from side to side as she writhed beneath me. I lost myself in her, in a maelstrom of pleasure almost too much to bear, until Rihanna climaxed again, this time, sweeping me away with her.

I slammed myself home with a feral roar, liquid bliss

shooting out of me into my mate. My vision blurred and the room spun as wave upon wave of ecstasy crashed over me. Still buried deep, I wrapped my arms around my female's trembling body, keeping her on top of me as I turned onto my back while my bulb swelled, knotting us together. Voluptuous spasms continued to course through me for a while longer as the last of my seed shot out in generous spurts inside my mate.

Destroyed, her breathing labored, Rihanna remained still on top of me. Her head rested on my chest while I gently caressed her back slick with sweat. For the next thirty minutes to one hour, we would be physically locked, my knot seeking to increase the chances my seed would take root.

"Sleep, my little sylphin," I whispered before kissing the top of her head. "You are safe."

CHAPTER 6

RIHANNA

E merging from the best sleep I could recall having in a long time, it took me a second to realize where I was. To my surprise, I was disappointed to find Zatruk no longer present in that mammoth bed of ours.

My face flushed and my body heated as memories of last night flooded my mind. To think I had dreaded my wedding night. Zatruk was a beast. I'd worried he would involuntarily hurt me, if only because of his insane strength and size. Sure, I could still feel a certain soreness from his crazy girth and from when he'd unleashed his passion on me. However, the gentle and careful way he'd handled me still blew my mind.

It was such a contradiction with the violent behavior of his people, clearly eager to come to fists at the first pretext. Zatruk was a teddy bear. A cuddly, fluffy teddy bear trapped in the body of an intimidating, beastly mountain of muscles. While I wasn't sure how I felt about his people, I could see myself falling for my husband in the long run. But it was much too soon to entertain these types of ideas.

However, a different thought demanded my attention. Considering how amazing last night's sex had been, I suspected my mate would frequently want an encore, with me as a more than willing participant. But once we'd both climaxed, Zatruk had knotted with me. In my lust-filled daze, I'd been too far gone to really reflect on that. Frankly, I hadn't expected it. As far as I knew, species with canine traits were the only ones that knotted. And they did so to lock their semen inside their females after release to increase the chances of conception.

I wasn't ready to get pregnant.

Sure, I wanted kids. If I ended up falling in love with Zatruk, I'd have no problem having a few with him. I'd always assumed I'd marry an alien at some point, so having non-human babies didn't trouble me. However, I wanted my children with the right person, with someone I intended to settle down with for the long haul. Now was much too early to make that call about Zatruk. Then again, were we even compatible? Kayog had stated that Zatruk and I were a perfect personality match, but that didn't necessarily mean that we were compatible from a reproductive standpoint.

For now, there was no reason for me to panic. I had a contraceptive implant with still almost two years to go. The question was whether it would be effective against a Yurus. The galactic database got regular updates as to which contraceptives worked with which species, as well as the species for which condoms were the only option. Recently, I had seen such an entry about a primitive species I'd never heard of before: the Ordosians, snake-like people... well, Nagas. Apparently, not only did their semen not care about contraceptives, it even made the female's body consider her contraceptive as an invasive toxin that her immune system attacked as a threat.

We knew too little about the Yurus to say if something similar could happen. In the next couple of days, I would need to go see the human colony's doctor to discuss my options. And then Zatruk and I would have to discuss the subject. Hopefully, that would go down well. At least, I wasn't in the fertile period of my cycle. So, whether my contraceptive worked or not against Zatruk, it wouldn't be an issue for the next few days.

Hoping out of bed, I glanced outside the window, the brightness indicating morning bowed to afternoon a while ago. Sure enough, it was already almost 1:00 PM. I normally woke up early, but it would take me a few days to adjust to Cibbos' time zone.

After a quick visit to the hygiene room to freshen up, I got dressed and went hunting for both food and my husband. The loud sound of voices emanating from the entrance hall immediately had all my senses on high alert. It didn't sound like a brawl, and no one was shouting. However, I could feel the tension all the way from here.

I hastened through the living area, my steps faltering as I caught the silhouette of one of the strongest Yurus I saw fighting yesterday, called Tarmek. I didn't know the name of the other one. Both their expressions were clearly disgruntled. I moved further ahead so that I could also see Zatruk through the large archway leading from the greeting hall to the living area. I wasn't trying to hide my presence, but it didn't feel appropriate to interfere.

"...are growing restless. The Vradrak Clan has initiated some skirmishes against the village of Konruk," Tarmek said, forcefully, his yellow eyes contrasting sharply with his coal skin and almost black fur.

"Your plans must move faster," the other Yurus added. "If a war starts between those two clans, it will spread through the other clans, and it will not stop until massive bloodshed gives us no other choice."

"I am well aware, Gulkis," Zatruk snapped. "You seem to forget *I* have been warning of the looming signs of another Great War."

"Then *act* on it!" Tarmek snarled. "You've been warning about it long before Vyrax's fall, but what have you done about it besides pretty plans on your technology? At least Vyrax tried to take steps!"

My jaw dropped at that attack, and I barely reined in my instinctive urge to step in and defend my man. But Zatruk didn't need me for that, especially since I didn't fully understand what was at stake.

"What Vyrax did was idiotic," Zatruk hissed. "Besides humiliating himself and our entire clan with him, he depleted our resources, burned our bridges with potential trade partners, and weakened our position in Cibbos. We cannot afford another failure, or the bloodbath of another Great War will be the least of our concerns."

"So, we do nothing while you ponder? While half of our clan is spoiling for war? While many are considering challenging your leadership?"

My blood turned to ice as a sense of dread washed over me. If other clansmen were indeed looking to dethrone Zatruk, I didn't doubt for a minute that Tarmek featured among them. And by the murderous expression on Zatruk's face, I could tell he knew it as well. The anger of the other Yurus, apparently named Gulkis, appeared to turn to wariness, as if he expected his Chieftain to lunge at his companion. I held my breath, waiting for the same.

Instead, his gaze never straying from Tarmek's face, my husband reached for a small pouch on the belt of his loincloth. He retrieved a tiny, whitish thing that resembled a petal from where I stood. He brought it to his mouth, and started slowly chewing it. Tarmek's aggressive stance shifted to contempt as he gave Zatruk a slow once over. Fury boiled in my veins. If I had a dagger or blaster handy, I'd have the son of a bitch become intimately acquainted with it for such disrespect.

"Praxilla... always praxilla," Tarmek said with disdain. "You may hide behind it, but beware how much you try to push it on the rest of us. We are warriors! That thing makes us weak!"

"That *thing* is the only reason why that ugly, overly inflated head of yours is still attached to your neck," Zatruk said in a cold and controlled voice that gave me chills. "With or without praxilla, I will gladly take on any who would challenge me and take great pleasure in demolishing them. And the day *you* do, be warned that I will show you no mercy."

Tarmek grimaced in anger. Although he didn't back down, a sliver of hesitation flitted through his yellow eyes. I realized then that he wasn't certain he could win against Zatruk. He opened his mouth to respond, but stopped himself, his eyes flicking towards me as he finally noticed my presence. I swallowed hard, resisting the urge to squirm when the two other males turned to look at me.

"We shall leave you to your new mate," Gulkis said, looking almost relieved things didn't escalate further.

"Indeed," Tarmek said, anger still brewing in his voice. "But remember, Great Chieftain, we can only brawl among ourselves for so long."

Without another word, he turned on his hooves and walked out, Gulkis on his tail, quietly closing the heavy front doors behind him. Zatruk continued glaring at the doors for a few more seconds before turning to me, his face taking on a troubled expression when he noticed the worry on mine.

"What was that?" I asked, making no effort to hide my concern.

He sighed and waved a dismissive hand. "I will tell you in a minute. How are you feeling this morning?"

I wanted to insist but let it go, since he stated he would enlighten me soon. "I'm fine. I'm great. I slept wonderfully."

He was hinting at more than that, likely wanting to make sure he hadn't roughed me up too much, but my answer appeared to satisfy him.

"I'm glad to hear it. I... also slept wonderfully."

I smiled, suddenly feeling a little timid at what I believed was his indirect way of saying he enjoyed our night together. His ears flicked, and he averted his eyes for a second, making me wonder if he, too, was feeling a little embarrassed.

"But you must be starving. It's already quite late in the day," Zatruk said.

"Yes. I could probably eat an entire krogi by myself," I conceded, sheepishly.

He smiled and came towards me. "Good. Your meal has been waiting for you on a plate heater."

He carefully took my hand and led me to the table in the living area. He made me sit in front of three temperature-controlled covered plates. To my surprise, Zatruk caressed my hair with the softest expression I'd ever seen on his face. He leaned down, kissed my forehead, then uncovered the dishes for me.

"Eat, my mate," he said. "I'll be right back."

He went to the bar located at the back of the room, and poured himself some kind of drink in a metal mug bigger than my head. I took a bite of the juicy, spicy red meat on my plate, while observing my man. Then a large ornate trunk on the counter drew my attention.

"What is that?" I asked, gesturing at it with my chin. "I don't recall seeing it before."

Zatruk looked at the trunk and nodded. "Because it arrived for you this morning."

"For me?" I exclaimed, my eyes widening with curiosity. "From who?"

Picking it up with one hand as if it weighed nothing, his drink held in the other, Zatruk came back and placed the trunk on top of the table. He then sat next to me.

"It's a wedding gift from Luana Torres. She's the human colony's doctor, and the daughter of their leader, Mateo Torres."

"Really?! Wow, that's super sweet of her," I said, rising to my feet to go check out what goodies I'd received.

Zatruk frowned. "You should finish your meal."

"Pfft, eating can wait. Do you really think hunger could supersede a woman's curiosity? MY curiosity?"

Zatruk chuckled. "Fair point."

The craftsmanship on that wooden trunk, highly ornate with swirling bas-relief pattern, was simply breathtaking. In itself, the box was a worthy gift. A simple rotating lock mechanism on top allowed me to open it. To my surprise, the top folded on the side, revealing two compartments which, when slid sideways, became trays that gave access to two more compartments at the bottom.

Each of the four sections contained themed gifts. The first one was medicine, from painkillers, to hyposprays against severe allergic reaction and the most common poisons, healing creams, and intelligent bandages, to name a few. The second one contained hygiene items from natural soaps and hair products, to skin, nail and dental care, including antiperspirant and tampons.

Judging by the confused look Zatruk cast on some of these things—especially the feminine hygiene stuff—he had obviously no clue what purpose they served. But he was pleased by my reaction to seeing them. It made me all the happier to have this human colony nearby that could cater to the needs the Yurus probably wouldn't be able to. As tiny as I was, when my period came rolling in, it was a freaking deluge. Tampons couldn't be a greater blessing.

The third compartment contained a couple of summer dresses, perfect for the warm weather of Cibbos, and a couple of nightgowns—sexy enough to want to parade in it in front of my man but not so much they'd be deemed vulgar. I instantly got a gut feeling Luana would have included panties and bras but didn't want to push it. Considering the clothes she'd sent were exactly my size, either the stuck-up Counselor Allan had informed her—which I highly doubted—or Kayog had spilled the beans.

I was convinced of the latter. He wanted peace among the

local population. What better way than for a friendship to blossom between the daughter of the leader of one faction and the wife of the leader of the other?

But the last compartment was actually the one that made me squeal with joy. Chocolate! All kinds of chocolates! Pralines, nougat, and a variety of sweets. Did I say chocolate? Yep, Luana and I would definitely become besties.

I picked up the little holocard included in the package. I activated it, and a holographic projection of a pretty woman appeared.

"Hello, Ms. Makeba.

My name is Luana Torres, the medical doctor of Kastan. On behalf of the people of the human colony, please accept our warmest welcome to Cibbos. We hope you will find this little gift useful as you adapt to our world. Should you ever require medical assistance catering to your specific human needs, I will be more than happy to be of service. Similarly, we will gladly provide you with anything else you may require that could otherwise not be available to you, including and beyond the products included in this gift.

We wish you great happiness in this new life you are starting and extend our friendship to you. Feel free to visit us whenever you wish.

Best regards."

The image of the hologram faded, and the card auto-deactivated.

"That is so very nice. I can't deny that it's great for me to have humans nearby, and especially a doctor," I said sheepishly, while putting everything back inside the trunk and carefully closing it.

"Indeed," Zatruk said with a nod. "She could make a very good friend for you."

I tilted my head to the side, intrigued by the way he

continued to stare at the trunk. "What is it? Does something about this bother you? Do you think it's not genuine?"

"No. While it is undoubtedly a smart political move from the humans, I am certain Luana would have sent you such a package and invitation regardless. She is a nurturer. Taking care of others is a visceral need in her, even the enemy who sought to enslave her people."

"You mean your ex-leader? Vyrax, I think?" I asked.

Zatruk nodded, took a large sip of his drink, then heavily sat down.

"That bad?" I asked in a commiserating voice, before resuming my seat in front of my plates.

He grunted. "No worse than it's been before. Just the same pathetic cycle repeating itself."

"You mean, that Great War Tarmek was alluding to?" I asked before taking a bite of my food, which was still surprisingly warm.

He nodded. "The Yurus are restless. When my people get bored, they fight. And if they get too bored, they war. We have a genetic need to battle."

"Genetic?" I asked, baffled.

"Have you noticed how none of us wear armor?" he asked.

"Yeah, but you're all at home. Sure, you brawl, but there isn't a war."

"Even during wars, we do not wear armor. We'll have bracers, a weapons belt, and other accessories that may hold more weapons, but no armor," he explained. "We don't need it, because our bones are stronger than your Kevlar. The more we fight, the stronger we get. We also regenerate quickly, and our wounds and bruises mend in record time."

My eyes widened as I gazed at his chest, as if I could see those unbreakable bones through his flesh.

He chuckled at my reaction. "Each blow we receive triggers

the release of testosterone and serotonin, which reinforces our bones and grows our muscles, but also fuels our aggression."

"You mean, you guys are mountains of muscles like that not because you're pumping iron all day, but because your hormones make them bulge every time you get slapped or punched?" I asked, disbelievingly.

Zatruk snorted. "I'm not sure what pumping iron means. And while you oversimplified it, yes, fighting makes our muscles grow. When our testosterone levels become too low, we get the instinctive urge to fight to get our levels back up. The more we fight, the bigger and the stronger we become."

"But you plateau at some point?" I argued.

"Not quite. Technically, we could keep going indefinitely. However, the stronger we get, the more powerful the damage we receive must be in order to trigger the testosterone release," Zatruk clarified. "For example, even if you punched me with all your might, it wouldn't be enough. But if you shot me, that would."

"Jeez! So, that's why they're always brawling? They need to get roughed up by a bunch of strong, adult males to get their hormones going?"

Zatruk nodded. "Yes. But the closer a male gets to the mid-thirties and early forties, brawling no longer suffices, which causes them to enter into blood rage. As you likely noticed, we do not brawl to maim or injure, merely to render unconscious or to beat into submission."

"Yeah, as much as all that fighting baffles me, I was relieved to see the males still exercised some restraint," I conceded.

"Well, we are entering the generational period where a majority of our males are reaching the blood rage phase," Zatruk said with a tired voice. "Their need to fight will transcend everything, even the bonds of friendship and family. They will battle to the death if needed, until they've managed to maintain their hormonal levels high enough for at least ten days to break the rage."

"My God," I whispered. "This sounds like drug addicts going through severe withdrawals who will do anything for their next fix."

"An apt comparison."

"But how do you contain it?" I asked, even though I could already guess where this story was headed.

"We don't. The first clan to give in will turn its rage on another clan. That will spread to another, and then another, and then all the clans will be engaged in a Great War where they will slaughter each other. During that time, our females will hide with our juveniles looking after them."

"What's left after that?"

"Death and ruins," he said, sounding tired. "Our males are too violent and too busy fighting to study, to focus on things such as science, philosophy, and art. Aside from brawling, our males are all adept at smithing, building, and hunting as they are the type of physical exertions that can compensate, at least for a while. Therefore, almost everything we have achieved technology-wise is thanks to our females. They are our brains. But every advance they make is set back by the raids and the wars that kill my people."

I reached for him and gently caressed his forearm in a comforting gesture.

"Surely, there is something, a treatment that can help control that rage?" I asked.

He fished out another white leaf from his pouch to show me. "This is a praxilla petal. It helps silence the rage and the urge to battle. Our head scientist, Jerdea, was the one to discover its pacifying properties. She tried to prove that, thanks to it, we males could also become thinkers instead of brawlers by giving it to her son as he was growing up."

"Oh boy, why do I feel a tragedy coming?" I asked before eating some of my vegetables.

"Well, it worked to the extent that he did study instead of fighting. However, it impeded his growth. It made him weak and prone to injuries, including bad fractures. You see, while large amounts of testosterone make us strong and muscular, an extensive deprivation before we reach maturity makes our bones brittle, our fractures slow to mend or heal badly, and causes us to remain scrawny. Lack of fighting actually causes deformity."

"Oh no! So, her son is deformed?" I asked, my heart breaking for both the boy and his mother.

He hesitated. "Not in a visible way. After a really bad injury that almost left him permanently disabled, Jerdea stopped giving praxilla to him. Her son went to the other extreme, fighting and brawling at every opportunity. But it was already too late."

"He remained scrawny?"

Zatruk shook his head. "No, he did grow big and strong, but the injury didn't properly heal, and our healers cannot mend him."

I froze, understanding suddenly dawning on me. "Wonjin? Wonjin is her son, isn't he?"

"Yes."

"Oh God," I whispered to myself. I pressed my hands to my cheeks, feeling even more horrible I had exploited his disability to make the point that I wouldn't be bullied.

"As you can guess, that situation has made our males extremely reluctant to use praxilla. But it is safe when used wisely and parsimoniously instead of constantly like Jerdea had done with her son. Its consumption should also be scaled over time based on age. For mature adults like me, pretty much at the maximum of our strength, taking it all the time isn't a threat. It doesn't affect our ability to battle, it simply dampens the urge to do so."

Unable to swallow another bite, I pushed my plate, still

partially full. "Is that the plan Tarmek was referring to? Are you trying to convince the Yurus to eat praxilla to prevent the next Great War?"

Zatruk shook his head and ran his hand over his beard. "No. Our males *need* to battle. *I* need to battle to a level higher than what brawling can provide. I suggested building a massive arena where we could run the most brutal gladiator battles. We would hold a series of themed galactic tournaments where we could face off against the best off-worlder warriors."

My eyes widened when I heard the simple but elegant solution. "That totally makes sense. I've seen some of those gladiator tournaments, and they are *savage*! I can't think of a better way for you guys to get that aggression out on people who can dish out as much as they can take. So, why didn't you guys proceed with that?"

"The prize," Zatruk said, sounding a little discouraged. "We have nothing of value to offer the people in order to lure them here. We thought deutenium weapons and armor would suffice, but the mercenaries said they wouldn't do. They convinced Vyrax that the Zelconians's crystals would guarantee our success."

"*That* was the reason behind the war?" I exclaimed, disbelieving.

"It was more the excuse. Vyrax was interested in the arena, but he was impatient. Even if all the clans came together to build the arena, it would take months. Months during which he would have to negotiate an agreement with the birds. As he didn't have a single diplomatic bone in his body, he figured it would be easier to simply take what he wanted. First, enslave the humans so we didn't have to waste time with battle free raids to steal their produce. Second, use their stable of zeebises to launch an attack on Synsara, the Zelconian mountain city, to take possession of their crystals."

"And I'm guessing that didn't work out how he planned," I said, grimacing.

"It never had a chance. It was a dumb plan from the start. Even with us riding zeebises, the Zelconians are masters at air combat. And then, you need a specialized Zelconian to imbue the crystals with the powers we would have wanted," Zatruk said with annoyance. "Sure, we can still make the crystals without one of them, but they would have been subpar. And you can't enslave a Zelconian. Not only are they empaths, with a simple stare, they can plunge you into the most horrendous nightmare that will have you clawing your own eyes out. And that's not even mentioning their technological advances, which are far superior to ours."

I whistled between my teeth. "Doesn't sound like people you would want to get on the bad side of."

"Exactly. And then Kayog orchestrated a marriage between Luana and a Zelconian hybrid a week before Vyrax's planned attack," Zatruk added.

"And that alliance made victory against the humans impossible!" I exclaimed, finally getting a clear portrait of the situation. "Where does that leave you and the plan for the arena?"

"Even further behind than where we started," Zatruk said, matter-of-factly. "Although we have a truce with the humans and Zelconians, we're not exactly on friendly terms. The mercenaries no longer wish to do business with us. We still do not have any type of prize that could lure people to our arenas. Our deutenium is apparently worthless, and the Yurus currency even more so on the galactic stage. Until I can convince my people that gladiators will come, they will refuse to start building the arena. But with each passing day, we get closer to the start of the next Great War. I must figure out that reward, and fast."

I nodded slowly, my wheels spinning. "Deutenium isn't worthless. That I know for a fact. Scaled to galactic standards, there will be demand for your weapons. But will it be enough for a battle arena prize? I don't know. Give me a couple of days to get in touch with some of my contacts. Worse case, you can always trade your weapons or sell them in exchange for something that could make a good prize. Either way, we'll figure it out. Kayog paired us for a reason."

Zatruk smiled and gently caressed my cheek. "Kayog did say that both you and your dowry would help us solve our issues. But it is my duty to fix this, not yours. While I am not too proud to accept genuine assistance when offered, this is not why I married you, my little sylphin. I accepted this bond because you are my soulmate. In that, a Temern is never wrong."

"What's a sylphin?" I asked, touched and embarrassed by his words.

A strange expression crossed his features, quickly replaced by that fiendish grin I'd come to recognize as him preparing to make a smartass comment. "A sylphin is a tiny little creature from the forest."

I glared at him and opened my mouth to reply, but a powerful knock at the door silenced me. I stood up while Zatruk headed to the entrance.

"A shuttle from the United Planets Organization is approaching," said a Yurus male voice I didn't recognize, the sound muffled by the distance.

"Probably my mate's belongings," Zatruk said. "We'll be right there."

I hurried to the entrance hall. My husband extended a hand towards me. I took it and let him lead me outside, my head buzzing with a million thoughts about prizes. Kayog believed I could help. Somehow, I would. And first, it started with finding out why the mercs had not wanted the deutenium.

CHAPTER 7
ZATRUK

How humiliating to have to confess to my mate just how pathetic my people were. And yet, it had been a necessity. Not only did I not want to keep any secret from Rihanna, I owed as much to her. The upcoming weeks and months would likely grow quite tense and volatile. I couldn't risk having her blindsided if violence erupted.

Still, my heart warmed with affection for my tiny human. I had feared horror and contempt from her as I revealed how the species whose males prided themselves as being the greatest warriors of the galaxy were in fact slaves to their endocrine system. But not my Rihanna. She had only expressed compassion and a genuine desire to help me find a solution.

My clanmates would mock me for entertaining the idea of a female's assistance in solving matters of war and combat. They were fools. Aside from the fact that my mate had proven her knowledge both by putting Wonjin on his ass but also in evaluating my weapons, she knew things we didn't and sorely needed. She had lived her entire life with off-worlders, had precious contacts that could be valuable to us, and could enlighten us in ways of luring competitors here.

But beyond that, our females were the sole reason the Yurus still had an even remotely functional society. I valued their insights and advice as they were the only people here I could have any type of serious brainstorming with that didn't quickly devolve in how best to crack skulls. And although I'd just met my little sylphin, I already knew that with her, too, I could have meaningful intellectual conversations... when I wasn't too busy pestering her.

The UPO shuttle began its descent as we were approaching the plaza. Its size surprised me, and I immediately began wondering just how many items my mate had brought, and especially their nature. Would she fill the house with pretty flowers, cute paintings, and other delicate and pointless things my research on human females hinted at?

The pilot made a flawless landing while the clan gathered around with undisguised curiosity. My eyes widened in shock when Wonjin approached us with a hovering platform. A nice forethought as it would allow us to more easily carry Rihanna's belongings to my dwelling without holding the UPO agents longer than necessary. I gave him a stiff nod by lifting my chin up. He responded in a similar fashion, although the flicking of his ears revealed his embarrassment at my approval.

Two far-too-handsome human males—identical twins—disembarked from the shuttle, beaming at my female. For the dumbest reason, I wrapped a possessive arm around Rihanna and drew her to my side. By the way the edges of their identical eyes creased with amusement, the wretches had obviously guessed as to what had prompted my gesture. I wanted to bash their pretty faces in. But I plastered a neutral expression on my face as they approached us.

"Hello, Mrs. Makeba. I'm Evan, and this is my brother Eric. The Prime Mating Agency has requested we bring you your personal belongings."

"Yes, thank you so much!" Rihanna replied with a grin.

"Would it be okay for us to unload them onto this hover platform?" he asked, pointing at it with his chin.

Rihanna hesitated.

"Yes, thank you," I replied in her stead.

"Very well. Coming right up," he said with the same enthusiasm.

They had a tanned skin that made their piercing green eyes stand out. Although muscular, they weren't bulky with bulging muscles like ours. They were shorter than me, but likely what Rihanna would have deemed a more comfortable height for a partner for her. And their golden mane framed their pretty faces like a halo, the wavy locks bouncing over their shoulders as they walked.

Although my female stared at them as they opened the hold of the shuttle, the glimmer in her eyes held none of the heat they usually contained as she gazed upon me when we coupled. The excitement she currently displayed had nothing to do with those males, but with recovering things she valued. My unusual reaction baffled and embarrassed me. I'd never been the jealous or possessive type. But then, I'd never been married, least of all to a fascinating human who could possibly leave me in a year's time.

I would make sure that never happened.

I stared in disbelief at the number of containers the twins had managed to pack in that hold. With an unexpected strength and efficiency, they brought out the crates and carefully laid them on the hover platform. Squealing and clapping her hands with an almost juvenile enthusiasm, Rihanna circled around the platform to start reading the labels on each crate, muttering joyful comments about each. I couldn't help but smile at such silly happiness.

When Evan pulled out a silver crate, my mate nearly lost it. As soon as he had it down, she opened it and pulled out two blades. The amused expressions of the clan quickly switched to a more focused attention. Weapons were a language they spoke and a topic that highly interested them. As every single Yurus male trained as a blacksmith, seeing new blades and the technique used to craft them always drew us.

"Now *that's* what I call a properly-sized blade!" Rihanna exclaimed before starting to manipulate them with great dexterity.

She spun them around, performing some kind of acrobatic gestures with them, even tossing one in the air then flawlessly catching it before flowing into more acrobatics. It was impressive, even though she was clearly showing off.

I approached the crate and picked another blade inside the neatly organized container. I grunted in approval at the obvious care and respect with which my female treated her weapons. I admired the blade under every angle.

"The craftsmanship is better than decent," I mused out loud, "but far from perfect. However, it is impressively light."

Tarmek snorted. "It looks baby-sized, like a child's training weapon."

Rihanna stopped performing her acrobatics to glare at Tarmek the way you would someone who'd just said something completely stupid—which was likely the case.

"It's not baby-sized," my mate replied in a stern voice. "By galactic standards, this is the normal size and weight for a blade of this length. This is the most-commonly sought-after model for throwable blades."

Tarmek huffed with contempt. "Then it sounds like galactic warriors are nothing more than suckling babes, if that's all they can handle."

The spark of anger ignited low in my belly, not only because he was trying to mock my mate by his comments, but also because he was trying to undermine my efforts to bring the battle arenas to Cibbos by implying that off-worlder warriors wouldn't be worthy opponents.

However, before my mate or I could reply, Wonjin intervened.

"What *you* think is irrelevant, Tarmek. What matters is what *they* want. If the majority of planets in the allied galaxies think this is the ideal size and format for those blades, then they must have a reason that clearly escapes you."

"Shut up, idiot!" Tarmek snapped, shoving Wonjin who stumbled back but managed to remain standing.

As was his wont, Wonjin rushed Tarmek, even knowing he didn't stand a chance against him.

"Cut it out!" I shouted as the two males exchanged a couple of punches.

They complied with much reluctance. But just as Wonjin was stepping away, Tarmek smacked him one last time behind the head while mumbling some insult in Yurusian. Wonjin turned back to hiss at Tarmek baring his fangs, although he didn't attack again.

I took a step forward with a low, menacing growl, my furious gaze leveled squarely on Tarmek. He lifted his chin defiantly, but kept his mouth shut. He was becoming a problem that I would soon need to address. The sad part was that Tarmek wasn't necessarily rotten. However, blood rage was slowly getting the best of him, drowning any rational thought or shred of decency he once possessed. If only he would eat praxilla petals...

"Check this out!" Rihanna suddenly exclaimed, deliberately pulling our attention away from the thickening tension. "I'm going to rock your hooves!"

Rock my hooves?

That expression made no sense whatsoever, but the way she'd spoken it implied she intended to impress me... or the clan as a whole. She put down her blades and retrieved some kind of extensible wooden pole one of the twins had brought out of the shuttle. My female walked a short distance away, and placed it on the ground. Some kind of base deployed around it, keeping the pole upright.

She came back, picked up the two blades she'd been showing off with and an additional two, holding a pair in each hand. Rihanna went to stand about ten meters away from the pole. She winked at me, then threw all four blades at it in quick succession, alternating between hands. Not only did the weapons find their mark on the narrow pole, they were perfectly aligned, with the same five-centimeter gap between them.

My brows shot up, reflecting the stunned expression on the faces of my brethren. "Impressive," I conceded in all sincerity.

Sure, the target had been stationary, but it still displayed her great aim, the difficulty further increased by the speed at which she threw them, and the fact that she used both her left and right hands. Few people showed this much accuracy with their non-dominant hand.

"I told you that with proper weapons, I would rock it," she replied smugly.

Her use of the word "rock" was totally confusing to me. When she first said she'd rock my hooves, I'd assumed the expression meant impress me. But now, she was saying she'd rocked throwing the blades. Clearly, she didn't mean 'impress' them.

However, another excited shout from my female put an end to my musings as to her weird speech.

"Oh, my God! YOGI!!" Rihanna shouted, hopping on her feet while clapping her hands. "I can't believe they got my speeder back, too!"

For a split second, I wondered if my mate was referring to some sort of a pet. Then I saw one of the twins leading some kind of small hovering metal vessel.

"Speeder?" I asked, baffled as to the purpose of the vessel.

"One of the most popular solo transportation devices in the galaxy," Rihanna replied enthusiastically. "Yogi cost me a fortune. It can attain a maximum altitude of twelve meters, two more than the standard ten. It can reach a speed of four hundred kilometers per hour. It has state-of-the-art stabilizers, a 360 degrees environmental and thermal shield to keep you comfortable even in the harshest environments, and an autopilot that can hook to pretty much any GPS system."

My people and I stared at her with the same confused look as she gushed over what apparently were great features for the device.

Eric—or was it Evan?—whistled with admiration. "Wow! I thought it looked pretty awesome, but I didn't realize you truly had it fully decked out. You got the shield, but did you get the beam upgrades, too?"

"You bet! Well... I had the beams ordered. The ports and hooks are already in place, as you can see," she added, pointing at the front of the speeder. "I wanted some customizations done. Sadly, things kind of got complicated before I could receive them."

The male chuckled with sympathy. I instantly wondered just how much he knew about what had led Rihanna here.

"Well, you're really lucky to have recovered it," Eric said. "Gems like these usually 'vanish' the moment they arrive in an impound."

"I know! That's why I can't believe it's here. I've really been blessed."

"That you are. Well, this completes our task. We wish you the very best, Mrs. Makeba," the male said while his brother closed the hold.

"Thanks a lot, guys. I really appreciate it," Rihanna said with genuine gratitude.

They waved, hopped back inside their shuttle, and took off.

"So, how does that work?" I asked, indicating with my chin the speeder she called Yogi.

"Watch and be amaaaazed!" she said teasingly before turning to look at the crowd gathered around us. "Clear the way!"

Everyone complied, moving all to one side to make room for her. Rihanna straddled the machine, placing her feet on some sort of supports on each side, and leaning forward to hold on to a pair of handles near the front.

The speeder made a discreet whooshing sound before hovering a little higher above ground, then it darted forward. A collective gasp escaped us at the speed with which it took off. For half a second, I feared my mate would crash into one of the buildings ahead, but she smoothly made a sharp turn right less than a meter from it. She turned around and came back our way, rushing past us at dizzying speed, while climbing ever so higher. I had to bend my neck all the way back to be able to watch her fly above us. She then hovered back down while returning to the center of the square, then dismounted with a smug grin on her face.

"It is an interesting device. Certainly fast... But a krogi is better as it can battle with you," Gulkis said.

Rihanna shrugged. "If you need help fighting, sure. But when traveling long distances in hostile places, this is far better. It auto-drives while you sleep. It automatically avoids obstacles. It can fly over bodies of water, difficult terrains, including mountains. It regulates the temperature when you activate the thermal shield to protect the rider from extreme cold or heat. Unlike a krogi, it doesn't need to eat, pee, or rest."

"Would galactic gladiators be interested in such a device as a prize?" Wonjin asked.

"Gladiators want weapons, you idiot," Gulkis said, smacking him in the back of the head.

Wonjin punched him in response, making him stumble back into Trogar. Immediately triggered, Trogar shoved him away, prompting Gulkis to turn around and backhand him. Within seconds, a dozen males had joined the melee as another brawl began.

I rolled my eyes and shook my head in discouragement while Rihanna gaped in shock. "Let's take your things home," I said, setting the hover platform to follow.

I took my mate back to our dwelling, temporarily leaving the hover platform carrying her crates inside the great hall. I then led her back out to show her the side entrance to the forge through which I normally had deutenium ore delivered. As it didn't make sense to stable her speeder with the krogis, I made some space for her to park it here instead.

The whole way there, and as my female secured her vehicle inside the forge, I kept stealing glances at the device, Wonjin's words replaying in my mind. Could gladiators truly be interested in something like that? It was undeniably a fast form of ground transport. Some of the benefits Rihanna outlined sounded very handy. But how was transport appealing to a warrior? My mate said she paid a lot for it, and the reaction of the UPO twins expressed serious envy and admiration. Still, I wasn't entirely convinced it would suffice to lure the type of fighters we wanted.

At a glance, I believed I could build something similar with deutenium, at least the chassis, frame, and all of the metal parts. Could Jerdea reverse-engineer the engine and onboard computer? I would need to discuss it with our head scientist.

However, Rihanna's weapons held my attention far more than the speeder. They were extremely light and thin, yet sturdy. Deutenium often proved ridiculously temperamental to work with. It required a great deal of strength and mastery to mold. Could that be the reason the mercenaries hadn't wanted it? Had their smiths been unable to bend the metal to their will? Even among us, many Yurus would struggle to craft flawless human weapons... or rather weapons meeting galactic standards in terms of lightness and size.

A worthy challenge.

If Rihanna was right in saying deutenium was sought after, but that off-worlders simply didn't know how to manipulate it, this could be the opportunity I needed... *we* needed. This gave me new hope. I would build a set of such weapons and see how my mate responded to them.

But first, I helped her unpack her belongings, gladly showing off my strength as I carried her crates around the dwelling. I offered to use one of the guest rooms to turn it into an office for her, but she declined, more than content to simply have a small workspace in my own office. Anyway, according to her, she usually slouched somewhere while working on her laptop.

I rearranged part of my armory to accommodate her impressive weapons collection. Having them nearby would further help me in recreating an enhanced version of them. I was already planning an expansion of the armory for all the new weapons I would be crafting.

The number of clothes, undergarments, and footwear my mate possessed left me speechless. I stopped counting the number of crates I carried up to our room, stacking a couple inside the walk-in closet and lining the others by the walls.

"Hmm, don't worry about these. I can handle them," Rihanna said, looking self-conscious after I picked up one piece of garment from a crate.

I stared at the mostly transparent, flimsy piece with see-through patterns my mate had called lace, before looking back questioningly at her. "I do not mind assisting you."

"Yeah, I appreciate that but... hmm... A woman prefers handling her unmentionables on her own."

"Unmentionables? Is that what this tiny piece of garment is called?" I asked, lifting it up before my eyes to better study it. "It looks meant to cover your breasts, although the lack of opacity wouldn't hide much."

"It's a bra! It's meant to be sexy while providing boob

support. People aren't supposed to see it," Rihanna said, looking mightily embarrassed before yanking her bra out of my grasp.

"What's the point of making it sexy if it isn't meant to be seen?" I asked, tilting my head to the side.

"It's supposed to be seen by our partner or lover only," she said, shoving it back into the crate that contained a slew of similar tiny strips of see-through clothes, some of them in luxurious fabrics. "Otherwise, it's covered by our regular clothes."

"Does that mean you are wearing a sexy bra for your husband beneath your regular clothes?" I asked, my voice dipping lower as my gaze settled on her breasts.

Rihanna had not stripped in front of me last night. She'd gone from her full clothes to that sheer nightgown after she showered. With the leather top she had worn yesterday, and the different leather one she had on today, it was hard to tell what hid beneath it.

"A woman always wears a bra if she wants to avoid the detrimental long-term effects of gravity," Rihanna mumbled, looking embarrassed.

"You're avoiding the question," I teased. "Do you have a sexy bra on for me, my mate? Show me?"

My female gave me an aggravated look laced with embarrassment that made me want to chuckle and further needle her.

"In case you haven't noticed, we're here to unpack these crates, not for me to strip for you," Rihanna said with a frown, turning away from me to pull out yet another leather outfit from the crate she'd been working on, then hanging it next to the previous one.

"Why so timid?" I asked, both because I was having a blast teasing her but also out of genuine confusion. "Why are you so reluctant to show me your breasts covered with a bra? As I recall, I saw them naked last night. I also played with them with my hands, mouth, and tongue."

"Zatruk! That's enough out of you!" Rihanna snapped, her

fists on her hips as she glared at me.

Jaafan! I loved that fire in her eyes. I wished she would jump on me. Too bad she didn't have claws to 'teach me to behave.'

I held her gaze unwaveringly, a slow grin stretching my lips. "Just so you know, I will lick them again tonight."

"That's it. Get out!" she shouted, pointing an angry finger outside of the walk-in.

"But I'm merely stating the truth!"

"I said out!" she exclaimed, throwing one of her leather pants at my face.

I caught it and burst out laughing. I set it down on top of one of the crates only to have Rihanna shoving me out. She might as well have tried to push a mountain, but I played along, pretending like her strength actually sufficed to make me move.

"Fine, be that way," I said, still laughing.

Looking mockingly at her over my shoulder, I flicked my tail upwards so the bristles at the tip tickled her cheek.

"ARGH!" Rihanna shouted, giving it a solid swipe.

The wonderful sting resonated directly in my loins. I wished she'd do it again. But I knew better than to press my luck further... this time.

"Next time, I'll chop it off," she said, watching me leave.

I turned around to look at her, arms spread as I continued to walk backwards towards the door. "Come at me anytime, my mate. I look forward to that tumble."

The aggravated expression on her face had me turned on beyond words. Yes, I really liked that compact bundle of sass and attitude that was my little sylphin. I couldn't wait for us to have angry sex.

On my way out, I paused one last time. "Dinner should be served in the next twenty minutes or so. See you then, my mate."

She uttered under her breath a series of curse words in whatever her native language was and went back to work as I made my way downstairs.

CHAPTER 8
RIHANNA

As much as Zatruk had annoyed me, I wasn't actually mad. I couldn't decide if I wanted to kick his ass or kiss him. There was always something sexy in the way he teased me. And the way he looked at me when I ordered him to get out, I could have sworn he'd considered further provoking me so that I would jump him. Was that what he wanted?

However, it was my own prudish reaction that baffled me. As he'd so accurately pointed out, considering all the naughty things we had done last night and all the places his hands and mouth had been on me, blushing over undies was silly. And yet, I kind of had reasons to.

I examined my clothes, and it once more dawned on me how unsuitable they were for Cibbos. I'd bought the sexy negligee I wore last night on the fancy transport ship Kayog had booked for me. But now, as I gave my existing undies collection a critical assessment, I could see how unsexy and mostly tired half of it was. I'd been single for a while, and it showed. The rest of my clothes were functional hunter stuff. With my petite stature, I'd mostly bought outfits with a hard edge to make me look badass instead of cutely feminine and delicate.

The couple of dresses the human doctor had sent me were beautiful and better suited the Cibbos' hot climate. While I didn't intend to go all girly-girl all of a sudden, I could use a change of style. The Yurus females all looked super sexy with their crop tops and loincloths. I looked like a pocket-sized armored tank.

In the morning, I'd check in with the Yurus seamstresses and go visit the humans. For now, I hurried to put away all my granny panties and other undies to spare myself further teasing from my wretch of a husband. I put away a few more things then called it good for now. Between my stomach clamoring for food and the lingering jetlag manifesting itself, I would take it easy for the evening and finish unpacking in the morning.

I made my way down to find the head cook Relven on her way out. She waved me goodbye with a gentle smile that warmed my heart. I had wondered what kind of welcome the Yurus females would grant me. I hadn't really had a chance to interact with them, only from a certain distance. The real test would be tomorrow. But so far, I'd thankfully not perceived any hostility from them.

I eyed Zatruk warily, wondering if he would continue teasing me, but he merely gestured at the covered dishes on the table. The delectable aroma emanating from them had my stomach rumbling with anticipation. Zatruk sat down as I approached. I settled next to him in the same seat I'd eaten breakfast at this morning. He gave me a strange look.

"What?" I asked.

He stared at me with an unreadable expression for a few seconds before shaking his head. He uncovered the dishes, and my mouth watered.

"You know, I can get used to having gourmet meals home delivered daily," I said, eyeing greedily the bounty laid out before us.

Zatruk snorted. "There's no reason for you not to."

"Tell me about yourself," I asked. "I want to know everything about how little Zatruk grew up into the fluffy mountain of muscles that now rules the Yurus of Cibbos."

He gave me a mean sideways glare that made me grin at him before I started filling my plate with a mix of everything.

"My youth was pretty standard. Study, fight, train blacksmithing, fight some more, and hunt. Repeat everything," Zatruk said with a shrug. "Things only changed once I reached puberty, since I have albinism."

I stiffened, outraged anger on his behalf ready to surge to the fore. "Why? They bullied you for being different?"

He chuckled. "No, I didn't get bullied for it, but I did get attacked more frequently."

I frowned in confusion. "How is that not being bullied?"

"According to my people, a person with albinism is either blessed or cursed," Zatruk explained. "Once I matured, many attacked me in the hopes of earning the title of having defeated the 'Chosen One.' But they all failed, making me stronger instead. I even had people from other clans come challenge me."

He laughed seeing my horrified expression and gently caressed my cheek with the back of his hand.

"It *was* a great honor," Zatruk insisted. "My reputation as invincible spread throughout the clans, therefore reinforcing the idea that I was indeed the Chosen One. It's also the reason why Vyrax never challenged me."

"Could you have beaten him?" I asked, genuinely curious.

"Of course," he replied, looking at me as if I had said something offensive, which made me smile. "I didn't challenge him back then because he had the loyalty of the other clans and was open to finding a solution to our blood rage issues. His father was only one of four adult males that survived the last Great War, which occurred when we were barely five years old. He made all of us younglings and juveniles swear back then that we would end this. But Vyrax was an idiot."

"A bona fide idiot or just a victim of blood rage?" I asked.

"I do not know the meaning of that word, but yes, a real idiot, although the onset of blood rage made it worse," he replied. "And now that I am the Great Chieftain, that Chosen One superstition is resurfacing."

I nodded in understanding. "If you find a solution, you confirm that you were indeed the Chosen One. But if you fail…"

"I am a Curse," he finished in my stead.

"Well, Fluffy Chosen One, you've got your work cut out for you! Make it happen!"

Right on cue, he gave me what should have been a terribly intimidating glare. Instead, it made me grin and got my girly bits standing to attention.

"You know, I will spank that bad habit out of you," he said in a growling tone.

I shamelessly batted my eyes at him and spread my arms wide in a provoking way. "How did you say that earlier? Oh yeah… Come at me anytime, my mate. I look forward to that tumble."

Zatruk burst out laughing and shook his head at me. "Remember you said that when I come collecting on that dare."

"Any time, my dear. Any time!"

We finished eating while enjoying an amiable conversation. Once more, Zatruk surprised me by bringing the empty dishes to the kitchen—which I helped him with.

"I was planning on taking you on an evening walk in the surrounding woods. Cibbos is quite stunning at night," Zatruk offered while rinsing the dishes and putting them away in the dishwasher.

I gave him a sheepish look, feeling guilty as I prepared to decline. "That sounds wonderful, but could we do that tomorrow? I'm still struggling with jet lag. I figured I would read for a while before calling it a night."

"Of course," he said, understanding. "We'll go tomorrow or another day, when you feel up to it."

I smiled gratefully, and we quickly wrapped up in the kitchen. I truly hadn't expected that side from him. I'd figured he would be the super macho male, above such menial tasks as cleaning up after himself. But then, I was starting to realize that although my husband wasn't a germaphobe, he was quite the clean freak.

Zatruk sat down in the massive stone chair I'd taken to calling 'the throne' while I went up to our bedroom to recover my tablet. I came back down to find him focused on his own reading. By the slight frown marring his brow, it appeared to be some serious stuff. I headed for a massive cushion that vaguely reminded me of a giant bean bag and plopped myself on top, curling up to the side in an almost fetal position.

I no sooner started reading than I felt the heavy weight of Zatruk's gaze on me. I looked up to find him frowning at me.

"What?"

"Why do you sit so far away? I don't bite," he said in a grumpy tone.

My eyes widened, then I looked at the number of seats between us. I hadn't thought of it that way. I just liked slumping on comfy seats, and the 'bean bag' had looked appealing. However, it was indeed closer to the other end of the room, with a three-cushion couch next to Zatruk's throne, a matching chair left of it, and then my bean bag.

Although disgruntled to leave my current comfort, I got up and went to sit at the end of the couch. Before I could kick my slippers off and curl up again, Zatruk's deepening frown clearly broadcast he still considered this too far. I rolled my eyes and moved to the other end of the couch, the position closest to his throne.

"Happy now?" I asked while letting myself drop onto the cushion. I looked at him disbelievingly when the same grumpy expression remained plastered on his face. "Oh, my God! This is the closest I can get. I mean, what else do you want me to do?! Sit on your lap?"

"Why not?" he grumbled.

My jaw dropped. Seriously? He wanted me to just sit on his lap because…? Zatruk's ears flicked as I just continued staring at him, speechless. He then scrunched his face and turned back to resume reading on his tablet. By the slight pinkening of his pale skin, I realized he was blushing.

He's embarrassed. He thinks I rejected his request.

I had not. I'd just been stunned speechless. But then images of the Yurus females sitting on their mates during our wedding feast flashed through my mind, as well as the strange way he had looked at me earlier when I sat down next to him for dinner. Had he wished me to sit on him then, too?

I rose to my feet, and came to stand in front of him. "You better be comfy," I muttered.

He looked up, appearing a little stunned. I kicked off my slippers while shoving his hands aside, then climbed on top of him. His surprise gave way to the strangest expression as he watched me wiggle and jiggle while I sought the perfect half slouching position on his lap. He slipped an arm behind my back for support as I sat partially sideways on him.

I folded my knees on his lap and rested my head on his shoulder. His arm tightened around me as I looked up at him.

"Comfy?" he asked, in a rumbling voice.

"Warm, fluffy, and comfy. You get a passing grade," I said, snuggling a little deeper against him.

His chest vibrated with a purr, and he gently rubbed his temple on my forehead, marking me with his scent. My heart clenched when I stole another glance at him and saw the happy and content expression on his face as he turned back to read his book. My beast was a cuddler who simply didn't know how to ask for it.

I ended up not reading a single line, soon falling asleep to the soothing sound of my husband's steady heartbeat and his comforting warmth all around me.

To my utter annoyance, although I woke up at a normal hour this time, I found Zatruk's side of the bed once more empty. I didn't recall him bringing me upstairs, let alone stripping me of my pants and top. However, finding myself still wearing my panties and bra left me both feeling touched and embarrassed. The latter because, although it wasn't my ugliest lingerie, it didn't particularly scream sexy either. And the former because, even though he'd already seen my goods, Zatruk had shown me enough respect not to fully strip me without my permission.

That grump was truly growing on me.

After a visit to the shower, I dressed and went hunting for my husband. He was nowhere to be found, but a hearty breakfast waited for me. Considering it was just eight in the morning, where could he have already gone to? I finished my meal, cleaned up, then decided to go back to our bedroom to finish unpacking.

Inside one of the last crates, I noticed a large box that I didn't recognize. I took it out and went to sit at the edge of the bed to open it. My eyes nearly popped out of my head at finding a holo-card on top with the credentials to log on to the restricted hub of the UPO as well as the instructions to set up a network so all of the Yurus clans could also access it.

This was a major gift that I knew for a fact came from Kayog. The Yurus had limited connectivity. But this constituted a *huge* expansion now that we could browse the massive galactic hub. It would also allow us to easily contact my connections, have access to many databases, including specifications for weapons, armor, and countless other things that could become the perfect rewards for Zatruk's gladiator arena. Then again, it was only fair considering the human colony and the Zelconians had benefited from a similar advantage after the PMA had brokered a union between their two species.

Excitement bubbled inside me as I looked for what other goodies Kayog had included. Some kind of device took up most of the box. I carefully removed it, my lips parting in shock when I recognized it as a nanobot encryptor, and next to it, a smaller container filled with self-reproducing nanites. This would allow us to create an endless supply.

But what were we supposed to encrypt with it? And did the Yurus have strong enough programmers to achieve that task? I had some functional skills, but I usually hired top notch hackers or used one of my hacking devices when needed.

As I pulled up the holosheet describing the encryptor, my jaw dropped when I realized which model Kayog had actually sent us. The Pulsar was the most advanced encryption system currently available on the market. It wasn't just extremely high tech, it was beyond idiot-proof. It possessed a bank containing all of the most popular functions people usually wanted encrypted, from medical, to technical, to pure convenience.

You didn't even need any programming skill. You simply chose the program you wanted, indicated which type of matter would host the nanites, such as organic or inert, and the encryptor would take care of the rest. You could even select a few templates that you wanted to combine. As long as their functions were complementary, the encryptor would handle it for us.

This machine cost a freaking fortune. I needed to figure out what the Temern had intended us to use it with. The final item of the Prime Mating Agency's wedding gift to us was a fancy tablet which opened on a browser page to the UPO's study on the Zelconian crystals. It was quite thorough and would take a while to read through it all—which I fully intended to do.

I'd negotiated enough deals in my past life to recognize when my counterpart was giving me hints as to what would be needed for the deal to go through without fully showing his hand. Kayog was spreading breadcrumbs and giving us tools to figure it out on our own. While a part of me wished he would simply come right out and say it, I also understood the political game the Prime Mating Agency and the United Planets Organization were playing.

They couldn't directly interfere in the direction primitive planets would evolve. But the UPO never did anything that didn't benefit it somehow. Keeping the Yurus busy and content would keep them from causing further unrest with the humans and the Zelconians. And the UPO wanted the Zelconian crystals.

But why send me a link to them?

I would need to discuss all of this with Zatruk so we could figure it out. I carefully put the encryptor and tablet on the dresser, quickly finished emptying the remaining crate, then headed outside when my husband still had not returned.

To my surprise, the village was oddly quiet, no males loitering around or bashing each other's faces in, simply because someone had given them a funny look. I didn't know if I would ever get used to that type of random violence, even though I now understood the cause. As I hadn't gotten a proper tour of Mutarak yet, I decided now would be as good a time as any to take a gander while trying to find out where everyone had gone.

My stroll didn't take me very far. I spotted a group of females as soon as I turned the corner past the large building that bordered the town square to the west. I immediately felt intimidated when their conversations halted, and they all turned their attention towards me.

One of them detached from the group and headed towards me. I silenced my instinctive urge to bolt and also advanced towards her. However, her smile and friendly demeanor reassured me. She was tall and slender, with reddish-brown fur and brown skin. Her obsidian eyes with long lashes observed me intently. She came to a stop in front of me, flicking her long, reddish hair over her shoulder. Like Zatruk, she had a single braid on each side of her face. I couldn't quite tell her age, but she was definitely older. Probably in her fifties.

"Hello, Rihanna," the female said in a soft voice. "My name is Jerdea. I am the Head Scientist of the clan."

"Wonjin's mother!" I blurted out upon recognizing the name.

I instantly kicked myself for it when she stiffened, some of her warmth fading to be replaced by an emotion I couldn't place, mixed with embarrassment.

"Yes, Wonjin is my only son," she said, matter-of-factly. "I should thank you for not unduly prolonging his shame."

"I had no idea that fight would have made him my slave," I said in an apologetic tone. "I didn't mean for that to happen."

She waved a dismissive hand. "He brought it on himself. Wonjin is a good male, and *very* smart. But my prior poor choices cause others to treat him like an idiot. He's not," she added forcefully. "If they listened to him more often, we'd be in a much better situation than we are right now."

The anger, bitterness, and frustration in her voice took me aback. Seeming to realize how she'd let her emotion shine through, she gave me a sheepish grin.

"Will you walk with me, Rihanna?" she asked.

"Sure, I'd love to," I said sincerely.

Jerdea led the way through the streets of Mutarak, and I fell into step with her.

"Has Zatruk told you anything about our people?" she asked.

I nodded. "He told me about your cycle of Great Wars, his plans for the gladiator arena, and how praxilla petals could help your people."

"Good. We pray to the Goddess that he is our Chosen, and that he will make it happen for us. We'll do anything for it. Anything!" Jerdea said, fervently. "We're tired, Rihanna. We're tired of the wars, of being widowed while our males are still in their prime, of raising fatherless sons, only to bury them thirty years later. Every generation, we make a few steps forward only to take half of them backward again when the war destroys what we have built. We want peace and not to worry if today or tomorrow will be the start of the next Great War. We want to live in harmony like the humans and Zelconians. Is that too much to ask?"

My throat tightened and tears pricked my eyes as I listened to this heartfelt plea from Jerdea. I couldn't imagine living through such a horrible cycle of self-destruction. It was all the more heartbreaking that their genetics dictated such wanton rampage and violence.

"No, it is not," I said in a soft voice. "Nobody wants to live like that."

Jerdea took in a shuddering breath. "Even though they often act like idiots and primitive barbarians, our males are actually quite smart. They could be so much more if they would only take praxilla. But I made a mess out of that."

She stopped in front of a building that resembled a green house, the first place, aside from a public forge and the stables, I had seen in the village that appeared devoted to business rather than being merely residential.

"You know the outer worlds," Jerdea said in a voice both urgent and pleading. "You know what would appeal to them. Help us build Zatruk's dream before our males lose faith."

"Do not doubt for a second that I intend to," I replied with conviction. "I don't have a magic wand to turn everything around, but I'm determined to help Zatruk and all of you change things for the better. In fact, here's the first thing." I drew the holocard out of my pocket and extended it to her. "As part of my wedding present, Kayog sent me this so that all the Yurus on Cibbos can access the UPO's restricted network."

"Restricted?" she asked, her eyes lighting up as she took the card.

"It's restricted to the extent that, as a primitive planet, Cibbos cannot be given open access to technologies far beyond what the native population has achieved on their own," I explained. "But it is still a huge network that will also give us access to the portals of other gladiator championships, so that we can see the type of prizes offered, the type of tournaments, and their popularity. It will also allow us to contact potential external partners that can help us make this come true."

Jerdea looked at the card as if it was the most precious gem in the world before pressing it to her chest with both hands. Her eyes flicked from side to side as her mind raced with countless possibilities.

"This is wonderful! I will work on setting up the network right away. But I will only make it accessible to our females for now. Our males might unknowingly sabotage it," Jerdea said.

I snorted and nodded. "Just so you know, I haven't told Zatruk yet. He's been gone all morning, and I only found this after breakfast."

"He will understand and fully agree for us to proceed. This will help us learn so much! I should get started right away!"

Her enthusiasm was contagious.

"Well, I won't hold you. But before you go, I've got a couple of questions for you. Do you know what a sylphin is?"

"Have you seen one?!" she exclaimed.

I recoiled. "No... I don't think so. I'm just wondering what it is."

Jerdea's shoulders slumped. "Oh. Sylphins are magical forest creatures. Extremely rare. They're very small, enough to fit in the palm of your hand. They would be somewhat like the human fairies. Seeing one is a sign of imminent good luck. But if you manage to touch one, or even better, if you are touched by one, it grants you a huge blessing."

"Oh wow!" I whispered under my breath.

Is that how Zatruk sees me? A good luck charm? A blessing?

"People wrongly assume they are skittish creatures that hide from others. But my mother used to say they are just very picky about who they interact with," Jerdea said wistfully. "They can see the goodness in your heart. If they love you, they will be quite bold in their affection."

"Well then, I hope I'll get to run into one of these mythical creatures," I said sheepishly.

"I wish it for you as well, Clan Mistress. Any blessing you receive is bound to trickle down to the rest of us. But you had another question?"

"Yes! I want to go see Luana, the human doctor in Kastan. Do you think Wonjin would agree to escort me there?" I asked.

Jerdea recoiled. She first appeared shocked then her expression melted into one of incredulous wonder. "It would be a tremendous honor for my son to be the bodyguard of the Great Chieftain's mate. Let me take you to him!"

To my surprise, Jerdea took me to a small, reinforced door by the city gate, then took me down a short path outside of the wall which led to an outcropping of trees that hid a peaceful pond. Sitting on a large rock by the water, Wonjin appeared engrossed by whatever he was reading on a tablet.

His ears flicked, and his head suddenly jerked up before turning in our direction. Shock, disbelief, and then embarrassment flitted over his features. He quickly rose to his hooves, partially hiding his tablet to his side, like a guilty child caught watching something he shouldn't.

"Wonjin, my son, the Great Chieftain's mate would like you to ensure her safety on her journey to Kastan," Jerdea said, proudly.

"If you don't mind, that is," I added softly.

CHAPTER 9
RIHANNA

A million different emotions battled over Wonjin's features as his gaze flicked between his mother and me, disbelief and confusion tugging at each other for dominance. When the silence stretched, his mother cleared her throat, her face clearly indicating for him to respond. That seemed to snap him out of his dazed shock.

"Yes. Yes, of course," Wonjin replied.

Jerdea's shoulders relaxed with relief. "Excellent. He will take good care of you, Rihanna. I will leave you now and go take care of this," she added, waving the holocard with excitement.

She nodded at me first then at her son in goodbye before hastening back to the city. I waved her goodbye then turned back to her son. Wonjin was staring at me, his brow creased with confusion and a sliver of suspicion.

"Why do you wish *me* to escort you?" he asked in a grumpy tone.

"Zatruk isn't around, and I'll feel safer with an escort while traveling in that unknown forest. You're strong, you know the area, and you're not afraid to fight."

He huffed with disdain. "So strong that you defeated me."

My face softened, and I shook my head while giving him a gentle smile. "I did not *defeat* you, Wonjin. I never could. You're too strong and too fast for me. I issued a challenge I knew I could win, which was simply to make you fall. I knew I could accomplish that in less than ten seconds by using a certain advantage against you. In a real battle, or had that one lasted longer, you would have crushed me, guaranteed. When you are small and physically weaker like me, you learn tricks to survive."

His nose and ears twitched, my words having clearly mollified him and soothed some of his wounded pride. "What advantage did you use?"

I shifted uneasily on my feet, knowing there were no real ways of diplomatically explaining it. "Well, I did what everyone else here does. I exploited your vulnerability," I confessed sheepishly, touching my right kidney to show him. He clenched his teeth to repress the anger my words had ignited. "You could learn tricks to counter it. If you ever feel like it, I can help you figure out some of them."

"I don't need your pity," he snapped, his upper fangs showing between his tusks.

"I don't pity you," I said with my most unimpressed face. "Pity is for the weak and helpless. You're neither. Everyone has some form of handicap they need to juggle, some more pronounced and challenging than others. Mine is my size and height. I find work arounds to still achieve what I want. Yours is whatever is happening with your side."

He grunted as sole response.

I chewed my bottom lip, hesitating about asking the question that burned my tongue. "I have to ask you something. Knowing that people deliberately take advantage of your problem, why do you keep fighting them?"

"Because each battle makes me bigger and stronger. They

will not always be able to exploit this wound. And then I will crush them," he said matter-of-factly.

"Right," I said, realizing he was far more deliberate and calculating than he let on. "Anyway, if you're going to escort me, how about we get going before it gets too late?"

Wonjin grimaced, his grumpy expression turning back to embarrassment, which threw me. He appeared to hesitate, then reluctantly walked to what I'd initially taken for a natural rock formation near a bush. Instead, it turned out to be a beautifully crafted safe inside which he hid his tablet. He came towards me, looking mightily self-conscious, and like he was bracing for me to mock him.

"I also love reading," I said in a soft voice as we followed the trail back to the city. "You chose a great spot for that."

Some of the tension bled from his shoulders, but he merely grunted in response. I repressed a smile. Grumpy males were always a riot to me.

"Where are all the males?" I asked as we entered the city to still find it mostly empty.

"They've gone hunting and should be back in about two hours. I went on the night hunt. Those who hunted with me are still sleeping. We will hunt again tonight," Wonjin explained. "Tomorrow, we trade with the humans. They can't hunt the larger prey we do. In exchange, they give us grains, vegetables, fruits, and some of the smaller meats they raise, like chicken."

"It's pretty awesome that you managed to work out a trade deal with them after the war," I said, trying to keep the conversation going and to get him to open up more.

He nodded with a grunt. "Zatruk made the deal. Under Vyrax, we used to raid them. It was fun, but also not that much. Humans are too fragile to fight back. It would have been a massacre. We would just go in and take what we wanted. This trade is smarter in the long run. With peace, the humans produce more and in greater variety. With war, they would have left.

Yurus are not farmers. Our lands are not appropriate for it, and our people do not have the discipline for it either. It would fall on our females, who already carry enough weight on their shoulders."

"You're pretty smart, you know," I said as we reached the sideways door into Zatruk's forge. Wonjin glared at me, no doubt thinking I was mocking him. "I mean it. Yesterday, when the UPO was unloading my stuff, you asked some really good questions."

His nose and ear twitched again. "Nobody listens to me. They think I'm stupid," he muttered.

"Well, they're wrong," I replied, while grabbing my speeder and leading it out of the forge.

Wonjin eyed it with undisguised curiosity as we made our way towards the stable for him to get his krogi. "Would they? Would off-worlder gladiators like speeders as rewards?"

"Designed right, absolutely," I replied with conviction. "Deutenium doesn't rust and is as strong as Titanium. The question is whether it can be sufficiently light."

"In a master's hands, yes," Wonjin replied with certainty.

I smiled. "Then the challenge would be the technological add-ons and the power source. Mine uses a sidinium crystal, like our spaceships, for maximum power and speed. It's very expensive and sadly tends to eat the metal, which requires maintenance and patches at least once a year."

"Nothing damages deutenium. It can hold any crystal, even sidinium. Our females use them for our generators. We never need to repair the casings. The crystal runs out of power first," Wonjin said smugly. "But the birds have the best crystals. They are more powerful than sidinium, and they don't damage metal."

I froze and gaped at him. "You're a fucking genius! A maintenance-free deutenium speeder, impervious to sidinium damage, even with minimum upgrade would sell like hotcakes. But one with a Zelconian crystal would be insane. What's the Yurus relationship with the Zelconians?"

"There is no relationship," Wonjin said, resuming our walk, thus prompting me to do the same. "As long as we do not threaten the humans, they stay up in their mountains."

"Okay. We're going to need to fix that," I mused out loud while Wonjin took his krogi out of the stables for himself.

We took off at an impressive speed, although much slower than my speeder could have achieved. Still, the krogi could maintain a respectable pace, which allowed us to reach the Kastan village in less than twenty minutes.

As we closed in on the village, a human male riding a zeebis flew overhead, probably a scout assessing if we represented a threat. He remained at a respectable distance, having made certain we were aware of his presence in case we got any funny ideas.

As we cleared the tree line of the forest leading to the village, a series of tall metallic poles embedded with large crystals drew my attention. By the way they were evenly spaced along the perimeter of the village, I could only presume they activated some kind of energy field to keep danger out at night or to repel any incoming attackers.

Kastan didn't look at all like what I imagined. Considering the technological advances humanity had achieved, I had expected sleek buildings with state-of-the-art gadgets everywhere, displaying what they had to flaunt their status. But nope. Although the city was clean, the architecture rather pleasant to the eye, sturdy, and built with excellent craftsmanship, its simplicity bordered on that of some of the better refugee camps or religious colonies I had seen during my travels.

But recent additions to the structures indicated a clear shift towards a more modern approach. I couldn't help but wonder if surviving that war with the Yurus had prompted that change.

However, two human males standing in the middle of the

town square reclaimed my attention, one of them Counselor Allan who had presided over my human wedding to Zatruk. They were waiting for us. I slowed down my speeder, stopping about five meters from them before dismounting, the action imitated by Wonjin.

My companion's intimidating expression once more made me want to smile. Wonjin was taking his bodyguard role very seriously, his gaze alert as he checked for possible threats.

"Hello, Mrs. Makeba," the man I didn't know said as I approached. "Welcome to Kastan. I am Mateo Torres, leader of the colony. And this is Counselor Allan, who you already met."

"Indeed," I said, nodding at the Counselor, somewhat embarrassed by the less-than-ladylike first impression I gave him. "It's a pleasure to see you again, Counselor, and a pleasure to meet you, Mr. Torres. This is Wonjin, who was kind enough to accompany me so that I wouldn't get lost."

The two males nodded at Wonjin, who responded by stiffly lifting his chin.

From the corner of my eyes, I could see a number of gawkers coming out of the woodwork to see what was going on. There probably wasn't much drama happening here, and I suspected all of them were curious to see what 'unfortunate' woman had been conned into marrying one of the brutes that had terrorized their village for so long. The horrified and sympathetic look many of them cast my way seemed to confirm my suspicions.

I barely repressed the urge to laugh while imagining what kind of wild speculations were running through their minds as to the reason for my visit. Once they saw me heading for the doctor's clinic, they'd likely start spreading rumors that my beast had split me in half. The mischievous part of me almost felt like hobbling just to further fuel the ridiculous theories that would regardless result from my presence.

"The news of your union with the Yurus Chieftain was greeted with joy by my people," Mateo continued. "We wish you all the happiness in your union and hope that Great Chieftain Zatruk's union to a human female will foster a greater understanding, friendship, and peace between our people."

I smiled at the less-than-subtle underlying message. "Indeed. Zatruk has many plans, none of which involves a war with the humans. In fact, he is as pleased for me as I am for myself that there should be a human colony so close to Mutarak so that I won't feel so totally isolated from my own people. And that's not to mention the relief of having a human doctor within reach."

Mateo's face softened, my response having pleased him. "That must undoubtedly be a great relief for you. You are welcome here whenever you wish. And we also have many human goods you might enjoy."

"Don't mind me taking you up on that offer, especially where chocolate is concerned," I said teasingly, which made both men chuckle. "By the way, thank you very much for that generous care package your daughter sent me on behalf of your colony. That was extremely sweet."

"We want you to feel at home. There are far too few new humans on Cibbos," Mateo responded proudly.

"Thank you. As a matter of fact, I was actually coming to see the doctor, if she's available that is," I said.

"Absolutely. Luana has been looking forward to meeting you," Mateo replied. "As you might have heard, she also married a native."

"I did."

"This way, please." He gestured at one of the buildings located almost directly in front of the square.

We made our way to the clinic under the watchful eyes of the crowd, a few of them shrinking on themselves under the baleful glares of Wonjin when they stood a little too close. I wanted to fluff the fur of his forearm and tell him to relax.

The cool air inside the clinic reminded me just how hot Cibbos got, especially now that the sun was steadily moving towards its zenith. The door opened on a small waiting area with white walls, a few chairs, a play area for children and a large vidscreen. Mateo waved his hand in front of the panel by the double doors next to the vacant reception desk. Seconds later, the door swished open before us.

I remained speechless at the sight of the top-of-the-line medical pods lining the walls of the examination room. Few people could afford a single one of those models. And yet, this small human colony in the middle of bumfuck nowhere had at least a dozen of them.

I bet you this was Kayog's wedding gift to them.

With the looming war at the time of Luana's wedding, it made sense. The place was spacious, the pods neatly folded in an upright position while not being used, only two of them—both empty and their domes open—sat horizontally, ready to receive a patient. Two examination tables occupied the center of the room, and at the back a couple of desks faced each other in front of a counter filled with medical supplies.

A pretty woman with tan skin and a puffy head of curly hair leaned sideways from behind her desk to see behind her monitor who had come calling. Her eyes widened, then a huge smile stretched her lips when she spotted me with my furry companion in tow.

"Luana, you have a visitor," Mateo said to his daughter.

She rose from her seat and circled around her desk to come greet us. It was then my turn to be surprised at the impressive size of her belly. Either her pregnancy was very advanced, or Zelconian babies were beyond massive. That immediately raised the question as to how huge a Yurus baby would be.

Mateo quickly made the introductions.

"Hello, Rihanna, Wonjin," Luana said, warmly. "I didn't dare hope to see you so soon. Please, come in, come in!"

Mateo excused himself, leaving us in his daughter's good care.

"Is this a bad time?" I asked.

"No, not at all! Your timing couldn't have been more perfect since it's Saturday. The clinic is normally closed, except for major emergencies," she said with a grin.

"Oh, my God! I didn't realize it was the weekend. I'm still too busy adjusting to the time difference," I said sheepishly.

"I bet. Are you here for medical reasons or is this a social call? If the latter, we could go to a café, if you like," Luana offered.

I hesitated. "Actually, it's a mix of both, but there's definitely a medical component."

"Oh, okay," she replied, casting a furtive glance at Wonjin.

"I will wait in the other room," Wonjin said, looking as grumpy as ever.

"Feel free to turn on the vidscreen. We have access to a lot of channels, some of which might interest you," Luana said.

He grunted his assent and stepped outside.

The door no sooner closed behind him than Luana turned to me with a concerned expression. "How are you doing? How is Cibbos treating you?"

I instantly knew she meant how my husband was treating me. While I appreciated the concern, I also felt slightly offended on his behalf.

"New planet and new culture to adapt to, but I'm actually doing really good," I said with a smile.

She gave me a dubious look. "Really?"

This time, I frowned. "Yes, really. I realize your colony has had a rough past with the Yurus, but Zatruk is working hard to change that. He's a good male." The look on her face in response to that pissed me off. "What? What was that look?"

She had the decency to look embarrassed and gestured for me to take a seat near the consultation desk. I followed while she appeared to be gathering her thoughts on the way there. She sat down, looking a little relieved to be off her feet. I immediately felt guilty, even though I hadn't actually done anything wrong.

"I'm sorry," Luana said. "I admit to being quite biased where the Yurus—and your husband in particular—are concerned. It's not fair, if I'm honest, considering all of the pain we met at their hands was under the command of a different Chieftain."

"Yeah, I heard of the raids and the mess with Vyrax. But why my husband in particular?" I asked with genuine curiosity.

"I don't want to badmouth him behind his back," she argued, looking mightily uncomfortable.

"You're not. He gave me his version of the events, and I believe him," I said with a shrug. "But it's always good to get a different perspective. Like me, I'm certain you want permanent peace with the Yurus. Understanding the sources of friction can only help us, moving forward."

"Well, it's honestly more of a personal issue," Luana said, looking guilty. "You see, when the war ended, Vyrax was grievously injured, and the Yurus left him for dead in the forest. Our men brought him back here, and I healed him. Or rather, I was working on it. He was out of the critical phase but still had a loooong way to go. Zatruk demanded we return Vyrax to them before he would resume talks with us. I had no choice but to comply. And then…"

"And then he killed him," I finished for her when her voice trailed off. I smiled sympathetically at the angry expression on her face. "I can see you've had a very sheltered life, Luana." She recoiled, and eyed me with surprise. "Killing him while he was still unconscious was a mercy. You were fixing him only to send him back to the lion's den to get eaten alive."

"You sound just like Zatruk and my husband," she said bitterly.

I smiled once more with sympathy. "You're a healer, a nurturer. It is normal for you to try to protect life at all cost, even that of the enemy who made your life hell. But for warrior clans like the Yurus, this level of failure is not acceptable. And how they described Vyrax to me, he wasn't the type who would have relinquished power to another, even though no warrior would follow someone who had been so soundly beaten. He would have dueled to the death, and everyone would have pounded on him, one challenge after the next without reprieve until he broke, if only out of sheer exhaustion. He was doomed."

Luana heaved a sigh, her shoulders slumping in defeat as she nodded in concession.

"Whatever you think of Zatruk, he truly is a good male, in spite of his intimidating appearance. He's been extremely sweet, gentle, and respectful towards me since my arrival. He desperately wants peace and to get his people out of this senseless spiral of violence," I said with fervor. "Appearances are deceiving. The Yurus aren't just gratuitously violent or savage."

"I know," Luana intervened, a frown creasing her brow, taking me by surprise. "While tending Vyrax, I got to study the Yurus anatomy and physiology. I know that their violence is due to hormonal surges."

"And they're trying to control that," I replied, excited to see she understood the problem.

"With praxilla?" Luana asked, stunning me once more. She smiled at my reaction. "I saw your husband eating a leaf when he started getting irritated while negotiating with my father at the end of the war."

"Right, that makes sense," I said pensively. "I had been wondering if maybe some hormonal therapy—?"

Luana shaking her head interrupted me. "I wondered the same the minute I realized the source of their violence. The problem is fairly complex. It's not just a matter of regulating their hormonal levels. There's a whole lot of things happening inside their bodies when they fight. Beyond the testosterone and serotonin, they need the faster heart rate, the muscular strain from their physical exertion, and the adrenalin rush—among other things—to create the perfect cocktail. Believe me, if a testosterone shot sufficed, I'm sure the Yurus healers would have fixed it already."

"Well, that explains it," I said with a heavy sigh. "Just know that Zatruk is actively working on a solution, and that I'll do everything I can to support him in that."

"I'm happy to hear it," she said before tilting her head to the side and giving me a strange look. "You're fond of him."

My face heated. "Like I said, he's a nice guy."

She shook her head with a teasing smile. "No, it's more than that. Kayog's magic is striking once again. You'll be head over heels with your Yurus before your six months are up."

"Not six months, one year," I countered.

"One year?!" she exclaimed, baffled.

"Long story. Once we get to know each other better, I'll tell you how I ended up marrying through the PMA," I said, scrunching my face.

She chuckled. "Now, I'm curious. Your emotions are fascinating." Her smile broadened before my stunned expression. "I inherited some of my husband's empathic abilities after we bonded. I'm nowhere near as powerful as he is, but enough to sense you really care about Zatruk, and that you truly believe in whatever plan he's working on. If I can help in any way, let me know."

"Expect me to take you up on that," I said, grateful. "I do not want to get ahead of myself, and least of all speak on Zatruk's behalf. But in the not-too-distant future, I believe warming the relationship between the Zelconians and the Yurus would be greatly beneficial for all. When the time comes, if you can help with that, it would be highly appreciated."

"We'll cross that bridge when we get there," she responded in a non-committal fashion.

I snorted and nodded. "Now, on to the main reason I came here before Wonjin starts climbing the walls. Since I've had a full medical and a slew of vaccines before I came here, I should be just fine. However, I have a contraceptive implant, and I wanted to know how effective it is with a Yurus. Zatruk and I haven't discussed kids yet, but it's a little too early for us—at least for me—to have any right now. And I'd like to know what the situation is, and what our options are before I have that talk with him."

"Wise approach," Luana said with approval. "Let's run a few tests. These medical pods are an absolute wonder. And I was thankfully able to gather sufficient data from Vyrax that we should be able to get you answers immediately."

"Even Yurus semen?" I asked, raising an eyebrow.

Luana's face turned crimson. "Well… I had to do a thorough mapping of his anatomy when I first got him to have a chance at healing him. Then after he was executed, Zatruk left his remains with us. So…"

"You did a thorough autopsy," I said, amused.

"We knew absolutely nothing about the Yurus," she said in a defensive tone. "Not even the UPO had the slightest info about their anatomy. It felt like important scientific research in case of future needs."

I chuckled. "You don't have to explain. I understand."

She scrunched her face, mumbled something, then invited me to get inside one of the medical pods. For the next fifteen minutes, she ran a thorough series of tests, explaining that she was getting my medical profile at the same time so that if anything happened, she would already have the necessary information about my blood type, allergies, medical history, etc.

The medical pod did most of the work, quickly and efficiently, including drawing blood samples. At the end of all that, the conclusion was that yes, humans and Yurus could have babies together. And yes, my contraceptive would work with a 98.5% efficiency rate. That was good enough for me.

"Thank you for that," I said, grateful. "Before I leave, I have one last favor to ask."

"Sure. What can I do for you?"

"Actually, it's not for me, but for my companion, Wonjin," I said sheepishly.

Luana recoiled, her eyes widening in both surprise and curiosity. I gave her a quick synopsis of the mishap with giving him praxilla as a boy, and the permanent damage it caused.

"I haven't discussed with him the possibility of you examining him. I wanted to check first if this was something you would be open to or even capable of doing," I cautioned.

"I would be delighted to help, if I can," she said with a smile and an eagerness I found endearing.

She truly was a healer at heart.

I went to fetch Wonjin. To my surprise, instead of having found himself some extreme fighting show or horror movie, he was watching a documentary on the most revolutionary individual or compact transport systems on the galactic market. Once again, Jerdea's words about just how smart her son was echoed in my mind. What kind of things was he reading—and maybe even learning—when he went hiding by the pond?

"You're ready to depart?" he asked, rising to his feet.

"Almost. But first, I was wondering if you would be willing to let Luana have a look at your side," I asked carefully.

He recoiled and looked at me as if I'd grown a second head. "Why would I see a human healer?"

"She is not clueless about Yurus anatomy," I quickly explained. "She was healing Vyrax after the war. She also possesses the most advanced medical pods in the galaxy. I mean, the worst that can happen is that she can't help. But what if she could?"

Despite his obvious reluctance and doubt, a glimmer of hope sparked in his eyes. He begrudgingly followed me in.

"Rihanna explained the situation," Luana said. "I'd be very

happy to run a scan of your side to see if there's anything we can do to fix it. If so, I'll discuss the possible treatments with you, and then you can decide if it's something you want to do or not. These medical pods are phenomenal and should be able to give a fairly accurate assessment of the success rate of a treatment, if any."

"Very well," Wonjin said.

"I just want to reiterate that there are no guarantees we will have a cure," Luana cautioned.

He nodded. "Yes, I understand."

"Do you wish me to give you privacy?" I asked Wonjin.

"No, you may stay. The human doctor will feel safer with you here," he added mockingly.

She snorted and shook her head. "I know you wouldn't harm me. You wouldn't dishonor yourself and your clan by attacking a female, and a pregnant one at that."

It was his turn to snort. He then nodded in concession. I gave the doctor an admiring glance at how she'd handle the grumpy Yurus. Luana indicated for him to enter the pod. He complied.

"Would it be okay for me to run a few additional scans on you, purely for research purposes?" Luana asked. "You are the first healthy Yurus I've been able to examine, excluding that injury. It would be useful to further help your people in the future, should any of you so wish."

Wonjin cast an inquisitive look my way. For some reason, that touched me. I nodded with an encouraging smile.

"Very well, you may," he said, before looking up at the ceiling.

"Thank you, it shouldn't be long," Luana said with enthusiasm.

She closed the dome above the pod, pulled a chair in front of the pod's display screen, and started running the scans. I didn't understand half of what it showed, but the way Luana's face lit up, she'd seen something of interest. She tapped on a thumbnail image on the interface, and it blew up on a giant screen on the wall behind the pod. It was an X-Ray of Wonjin's side.

The doctor's fingers flew over the keyboard, and the image on the screen started rotating, a bunch of intersecting lines appearing, some sections of the bone highlighting in red. A series of medical terms appeared on the screen, and then a large 97% displayed in green beneath it.

"What is it? Is that good news?" I asked, tension in my voice. You'd think I was the patient.

Luana smiled, but didn't answer, instead opening the dome and inviting Wonjin to sit so they could discuss his results. Obviously, she couldn't discuss his case with a third party first.

"The good news is that we were able to identify the problem," she said, pointing at the giant screen. "This is your side. The issue is located right here along the lower part of your ribcage. During the time of your hormonal imbalance, your bones developed abnormally. There are three rather pronounced bone spurs on your ninth rib and another on the lower half of your costal cartilage."

Wonjin grunted his assent, seeming not surprised in the least.

"You already knew that?" I asked, although it was more of a surprised statement.

He nodded. "My mother scanned me before." He turned back to Luana, looking almost bored. "So, what's the bad news? You can't fix it either?"

"Actually, we can, and frankly we should," she said. "I'm surprised there is no internal bleeding, or that you haven't punctured an organ. The spurs are severely pronounced. Any major blow there essentially causes the spur to stab your liver or your kidney. With how frequently your people brawl, the 'right' hit could actually be fatal."

"How would you fix it?" I asked.

"*I* can't, but the medical pod can," she explained. "See these four things highlighted in red around these ribs? They are what we need to excise. But as a mature adult, Wonjin's bones are almost like titanium. We need a very powerful, and high-precision laser to do it, which the pod has. It should take about twenty minutes to complete the procedure, and the chances of success are 97%."

"That sounds very good," Wonjin said, finally showing a sliver of excitement and hope.

"It is," Luana said with a grin. "But the bad news is that once we perform the procedure, you cannot fight *at all* for the next forty-eight hours. I seriously mean *not at all*. The risk of grievous injury during the recovery phase could be life threatening. And yes, eating praxilla to control the urge would be entirely fine."

Wonjin frowned. "I have to go hunt tonight for tomorrow's trade with your colony."

Luana shook her head with a stern expression. "No hunting for you. Nothing that could possibly result in your getting struck on your ribs. Physical exertion is fine, just not fighting."

"Would smithing be okay?" I asked. "The Yurus often do that to work up their testosterone levels."

She nodded. "Yes, that would be acceptable."

"Problem solved. He'll be smithing," I said in a tone that brooked no argument.

"But—"

"No buts, Wonjin," I said, interrupting him. "You'll be smithing. Zatruk needs a few blades built to galactic specifications. There are plenty of others to go hunt."

He grunted in concession. With that, Luana had him lie back down in the pod, and set the machine to work. It was eerie watching the damn thing do everything, from cleaning the area to be operated on and performing the local anesthetic, to making three small incisions where long metal needles were inserted. I didn't quite understand which one was equipped with a camera, but we were able to witness the entire procedure on the giant monitor.

Luana had not been kidding by saying the medical pod would do everything. She merely sat there, bearing witness, typing some input from time to time. I didn't quite know what purpose it served.

Nineteen minutes and twelve seconds later, the pod had excised and extracted the four spurs. The dome opened on an amazed and emotional Wonjin. He immediately sat at the edge of the pod, fully alert, with his side still feeling numb from the procedure. Although he forced a neutral expression on his face, his overly bright eyes hinted that he was repressing what I assumed to be tears of joy after a lifetime of pain and abuse over this unfortunate deformity.

Luana gave him a painkiller hypospray with detailed instructions on what he could and couldn't do for the next couple of days, which she copied onto a holocard so he wouldn't forget. I demanded a copy to make sure he would follow them, which made Wonjin huff.

"The pod has injected you with some nanobots that will help stitch the bones where we shaved the spurs," Luana explained. "They will naturally be eliminated from your system over the next week through kidney filtration and subsequent urination. I have added my online contact to the card. You should be back to 100% and as good as new within the next two days. But if you feel any unusual pain or discomfort, message me at any time of day or night."

"I am sure it will be fine. Thank you, doctor," Wonjin said with a softness I'd never seen from him before.

"Glad to have been of service, although the pod really did all the work," she said timidly. She then turned to me as if remembering something. "Oh, and if you need or want anything we can provide you with, just give a note to the Yurus who will come do the trade or send me a message via my contact info, and I will include it with our produce tomorrow."

After the usual goodbyes, Wonjin and I made our way back home at a slightly slower pace to avoid his krogi bouncing him too much.

CHAPTER 10
ZATRUK

I reveled in the burning pain running the length of my arms and the influx of testosterone coursing through my veins as I slammed my hammers on the metal. It sang to me, telling me exactly where I needed to strike, and how hard to make it bend to my will, smoothing it out to make it ring in perfect harmony.

The physical strain of working with deutenium was the closest thing I had found to the pleasure of combatting a foe in a no-holds-barred battle. But it was even more enjoyable to the extent that each blow aimed at creating lethal beauty rather than destroying. And the challenge my mate had set with those galactic standards thrilled me.

However, thoughts of Rihanna reawakened my growing worry at her absence. I should have warned her I'd be leaving early for a hunt. It was such a well-known fact within the clan that it slipped my mind to inform her. As she'd been sleeping in quite late due to her jet lag, I'd hoped to be back before she awakened, or shortly thereafter. She'd looked so delicate and peaceful in our massive bed that I hadn't had the heart to wake her to tell her before I left.

Obviously, Jerdea had informed me of her visit to Kastan.

The path there was safe enough that Rihanna could have gone on her own. But it reassured me that she had a bodyguard, even though I didn't quite understand her choice of Wonjin. What was my mate up to? At least, I had no doubt he would keep her safe. She'd just been gone a really long time.

Still, my heart soared at the other news Jerdea had shared with me. She'd successfully connected to the UPO network and was diligently setting it up so that every household in Mutarak and every other Yurus clan could also access it. A number of our females were already lined up to scour through every relevant site to help me achieve my goal... *our* goal.

It would not only give my people a real chance at a prosperous future, but it would make a safer environment that my Rihanna would wish to live in and raise our offspring. The violent sense of longing that struck when the image of my pregnant mate flashed before my mind's eye left me reeling. How had she grown so much on me in such a short time?

The large side door opening startled me out of my musings. As if summoned by my thoughts, Rihanna walked in next to her speeder. Behind her, Wonjin, still seated on his krogi, nodded at me. I returned the gesture, and he rode off.

"You're back!" Rihanna said with an enthusiasm that warmed my heart. "How did the hunt go?"

Even as she asked the question, she continued to the back to park her speeder before returning to me.

"Very well," I said, still hammering the metal. "I do not mean to be rude, but deutenium is very temperamental. I cannot stop now or this work will be wasted. I need about ten more minutes to finish."

"No worries. Is it okay for me to stay and watch?"

It was more than okay! What Yurus male didn't want to show off his smithing skills, especially to a female he was trying to seduce? Naturally, I didn't say that out loud.

"Yes, it is fine," I responded in a gentle tone.

The weight of her gaze on me made me want to make a spectacle of it, but I reined myself in. Shaping deutenium was a show in and of itself as I worked the metal with a hammer in each hand. I felt bad about having to ignore her to focus on my task. And yet, I soon fell back into the smithing trance where I almost became one with the metal as I listened to its sound and felt the way each blow vibrated up the length of my arms to my shoulders.

There was something magical about bending such a wild metal to one's will, tempering it, giving it just the right heat treatment, then hammering, folding, hammering again until it became a masterpiece. By the time I finished, I was blown away by the lightness and thinness I had achieved with the blade.

As I intended to keep the spine more flexible and later add some adornments to it, I placed some clay in specific spots. I then quenched the blade in oil so that it would cool slower than in water, which would make it less brittle.

I wrapped the handle in a thick cloth and showed the weapon to my little sylphin, who had quietly observed with undisguised curiosity. I had feared she would have grown bored. But her eyes sparkled when I extended the blade to her.

"That's already freaking amazing!" she exclaimed with an awed expression.

She gestured around with it, whispering to herself as she praised the lightness and balance of the blade. My throat tightened at the way Rihanna looked back up at me, her eyes filled with wonder.

"You're really, really good at this," she said, incredulous. "I'm genuinely impressed."

With a will of their own, my stupid ears flicked, betraying my embarrassment, and my even more stupid pale skin started heating. At least, the heat of the forge and my recent exertion already had my skin flushed, which helped hide my silly reaction to her compliment.

I took the blade back to put it away. "Thank you, I will finish it tomorrow. But right now, what I am is extremely sweaty. I need a shower. You are welcome to join me," I added teasingly.

She made a face. "Are you implying that I stink?"

I chuckled. "No, I'm implying that I need help washing my back," I said, coming back then picking her up.

"Hey! I can walk!" my female exclaimed, even as she passed her arm around my neck. "And you're covering me in your sweat!"

"Well, I guess now you have no choice but to shower, too," I deadpanned. She glared at me, looking like she was trying to come up with a snarky remark, but I didn't give her a chance to. "I missed you."

Rihanna's fake anger instantly melted away, and she stared at me, stunned. Her face softened, and the strangest expression flitted over her features as she locked eyes with me. She gently caressed my face with her free hand, her fingers then sinking into my hair. I couldn't tell who kissed who, not that it mattered. Our lips met, and a burning desire surged low in my belly.

I had hungered for her last night, but she'd fallen asleep so trustingly on my lap, that I had merely removed her clothes and tucked her in bed. My female slept like the dead—a worrisome trait. Thankfully, I was here to look after her.

Our tongues mingled as I carried her upstairs to our en suite hygiene room, my arms tightening around her slender body. I would never tire of kissing my female. It wasn't just the taste of her, but the passionate way in which she responded, as if she couldn't get enough of me.

As soon as we entered the hygiene room, I sat her on the counter and feverishly worked on ridding her of all those silly layers of leather clothes she wore. We would need to address that. My lips only stopped devouring her mouth to remove her top, before reclaiming it.

The wretched thing Rihanna called a bra was trying my

patience as it refused to detach. My female eventually burst out laughing when I growled in aggravation. She batted my hands away, ridding herself of that abomination at mind boggling speed. My mouth watered at the sight of the dark brown halo around her nipples. I sucked on one while undoing the even more infuriating lower garment called pants that she wore. There would be no more of that. She would wear a loincloth or one of those human dresses from now on.

I could already hear her stubbornly arguing with me. I looked forward to it.

Without stopping to suck on Rihanna's breast, I lowered her pants. My mate rested her palms on the counter for support and lifted her behind to ease my task of ridding her of that second abomination. I took down her panties at the same time. Lifting my female up with one arm around her back, my face still buried in her chest, I quickly removed my loincloth with my free hand. I discarded it on the floor, and made my way to the shower.

With surprising dexterity, Rihanna had loosened the braids framing my face without me noticing. She loved playing with my hair and beard. I didn't understand why, but wouldn't complain either. I welcomed any excuse for her to touch me.

I turned on the water, letting it rain over us while I continued to kiss and caress my female. I lowered her back down to reclaim her mouth, and she wrapped her legs around my waist. My already stiff cock jerked in response as her core pressed against it. *Jaafan*, how she turned me on. The feverish way in which she returned my attentions further fanned the fire within.

The lukewarm water switching to soapy startled me. Of course, in my lusty daze, I had forgotten to set the shower to manual instead of my usual preprogrammed setting. But I didn't mind. The soap made my female's skin even softer as she rubbed herself all over me. The water stopped, soapy or otherwise, and would automatically resume to rinse me in five minutes.

Rihanna began grinding her sex against mine, clearly

needing some friction. I slipped a hand around her deliciously round behind, reaching for her clitoris. A strangled cry escaped her and she threw her head back, lips open as she gyrated in response to my touch. *Jaafan*, she was beautiful. She straightened, looking at me with hooded eyes, her hands caressing my face and my hair passionately. As she neared the edge, she leaned forward, rubbing her face all over mine, her labored breathing interspersed with needy moans acting as the most potent of aphrodisiacs.

She climaxed with a startled cry, burying her face in my neck, and her nails digging in my back half a second before the water rained over us. I rinsed us both, holding my mate at first until she regained her bearings, then put her down to thoroughly finish the job.

Crouching as I rubbed her legs, I suddenly slipped my arms behind her knees and lifted her up. Rihanna yelped with fear, instinctively holding on to my horns. A bolt of lust exploded in my loins, and I growled with need. I placed each of my female's legs on my shoulders. My face buried in my prize, I rose to my hooves while devouring my mate. She cried out, hanging on to my horns, threatening to tilt backwards in the throes of pleasure.

I walked a few steps towards the tiled walls of the shower, pressing Rihanna's back against it for support as I licked and lapped at her core. *Jaafan*, the way she sounded and whispered my name in an almost pleading fashion, had me almost spilling my seed. But I needed to prepare her further to receive me. Even as I sucked on her clitoris, I inserted two fingers inside her slit, working them in and out while stretching her. Soon, the trembling of my mate's legs around my face announced her impending orgasm. I intensified the movement of my tongue on her little nub, and crooked my fingers inside her, massaging her sensitive spot until she fell apart for me again.

With much care, I removed Rihanna's legs from my shoulders, letting her boneless body slide down the cool tiles, lowering her onto my aching cock. She arched her back against the wall, her taut nipples pointing impertinently at me. I bent my head to nip at one, my mouth trailing a path back up her chest and the line of her neck, while gradually inserting myself within her with shallow thrusts.

My lips reached hers at the same time her body yielded to me. Goddess, the way she squeezed my cock was the most exquisite of torments. Ancestors forgive me, but I couldn't wait anymore and immediately started moving inside my female. A growling moan of bliss poured out of me at the almost painful pleasure she gave me. With each thrust, the searing heat of her sheath stroked and caressed me in its greedy vise. Her inner walls clenched spasmodically around my length, spurring me on, as did her nails, digging in the fleshy part of my ass, as if begging for more.

And I would give her more...

Setting my *vylus* in motion to massage her little clitoris, I soon had my female crying out my name. I accelerated the pace, my skin burning from the liquid flame coursing through my veins and the inferno raging in my loins. My mate... my beautiful sylphin. I crushed her lips, swallowing the sound of the pleasure I was giving her as my own need to climax rode me hard. But I would see her scream for me one more time. I would feel her fall apart all over my cock once again.

I opened Rihanna's legs, spreading her wider for me, and surrendered to the unbridled desire she awakened in me. I took her hard and fast as I held her helplessly pinned against the wall. My mate's orgasm slammed into her with a violence that resonated directly into me. The moment her inner walls clamped down on my cock, a bolt of lightning ripped down my spine. I threw my head back and roared as my seed shot out into my female in an excruciatingly blissful flow of ecstasy.

I was nearly crushing Rihanna against the wall, kissing her, caressing her, wanting to be impossibly closer to her as I spilled every drop of my essence. *Jaafan!* She would be the death of me.

Feeling wobbly on my hooves, my head spinning from this pleasure overload, I turned us around, leaning against the wall for support while I kept my mate impaled on my cock. A part of me regretted that we weren't in bed so that I could knot with her.

But does she even want a young with me?

There was no question I wanted many with her. The image of a little Yurus female, with black horns the same colors as her mother's hair, dark brown skin, and Rihanna's lovely features, awakened a painful ache in my heart. We would need to address that matter. While I intended to do everything in my power to keep my female forever, should Rihanna decide to leave, any child of mine would stay.

Looking mightily groggy, my mate lifted her head to look at me. "You Yurus sure have an interesting way of showering," she said.

I snorted, kissed her forehead, the tip of her nose, and then her lips. "That was a first, my mate. And hopefully, not the last."

Rihanna emitted a purring sound as her sole response, while rubbing her nose against mine.

Feeling steadier, I reluctantly pulled out of my female, set her back down on her feet, and gave both of us a thorough rinse. I then led her to the nook with the drying fans—three on top, and two on each of the three side walls. Rihanna had used a towel on her first night here. While Yurus occasionally did as well, the fans did a better job with our fur. My woman's eyes widened when I picked up a comb and first detangled my hair while drying, then moved on to the same with the fur on my body.

"You don't want to see clumpy patches of fur," I said in a far too defensive tone, feeling self-conscious.

"That would not be very sexy," she concurred in a teasing voice. She smiled and pulled a curly lock of her hair. "My own hair is going to be a bit more challenging. This always happens when we wet it. But nothing a bit of care can't fix."

Her hair looked like it had shrunk by half, her curls now looking tighter than ever. It was adorable, and incredibly soft... like everything about her.

We picked up our clothes on our way back to the bedroom. I loved how carefree my mate seemed to be about her nudity as she headed to the walk-in. It partially saddened me when she put on a new set of underwear, but thankfully went for a short dress while I put on a new loincloth.

"So, how did your visit to Kastan go?" I asked as she headed back to the hygiene room, holding a large tooth comb and what resembled a small pot of ointment or cream.

"It went really well. Luana is a sweetheart. And the clinic is amazing. Their medical pods are insane. I bet you they were gifts from Kayog," she said with enthusiasm.

I watched in fascination as Rihanna stood in front of the vanity mirror and began parting her hair. She detangled it in small sections to which she applied some of the lightly scented cream from the pot she had brought. Then, she twisted two strands, turning them into the cutest 'braid' that showed the true length of her hair.

"Luana and I talked about many things, and she gave me a full medical exam," Rihanna continued.

The way she said that immediately set all of my senses on high alert. Averting my eyes from the mesmerizing work she was doing on her hair, I locked gazes with my mate through the mirror. Under different circumstances, I would have been impressed by her ability to continue to part, detangle, treat, and twist her hair without even looking. However, I could sense a serious conversation incoming.

"Among other things, we discussed whether humans and Yurus were genetically compatible when it came to conceiving," she said carefully.

My heart seized. The thought that our species might not be able to reproduce together had never entered my mind, only the fact that Rihanna might not want or be ready to take that step. A terrible sense of loss crashed over me.

"We're not?" I asked, already expecting her answer to be negative.

"Actually, we are," Rihanna said, her gaze intense as she studied my reaction through my reflection on the mirror.

It took every bit of my willpower to maintain a neutral expression on my face instead of shouting with joy. "I am pleased to hear it. I would very much like to have many offspring with you. But I suspect you do not share that sentiment," I said cautiously, my voice devoid of any anger or accusation.

Rihanna stopped working with her hair and turned to face me with a serious expression. "It's not that. I like you. At least, what I know of you so far. But we only met a couple of days ago. Children are a lifetime commitment. I want to make as sure as possible that the male that sires my kids is someone I want to spend the rest of my life with, and that he feels the same about me."

"So, you want more time to decide if I am that male," I said, matter-of-factly. She nodded, looking slightly worried as to how I would react. I smiled reassuringly. "I can already tell you that I am, as you are the one for me. But it is a fair request, and I shall honor it."

Rihanna sighed, her shoulders slumping with relief. "Well, that went better than I expected," she said sheepishly.

I chuckled and gently caressed her cheek. "There's nothing you can't discuss with me, my mate. I want you happy. Whatever the problem, we will find a solution together. We are soulmates. I don't need the Temern to confirm it. I feel it in my bones."

"You're really sweet, Zatruk."

I immediately frowned, which made her chuckle. "I'm not

sweet. As for this matter, I will have our healer give me a vasectomy before the day's end."

Rihanna recoiled, her eyes nearly popping out of her head. "You would do that?"

"Of course. It's a simple procedure and easily reversible. Why?" I asked, confused by her reaction.

"Sheesh. Men usually are such wimps and drama queens when anyone dares to suggest messing with their plumbing," she grumbled with annoyance. "But that's not going to be necessary. I already had a contraceptive implant before I came here. It's still valid for two years, but... you know..."

"I know what?" I asked, distraught we wouldn't have a chance to conceive before such a long time.

"If I decide I want to stick with your fluffy fur and cute ears for the long haul, I can simply remove it. It would take less than a week after that for me to be fertile again... Well, assuming I'm at the right time in my cycle," she said.

My heart soared again, and I drew her against me. She came willingly. "Then we can enjoy practicing until the day you do remove it," I said before kissing her.

"Someone sure is confident," she said teasingly after I broke the kiss.

"I am. You *are* my soulmate. Of that, I am certain."

She smiled, looking almost timid, then turned back to face the mirror as she resumed twisting her hair. "By the way, while you were gone, I found more gifts from Kayog than just the network access."

Rihanna proceeded to describe the encryptor and self-reproducing nanobots placed in her belongings, as well as the tablet opening on the UPO's site devoted to the Zelconian crystals.

"I'm stumped," my mate said with frustration. "Nanobots can be imbued in anything, organic or not. I figured it's for the deutenium, but to do what?"

I frowned, stumped as well. "I'm not sure. However, that and the crystals are clues well-worth following. Although the crystals might prove more challenging. The Zelconians and Yurus aren't exactly close."

"But you're not enemies, right?" Rihanna asked. I shook my head. "Good. Therefore, maybe something can be worked out when we've fully figured out what we want to do."

"Actually, Wonjin had echoed one of my thoughts. I, too, have been wondering if a speeder similar to yours would make a worthy prize," I said.

"A fully-decked one, that never gets damaged thanks to its deutenium frame, and especially powered by a Zelconian crystal?" she asked. "Anyone would kill for one. Assuming you can make it light enough to achieve great speed. It's called a speeder for a reason," she added, teasingly.

"And a speeder without a Zelconian crystal?" I insisted. "Don't get me wrong. I am not too proud to open a dialogue with the birds to see if a trade is possible. But it's a long shot. If they continue to refuse the UPO, despite the benefits they could reap, why would they trade with us? I rather have a base plan that we can achieve on our own, and only rely on the whims of others for our stretch goals."

Rihanna nodded. "Wise thinking. And yes, a deutenium speeder on its own would be appealing, if only for the fact that any crystal, even one as powerful as sidinium, wouldn't damage it—at least, according to what Wonjin told me."

I nodded. "That is correct. Our generators use sidinium crystals and sustain no damage."

"Yeah, that's what Wonjin said," Rihanna replied, finishing the last twist of her hair. She closed the cream pot, and turned back to face me. "Do you think you could build a speeder?"

"The chassis, frame, and other metal parts, yes. Jerdea's team would need to figure out the onboard computer and engine. Any chance they could study yours?" I asked carefully.

"As long as they don't dismantle it, sure," Rihanna said with a shrug. "There are plenty of databases online where we should be able to get some blueprints to build them. We're not going to find the specific one for my speeder, since they have a patent for that. But we should find something good enough."

"Then I'm going to start looking into it right away," I said, hope surging in my heart. "Time is of the essence. If I do not present a solid plan to the clans within the next two weeks, things will escalate quickly. In truth, I don't even know that I have that much time—not with the majority of the males refusing to take praxilla."

Worry settled on Rihanna's delicate face. "I know it's not exactly ethical, but human parents often find clever ways to include vegetables in their children's meal in a way they won't even notice. My mother used to make avocado chocolate mousse for me. Maybe Relven could *accidently* drop some chopped praxilla petals in one of the side dishes. You guys eat a surprisingly large amount of greens, vegetables, and fruits. And you're getting a fresh batch from the humans tomorrow."

By the careful way in which Rihanna said it, she clearly feared to shock or anger me with her suggestion. It was indeed unethical as it basically came down to administering drugs to our clan without their knowledge. If they discovered it, they'd be rightfully enraged.

"Relven and I have already discussed it," I confessed without the slightest shame. "As you can guess, we are reluctant to go that route, but have occasionally crossed that line when tensions grew too high. However, it cannot become the norm. I will continue to try and reason with them. At least for now. But if it comes to that, I will do it to save my people. Then I shall accept the consequences of my actions, once the danger has passed. After what has happened to Wonjin, and the permanent disability he suffers, nobody wants to mess with praxilla, despite me setting the example."

"Actually, about that..." Rihanna started, looking both sheepish and excited.

But she never had a chance to finish her thought. The sound of the doorbell being frantically pressed followed by a loud, powerful pounding on the front door immediately set me in combat mode.

Am I already too late? Has blood rage already taken over one of my brothers?

Gesturing for my female to stay back, I opened the hidden panel in our bedroom where I kept an emergency weapon stash, and picked up a bladed staff. However, before I could set the first foot on the stairs leading down, the intruder opened the door— which we always left unlocked during the day, as was the custom among the Yurus.

"Rihanna! Rihanna, are you home?" Jerdea's voice called out, sounding a little frantic, but not panicked.

Stunned, I cast a confused look at my mate, who gave me a guilty grin. She tapped my forearm in a reassuring fashion then ran down the stairs. I rested my staff against the wall and followed in her wake.

CHAPTER 11
ZATRUK

To my shock, Rihanna never got a chance to fully cross our living area before Jerdea rushed out of the Great Hall to pick up my mate. She yelped in surprise, and my jaw dropped as our head scientist covered her face with kisses before giving her a bone-crushing hug.

Jaafan, what's going on?

By the time Jerdea put Rihanna back on her feet, my female was giggling, looking shy, the way a youngling would be when showered with too many praises.

"You are truly a gift from the Goddess. A blessing to our Chosen One," Jerdea said, her gaze flicking my way before returning to Rihanna, "and to every Yurus. Thank you! Thank you so much for fixing my son!"

My brain froze upon hearing those words, while Jerdea cupped my mate's cheeks and resumed kissing her face, earning herself more giggles.

"What do you mean by fixed?" I asked, approaching the two females.

"*I* didn't fix anything," Rihanna said, looking a little over-whelmed when Jerdea released her. "Before we left Kastan, I asked Luana if she would mind having a look at Wonjin's side. She agreed, and so did he. Turns out he had some spurs, not in his side, but up in his ribs, that her super advanced medical pod was able to remove. So, I really don't have any merit."

"But the only reason my son is no longer vulnerable is because of *your* intervention," Jerdea insisted. "*You* made it happen."

"He's fully healed?" I asked, awed by the news.

Rihanna hesitated then shook her head. "The spurs have been excised, but he *must not* get into any fights for forty-eight hours until he's fully healed. The spots where the deformities have been removed are weak right now. Any blows there could cause severe damage."

Jerdea nodded forcefully. "He told me. If I have to chain or drug him so that he stays out of trouble, you can be certain I will. Anyway, he is obeying his Clan Mistress' order to smith weapons matching galactic standards."

I cast a questioning look at Rihanna, who gave me another guilty grin.

She shrugged. "Out of sight, out of trouble. He gets time to heal while helping with your project."

"And he has many, many ideas," Jerdea said enthusiastically. "He got ideas from the documentaries he watched at the clinic while waiting for you, but also from your speeder, and from your talk about the crystals, especially the energy field poles around Kastan."

I recoiled at the last part, which sounded nonsensical to me. "The energy field poles? Why?"

"Indeed, why?" Rihanna echoed. "I mean, I saw them on my way in and guessed they served to erect a safety perimeter. But I wished I'd seen how it actually worked."

"The crystals are harmonized," I explained. "When activated, they form an impenetrable energy field, safe on the inner side, but potentially lethal on the outer side, depending on the setting.

At the non-lethal setting, when the field or crystals are struck, it provokes a powerful repulsion area of effect on a…"

I froze, understanding suddenly dawning on me. Kayog's wedding gifts flashed through my mind as the pieces began falling into place.

"What? What is it?" Rihanna asked.

"I think I know what Kayog wants us to do," I mused out loud. "The Zelconians can nurture crystals into having specific abilities, be it healing, power, damage, focus, and so on. When they built the human defenses against Vyrax's war, they programmed whatever casing supported the crystals to make them act in a specific way."

Rihanna's eyes widened in understanding. "Because the crystals themselves cannot be programmed. Buuut… a nanite subroutine in their casing can control them however we want."

I grinned at my female. "Exactly."

"And that's where the encryptor Kayog gave us comes into play," Rihanna said, her wheels spinning. "With its infinite preprogrammed subroutines, we could get the crystals to behave however we want."

"Imagine having a portable, smaller version of Kastan's perimeter wall as your personal shield?" I said wistfully. "Whether in combat or as night protection on your small camp in the forest, it would be an efficient and highly desirable tool."

"The personal shield was exactly what Wonjin had in mind!" Jerdea exclaimed with pride.

Rihanna frowned and shook her head. "Repulsion shields have been tried before. They work on perimeter walls like in Kastan because there is a great distance between the wall and the closest building. But it doesn't work with personal shields because the wielder always also gets blasted by the area of effect."

I smiled and shook my head. "Not with Zelconian crystals. You can fully control the direction of their effect."

"That's badass, then!" Rihanna said, her face lighting up. "What about damage crystals? We could—"

"No," I interrupted, gently but firmly. "Assuming the Zelconians would even consider collaborating with us by providing any crystal to begin with, damage crystals are extremely unlikely. They wouldn't trust us or the winners with them. If we are to negotiate with the birds, we need to present them prizes and weapons they will be comfortable with us building, owning, and distributing."

Rihanna nodded slowly. "I see no potential threat in the speeder. With a deutenium frame, Zelconian power and healing crystals, we could make the perfect vehicle."

Jerdea scratched the back of one of her floppy ears. "But why would the Zelconians consent in aiding us at all? If they don't sell to the United Planets Organization that has much to offer them in exchange, why trade with us that have nothing really to give them?"

"First, to ensure peace," Rihanna said. "The whole point of this arena is to give your males plenty of worthy opponents to fight to sate their blood rage in a controlled environment. And second, because it will increase the demand for their crystals, but this time with far more bidders in the pool. Right now, the UPO is pretty much the only buyer talking with the Zelconians while cockblocking everyone else. Once the planet opens up, potential traders will have more direct access to the Zelconians, which will put them in a much stronger negotiating position with the UPO."

"You make a fair point, my mate," I conceded. "However, I do not want us to make plans based on what the Zelconians may or may not agree to. We need to be self-sufficient, have a plan that we Yurus can bring to fruition on our own. Zelconian crystals must only be a potential enhancement to make our offering even more appealing."

Jerdea nodded. "Agreed. Too many uncertainties with the

humans and Zelconians. We need certainties that will get all the clans to rally without the risk of potential partners pulling out at the last minute. My team is already all over the galactic sites. They are putting together a list that we can review tomorrow. Wonjin is also already smithing weapons that will hopefully be suitable. But the biggest challenge will be the speeder's engine."

"There should be various blueprints available online," Rihanna interjected.

"Yes. We have found a few, but they are rather basic. We will work on enhancing them," Jerdea replied. "Drenia is drawing a few speeder designs based on what our research so far has indicated as being the most popular shapes, colors, and patterns. Rihanna can help us select the ones she thinks will be best received. In the next forty-eight hours, we will have a detailed blueprint of the chassis and frame for you to build, Zatruk."

"Perfect," I replied, excitement bubbling within me. "I will have deutenium ore turned into sheets by then to do the work."

~

Three days later, I traipsed through the woods with a heart filled with hope and unexpected happiness. Arms around my neck, chin resting on top of my head, my tiny mate had stopped complaining about me carrying her in what she called *peeguee* back.

We weren't traveling such a great distance that she would have needed me to carry her, but Rihanna had finally come to accept that I simply loved holding her and feeling her body wrapped around mine. Walking hand in hand didn't offer enough contact.

As I could run quite fast, I also made a show of it, racing through the forest with her spurring me on, cheering and laughing while hanging on to my horns.

"You're the best mount ever," Rihanna said teasingly when I resumed a walking pace.

"You can ride me anytime, my mate," I replied, my voice dipping in a suggestive fashion.

"You perv!" she exclaimed, giving me a playful tap on the shoulder.

"I offered you to ride *me*, I didn't say *my cock*. Do not blame me for your own improper thoughts," I said with shameless fake innocence.

Rihanna gasped, making me chuckle. "Your tone clearly implied—"

"My tone implied nothing other than what my words said," I interrupted. "*Your* perverted mind *chose* to interpret my tone in a way that fit your fantasies. It's okay to admit you want me, my mate. How could you not? Anyway, I am yours to do with as you please."

I turned my head to look at her over my shoulders. As I had hoped, she was glaring at me in that way I so loved.

"I really want to kick your ass right now," she mumbled.

I shrugged. "You keep promising to do so but never deliver," I said with fake boredom, before flicking my tail at her behind.

"Hey!" she exclaimed, swatting at it.

"Missed," I taunted, flicking my tail at her bum again.

"You little...!" It was her turn to do some flicking, this time targeting the tip of my right ear. "Next time, I'll flick both!"

"Is that so?" I asked in a menacing tone.

Rihanna nodded while wrapping her arm back around my neck. An evil smile tugged at my lips. Moving quickly before she could react, I caught both of her wrists crossed in front of my neck with one hand, and used my free arm to hold her legs wrapped around me trapped against my body.

"What are you...?"

Rihanna's question died in a shocked yelp when I proceeded to whip her behind with my tail, not hard enough to hurt, but enough for a slight sting. She began squirming and wriggling against my back in a vain attempt at freeing herself. I burst out laughing as she showered me with invectives, first in Universal, then in languages I didn't know. However, I recognized a few swear words I'd previously heard used by the Kastan humans.

A sharp pain in my left ear cut off my laughter. The unexpected pain traveled straight to my groin, awakening my shaft as my female's blunt teeth held on to my ear.

"I'm going to bite it right off," she threatened, her words muffled by my ear still stuffed in her mouth.

My cock jerked in response, and I barely kept myself from telling her to go ahead. While I didn't actually want my ear bitten off, I wouldn't have minded my female giving me an even sharper bite. Yurus had fangs, but no venom. Our females' fangs were smaller than a male's, and they often used them on us. I'd welcome a bit more roughness from my mate.

"Fine," I grumbled, releasing her wrists and legs.

As expected, Rihanna let go of my ear and immediately tried to jump off my back. Naturally, I didn't let her, yanking her to my front instead.

"Hey! What are you—?"

I silenced her protest with a possessive kiss while my hand soothed the sting from the 'spanking' I'd just given her. Rihanna punched my shoulder twice in a token protest before melting against me. Desire surged within. For a split second, I considered sitting her on my shoulders, propped against a tree to make her first climax on my tongue and then on my cock, but thought better of it. Not only were we too close to the city, but tonight was about making her discover the nighttime beauty of Cibbos. There would be time to ravage her later in our bed.

With much reluctance, I broke the kiss and set her back down on her feet. "Come. I want you to see the night forest awakening by the cliff," I said, taking her hand.

She gave me a suspicious look but complied. Naturally, being me, I couldn't resist the urge to swat her behind one last time with my tail.

Rihanna gasped. "I'm going to chop it off while you sleep and use it to make bows to tie your braids with," she threatened, glaring at me with the most adorable fake anger on her pretty face.

"Hmm, tail bows," I said pensively. "That might make for a new, bloody fashion trend."

"Keep being a smart ass. You won't be so smug when…"

Her voice trailed off as the trees parted before us, giving way to a series of tall plants, and medium-sized bushes, slowly fading as they neared the cliff overlooking the valley and the river in the distance.

With a timing even more perfect than I could have ever scheduled, the flora awakened with the last rays of the sun vanishing on the horizon. As if activated by a light dimmer, the plant colors all around us appeared to start glowing from within. Bright, neon colors suffused their leaves and petals. Over the water, a million sparkles lit up from the shore, spreading further away, as the phytoplankton began to fluoresce.

Rihanna pivoted on herself, staring at the world around us with an air of pure awe. Aside from the stunning colors of the flora under the moonlight that appeared to make them glow, the flowers themselves morphed. Many deployed larger petals, leaves, or bark-covered limbs to reveal a bright and delicate part of themselves, too sensitive to be exposed to the harsh heat and rays of sunlight.

It changed the entire layout of the forest, giving the illusion we were now in a completely different place, different world even.

"This is breathtaking," Rihanna whispered at last, advancing slowly back towards the plants.

She carefully ran her fingertips along a glowing petal or a newly protruding limb. With the forest's colorful new look came a matching fauna, lured by the fragrant perfumes of the awakening plants. Luminous flying creatures soared from the bushes, hailed by growing chirps and chants all around us.

Rihanna gasped before laughing when a few of the plants she touched reacted, some folding in on themselves, others stretching as if begging to be petted some more. The plants in this area were safe, but deeper in the forest, carnivorous and poisonous ones needed to be avoided.

She approached a beranea, one of the dullest-looking plants during the day, with the appearance of a huge, green bulb covered in spikes. At night, it opened up, revealing a large flower inside resembling a lotus flower. Rihanna approached one of them, the red petals, still partially folded around the center, glowed with an inner fire.

My mate touched the petals. To both our shock, they parted as a small creature flew out. It made a couple of acrobatic spins before coming to hover in front of Rihanna's face. My brain froze and my heart leapt at the sight of a sylphin.

The small creature had two arms attached to a torso that ended in a weird tail instead of legs. Her big head with large eyes, a wide mouth, and no visible nose, was adorned with hair shaped like petals. Her diaphanous wings flapped at high speed with a musical hum as she hovered, occasionally moving swiftly left or right, up and down. She appeared to glow from within, the intensity varying based on her emotions.

"Goddess!" I whispered, my voice filled with awe. "Do not make any sudden movements. It might frighten her. Don't worry, she's harmless."

"Okay," Rihanna breathed out with an air of wonder.

Sylphins were extremely rare, almost a thing of legend. I'd never seen one in the flesh before. Her timing couldn't have been more perfect.

My heart filled to bursting when the little creature flew closer to Rihanna. She stretched her tiny, three-fingered hands towards my mate, cupping the tip of her nose before pressing her face to it. I could only assume it to be her version of a hug or a kiss. She flew away, repeating the 'kiss' on Rihanna's cheek and forehead before she started playing with her curly hair.

Her head, much bigger than her body, suddenly turned towards me. I held my breath as she let go of Rihanna's hair to come hover in front of my face. I thanked the Goddess for the promise of luck the sylphin's mere presence offered. But I could certainly use a blessing with all the craziness I was juggling to get my people out of their current predicament.

As if in response to that silent plea, the sylphin wrapped her tail around my left tusk and started playing with it, poking and pinching my lips around it, then pulling on strands of my beard. She flew up next to one of my eyes, probably drawn by their red color, which was presumed to be attractive to the legendary creatures. She ran her tiny hand over my brow before bumping her face against it in her weird version of a kiss. She repeated it on my forehead too before wrapping her arms around the top of my right braid and letting herself slide down its length.

Rihanna burst out laughing, quickly covering her mouth with her hand for fear of frightening the creature. However, the sylphin was too busy using my braids and then my horn as some sort of amusement park, making it harder for me to properly see how she was entertaining herself.

Just as she was dangling upside down, swinging back and forth by the tip of her tail wrapped around the narrower end of my horn, something startled her. She straightened, wrapping herself more tightly around my horn, her glow fading, her hands taking a pose that made them look like tiny tendrils stemming from her roots. Had I not seen her moving before, I would have been fooled into thinking a flower had grown on or been tied to my horn.

My ears flicked as I strained them to hear what had frightened the sylphin. At the same time I heard it, I grabbed Rihanna's arm, pulling her behind me. She gave me a worried look before glancing at the direction I was watching.

I recognized well the muffled sound of hooves on the ground, the intruder trying—and failing—at his stealth approach. I berated myself for not bringing any weapon. But then, I never would have expected any Yurus would dare stalk me here during my bonding time with my mate.

The sylphin unwrapped herself from my horn and flew away. Seconds after she vanished into the bushes, my eyes widened in shock when Doreg cleared the tree line. Our eyes connected, and the glazed appearance of his erased any doubt he was entering the first uncontrolled stage of blood rage, where reason flirted with madness. Abandoning any pretense of stealth, he marched towards me with a malicious grin.

"What are you doing, invading my privacy," I demanded while he continued to advance.

"It is time for Mutarak to have a better leader," he spat, lifting his chin defiantly. "I'm here to challenge you."

"Here?" I snarled. "You dare interrupt my bonding time with my mate for your stupid ambitions? I happily accept your challenge and look forward to teaching you your place. But not here. Not in the dark without witnesses."

"You're too scared to fight me, *hoodah*?" he asked, uttering the insult with contempt and provocation.

"Please, you idiot. The only way you even remotely stand a chance to defeat me is by murdering me from a distance," I replied with a disdainful gesture. "Either way, we will only fight in public."

Anger and an air of madness flitted over his face. "You will fight me now, you coward. And if you won't... If you won't..." My blood turned to ice when his face took on a malicious glee as it flicked to my mate behind me. "If you won't, I will shoot that human you call a mate. Swear to fight me!"

A blind fury descended over me that not even a praxilla petal could silence. "You dare?" I whispered, taking a step towards him. "You threaten a female? My mate?" I added, slamming my fists to my chest as I continued to advance.

A sliver of fear and rationality sparked in his eyes, vanishing almost immediately to give way once more to his bloodlust. It didn't matter. He had crossed a line that could not be forgiven.

"I do not need to swear," I hissed. "You signed your death warrant."

I gestured with both hands for him to come at me. He holstered his blaster even as he broke into a run, charging me. I rushed him as well, our bodies violently clashing against each other's. We remained tangled in a duel of brute force. Whoever came out on top once we separated would have an advantage difficult to overcome by his opponent. And I fully intended for that to be me.

I headbutted him, slamming my forehead on the bridge of his nose, and immediately swiped my left horn at his face. The smell of fresh blood rewarded my effort as his flesh gave way under the sharp tip. I didn't wait to see what damage I'd inflicted. Spinning on myself to gain momentum as he attempted to jerk away from me, I smacked my right elbow at the back of his head. As he stumbled forward, I rushed after him, ramming the bottom of my hoof in his back, sending him sprawling to the ground.

Before he could get back up, I was already on top of him. I grabbed him by the left horn, yanked him backwards before smashing his face twice on my knee. Doreg roared in pain and fury and viciously swiped his claws at me. I dodged, letting him drop as I stepped away. He charged me again, trying to punch me before we could get into another lock. I easily avoided it, blocking the flurry of kicks and blows he ineffectively threw at me, partially blinded by the blood trickling into his eyes.

I caught the fist he'd intended to punch me in the throat with and held on to it as I spun around behind him. I kicked the back of his leg, making him fall to his knees and grabbed his left horn, twisting his neck with it. I could snap it and end it all there, but it wouldn't sate my hunger to see him suffer. Instead, I further twisted his arm I still held behind his back, snapping it. He shouted in both pain and fury. The sweetest music to my ears...

Yanking his head to make him fall onto his back, I straddled his chest. Doreg tried in vain to buck me off as I rained an endless barrage of punches on his bloodied face, each blow painfully resonating in an almost orgasmic fashion against my knuckles and up the length of my arms. A mad laugh flowed out of me as the bone of his left cheek gave beneath my assault. Testosterone flooded my veins, and blissful euphoria washed over me as I beat my opponent into a pulp.

"Zatruk... Stop. Please, stop, Zatruk. Snap out of it. Zatruk!"

That voice, so sweet, so familiar... It awakened such longing that I wanted to go to it. But my prey...? I wanted to destroy him. He deserved to die. I couldn't even remember why, just that he deserved... that I wanted to hurt him... that I...

"Zatruk! I beg you, stop! You're frightening me."

My head jerked up as sudden movement entered my field of vision and the words penetrated my mind. I blinked, seeing the pleading face of Rihanna before me.

"Please, Zatruk. You won. Stop."

I looked back down and swallowed hard at the sight of Doreg's still form and damaged face. Shame swelled in waves inside me while bile rose in my throat. I got back up on my hooves, my skin, hands, and fur covered in blood. I could still feel my hormones coursing through my body, demanding I finish what I had started.

How could I allow myself to lose control like this?

And in front of my mate, no less. I'd frightened her. Swallowing hard again, I turned my gaze to her face, expecting disgust and horror.

CHAPTER 12
RIHANNA

Heart pounding, I stared at my husband in shock. I had known Zatruk would be a formidable fighter. Warrior species like his only followed the strongest and most vicious fighter among themselves. But he'd always been so careful and gentle with me, the extent of his potential savagery had never fully dawned on me.

I understood his fury at Doreg threatening me with a weapon. However, the murderous madness in his eyes, his sadistic glee at slaughtering his opponent was freaking me out.

Zatruk fumbled blindly with the pouch on his belt, shoving a praxilla petal into his mouth. He hadn't made eye contact with me again since my voice had snapped him out of his blood rage. Although he and Jerdea had explained it to me at length, I hadn't fully grasped the depth of the insanity that took them over. When he finally looked at me, I didn't know what expression he saw on my face, but relief clearly flooded through him.

And then it struck me.

He thought I'd be terrified of or repulsed by him, by the violence he displayed.

"Thank you for stopping," I said, immediately kicking

myself for it. *That* was the best I could come up with under the circumstances?

"I'm sorry," he said, shame creeping back onto his face. "I shouldn't have allowed myself to get this carried away. Please, do not be afraid of me, Rihanna. I would *never* hurt you."

"I know that," I said with conviction, taking a few careful steps towards him. "I mean it. I know beyond any doubt that you will never hurt me. Your violence scared me, but not for myself. For him *and* for you. Despite what he did, I know you didn't want to kill him. He wasn't in his right mind."

A million emotions crossed his features, each one breaking my heart. Something had shattered inside my husband, or at least seriously fractured. This fight had taken something away from him, and I suspected it might be his conviction that he would be the one to break the cycle of violence. How could he lead the others to a path of peace if he himself couldn't control his rage?

But he did. He listened to my voice and snapped out of it.

I carefully cupped his face between my hands and caressed his cheeks with my thumbs. "You stopped, Zatruk. Your blood rage didn't control you. *You* controlled *it*."

"Because *you* called me out of it," he replied, distraught.

"And you listened," I retorted. "You are not a machine. You are a male with the weight of the world on your shoulders, fighting your own demon while trying to ensure the survival of your entire species. So what you stumbled through this one battle? It happens. But you're going to win the war. You're still fighting, you've got a promising plan, and people who believe in you. *I* believe in you, and I'll be by your side every step of the way."

A powerful emotion settled on my husband's face as he showed a vulnerability I doubted anyone had ever seen before me. He picked me up and gave me a bone crushing embrace. Heedless of the blood on him, I returned it and gently kissed him. He responded with a fervor devoid of lust, but filled with tenderness and gratitude. After I broke the kiss, he rested his forehead against mine.

"You are everything to me, Rihanna. You are my light in the endless darkness I'd been stumbling around, blindly looking for a way out of this dreadful cycle. You are my sylphin, my blessing, my hope, and my heart."

A pained groan from Doreg kept me from answering. All tenderness melted away from Zatruk's face, and his eyes seemed to glow redder as he turned to glare at Doreg's prone form.

"Let's go back to the village," Zatruk said.

He put me down, removed the blaster from Doreg's holster, and handed it over to me. To my shock, he then grabbed my free hand and one of Doreg's hooves, and dragged him behind us as he led me back to the city. I bit my tongue not to argue. At least, he wasn't dragging him by a horn.

To my pleasant surprise, it was only an eight-minute walk back to the village. While I couldn't be certain, I believed Zatruk had taken a shortcut. With the night 'mode' of the flora kicking in, I didn't recognize the path we'd taken initially. I also believed we had wandered around a bit before heading for the cliff.

As soon as we approached the side entrance to the city, Zatruk released my hand long enough to speak something in Yurusian in his armband. I nearly jumped out of my skin when some kind of city-wide alarm went off. He took my hand again and led me to the town square, still dragging Doreg in tow.

People were coming out of every building like an army of ants with panicked or worried expressions. The murmur of speculating voices died as they started noticing our approach. The gathering crowd parted before us, casting horrified looks at the blood on Zatruk, the one that had transferred to me, and then at Doreg's messed up face and busted arm. I didn't even want to imagine the state of his back after getting dragged on such a distance.

Zatruk let go of my hand, pulled Doreg to the middle of the

square, then released his foot with a disgusted gesture. A savage expression settled on his face as he slowly pivoted, looking at every male in attendance with a dare in his eyes.

He talked in his armband again, silencing the alarm, then pointed at Doreg. "Is this what the Yurus have become? Has our blood become so diluted by Great Wars that usurpers would try to sneak up on their Chieftain during his bonding time with his mate in the forest, in the dark of night? Threatening to shoot a female, MY MATE," he shouted, slamming his fist on his chest, "to force a duel he could never win to begin with?"

Shocked and horrified mutterings rose from the crowd as they glared at Doreg with outrage. A few spat on the ground, hurling insults at the barely conscious male.

"You want to fight me, then you *jaafing* challenge me in *public!*" Zatruk yelled. "Challenge me so that I can enjoy crushing you. I see every single one of you *hoodahs* eyeing me, assessing your chances of defeating me. You stroke your cocks at the thought of becoming the Great Chieftain of Mutarak. WHAT FOR? What in a nyloth's ass do you hope to accomplish as Chieftain?"

A glance around the assembled crowd revealed more than one male was indeed eyeing his position. And that question had struck a nerve. It was easy to crave power. But knowing what to do with it, and especially how to keep it, soon became a completely different ball game.

"Not a single one of you has shown himself even *worthy* of contemplating the position," Zatruk continued, his voice dripping with contempt. "What are you going to do that's different than what you're currently doing? You sit on your ass all day and wait for blood rage to take over you."

"We're waiting for your plan that's never completed!" Tarmek shouted, earning himself some nods from many of the males I highly suspected coveted the Chieftain role.

"And how about *you* start helping instead of waiting," Zatruk snapped back. "You moan, complain, and make demands while time flies. Look around you, how few juveniles we have. If we go into another Great War, our young across all of Cibbos will have to merge into a single clan to survive. Is this what you want for your son?"

The same stunned and shocked expression descended on every face—including mine—except that of the Yurus females. The males looked around the square, clearly counting the far too few young heads in our midst.

"Most of us grew up without a father. Do you once again want your sons to console their mothers and sisters while we die by our own hands?" Zatruk challenged, every male avoiding eye contact with him. "Only four adult males survived the last Great War, one of them my sire's killer—his best friend. My mother left Mutarak because she couldn't stand to look at the face of my father's killer, her own brother. Is this what you want? To kill each other because you are slaves to your hormones?"

I covered my mouth with my hand, shock, horror, and pity constricting my chest. I had no siblings that I knew of. But I couldn't imagine having a brother that would kill the man I loved in an act of temporary madness. Having no real family to speak of myself, I hadn't brought up the topic with Zatruk either, assuming his parents had passed since he had never mentioned them before. But this...

"Are we truly going to put our females through yet another cycle of misery and sorrow? There's a reason I eat praxilla. It doesn't weaken me. Challenge me, and you'll see just how soundly I'll destroy any of you," Zatruk said with a dare in both his voice and his eyes. "I will end this cycle of war, even if I have to beat each one of you into a pulp."

Pride filled my heart as I stared at my man. For a brief instant in the forest, I had feared that he would throw in the towel. But he still very much had the fire and determination to see this through.

"And how do we know that praxilla will not damage you and the rest of us over time like it did with the idiot?" Tarmek shouted.

"Once again, here's Tarmek complaining, sowing doubt, while offering nothing in terms of solutions," Wonjin interjected. "Are you so eager to make your son an orphan?"

Flabbergasted gasps rose from the crowd, everyone eyeing Wonjin in disbelief that he should talk back to Tarmek. By all accounts, Tarmek was deemed the most likely successor to Zatruk, or at least the one with the highest chance at maybe defeating him in a duel.

"Shut up, idiot!" Torgal said in Tarmek's stead. "You've been hiding for the past days and now you show up giving lip? Where were you, anyway? We've all missed giving you the beatings you enjoy so much."

Mocking laughter rose from the crowd, the atmosphere shifting had anger soaring within me. They'd been having a long-overdue discussion about the state of their species, and all it took was for a moron to spew some bullshit for everyone to start looking for an excuse to brawl.

"I've not been hiding, but helping our Great Chieftain with a solution," Wonjin replied calmly. "Unlike you useless pile of krogi dung. You sit here, scratching your sweaty balls all day, and leaving our females to do all the work. You call *me* an idiot, but how many of you would even know how to fix the generator if it broke down? You of all people, Torgal, are the biggest idiot in Mutarak. When your sink overflowed, you didn't even know how to turn off the *jaafing* water. You were crying to my mother for help."

I couldn't help a chuckle, picturing that big, burly male in a total panic in front of a water spill. As offended as the others felt about Wonjin's attack, they also laughed at Torgal.

"SHUT UP!" Torgal yelled, taking a menacing step, his pride obviously stung.

"Or what?" Wonjin retorted in a daring tone. "Besides complaining, all you pathetic *hoodahs* do is hunt, eat, sleep, and couple when a female takes pity on you and settles for your limp cocks. The only difference between animals and you is that you know how to hammer metal... and each other."

"And you're about to get your *jaafing* ugly face hammered," Torgal said, marching towards the center of the square.

Wonjin shrugged. "You can try. But I'll have you on your back in less than ten seconds."

This time, I burst out laughing, catching myself immediately. Everyone else gaped at Wonjin in disbelief upon hearing him echoing my original challenge to him. Zatruk moved close to me, and Gulkis ran to grab Doreg, dragging him away while Wonjin walked towards the center.

He only got a few steps in before Torgal rushed him. The crowd erupted in cheers. Heart pounding, I held my breath and sent all the positive energy I could muster towards Wonjin. Seconds later, anger surged within me when, as expected, Torgal threw a vicious punch at Wonjin's kidney as soon as he reached him. But his target didn't flinch or bend in pain as he used to. A stunned silence fell over the crowd, reflecting the shocked look on Torgal's face.

A savage expression descended over Wonjin's features. He backhanded Torgal with such violence, it sounded like thunderclap, making him stumble. He then caught Torgal's horn to smash his face on his knee. Without giving him a chance to recover, Wonjin yanked his head back, grabbed one of his legs, and lifted him like he weighed nothing. Air rushed out of Torgal as Wonjin slammed him onto the ground, before stomping on his groin.

Torgal cried out, folding into two under the bewildered expression of the silent crowd.

"That was six seconds, I think," I shouted, breaking the deafening silence.

Zatruk snorted, while a few of the females chuckled. Pride filled my heart as I stared at Wonjin, spreading his arms wide while slowly pivoting himself around, looking tauntingly at the gathered males.

"I guess he's not so tough when he can't exploit a vulnerability, right?" Wonjin said. "Anyone else wants an easy round with the 'idiot'? No? Not so eager anymore, are you? Yes, you've had years of enjoying easy wins, but that's over. Science fixed it. *Human* science. Science *we* could have achieved, too, if we stopped fighting all the time. And we could with praxilla."

Disapproving grunts rose all around from the males, their faces taking on mulish expressions.

"You would have us all become disabled and at the mercy of a human healer to function again?" Gulkis asked.

"No, you fool," Wonjin said, shaking his head. "All those years ago, Mother did not *force* me to take praxilla. I *chose* to do so back then like I *choose* to do it again today. I always knew the risk of side effects and accepted it. It was *worth it* for us to learn what was safe and what wasn't. We have done that study. We *know* what is safe. Stop being *hoodahs*, and do your part to save our future. Stop being a burden to our females. Pick up a *jaafing* hammer and ask our females how you can help, for once. Or remain as you are, and end up like him," he concluded, pointing at Doreg.

He spat on the ground with disgust, then walked away, the crowd parting to let him through.

I watched him walk away, my heart overflowing with pride. I felt as if I'd just seen my baby brother turn into a man before my very eyes.

"You've called him an idiot for years. And yet, he's ten times the male any of you will ever be," Zatruk shouted. Casting a disdainful look at Doreg still prone form, he gestured with his chin at him. "Heal his ass, and let him challenge me again, if he so dares."

Taking my hand, he led me back to our house.

~

A major shift occurred after that night. While a majority of males continued to refuse to take praxilla, a non-negligible number of others started timidly doing so. But more importantly, the city essentially turned into a ghost town. Instead of taunting shouts and the cheers of the crowd during a brawl, the muffled sounds of hammers filled the air as every male went back to smithing.

The Yurus females buzzed with excitement. They'd done a phenomenal job of gathering a list of weapons, shields, armor, and speeder models from the UPO's network. They'd designed templates meeting galactic standards and assigned them to the males, based on their respective skills. With so many hands on deck, we'd ended up with a substantial, high-quality collection in barely a week.

I reached out to all of my contacts, sending them photos and videos. The first feedback was mixed. While they loved the craftsmanship of the weapons and would have no problem selling them for a nice lump of credits, they wouldn't make an appealing enough reward as is. They would need to be enhanced with special properties. That was fair enough. Enhancement would be the next steps of our work.

But even if that failed, the type of numbers my contacts were throwing around for selling our regular weapons and armor pieces would suffice for us to raise a large enough purse to offer a credits reward instead.

The speeders, on the other hand, they absolutely loved, even if we stuck with a simple sidinium power crystal instead of a Zelconian one. The designs were badass, and the maintenance-free deutenium made it a dream. Not only would they have plenty of buyers at ridiculously high prices, they confirmed it would make a more-than-worthy reward. The problem? The speeder's performance was pure shit.

Until we'd sold a few weapons and armor pieces, we couldn't afford to bring in a highly-skilled, off-world engineer to help the Yurus females figure out how to improve it. Naturally, we would do it, if it came to that. Although it was a long shot, I held hope that we might find a good engineer in the human colony of Kastan. With a bit of luck, they could assist us without breaking our bank.

As we had another trade with the humans happening this morning, I decided to join the convoy to go inquire in person. Wonjin tagged along.

The entire journey to Kastan, I kept stealing freaked out glances at our carrier creatures called nyloth. I couldn't decide if they were ugly beasts or giant creepy crawlers. According to Wonjin, a female didn't lay eggs or larvae, but gave birth to live mini versions of herself. The grayish-green nyloth looked like the offspring of a threesome between a centipede, a lobster, and a fly. A dozen spindly legs lined the entire length of its ringed body, its wide back slightly recurving on the sides, making it a perfect container. Large lobster pincers on his shoulders served as arms framing its massive fly-like head.

On its back, countless temperature-controlled crates contained the roughly butchered meats the Yurus had hunted for the trade. But it also included polished bones, tusks, horns, furs, and scales the human crafters could make use of.

When we reached Kastan, Wonjin and I made a beeline for the medical clinic, leaving Gulkis to handle the trade. To my shock, when we entered the clinic, the door between the waiting area and the examination room lay wide open. The first Zelconian I'd ever laid eyes on was crouching in front of Luana, his hands cupping her swollen belly while he gently kissed it.

I stopped dead in my tracks, wondering if we should

skedaddle back out. Before my brain could order my legs to move, the Zelconian turned his head to look at us.

"Come in, Rihanna Makeba," he said, his voice deep, incredibly soft, and musical, that gave me goosebumps.

He rose to his feet, drawing Luana against his side. She leaned against him with a happy smile welcoming us.

Good heavens, he was stunning! Unlike Kayog, who possessed a beak, Luana's husband had a very human face aside from his large, midnight-blue eyes that seemed filled with a constellation of stars. As a hybrid half-human, half-Zelconian, he had human legs, although his feet and ankles were covered in small scales. He was completely naked, a patch of down feathers, the same color as his blue skin, covering his naughty bits. I presumed they retracted inside his body as no bulge adorned his nether region. Similar but colorful feathers covered his chest while a massive set of majestic midnight-blue wings hung on his back. And on his forehead, a magnificent crest of golden feathers shaped like a fan, similar to Earth's royal Amazonian flycatcher birds.

He looked regal and a little intimidating.

A discreet but amused smile stretched his lips as he observed me, his tattletale empathic abilities having no doubt revealed to him just how breathtaking I thought he was. For all that, while I could stand there for hours admiring him like the visual work of art that he was, I didn't feel any sexual attraction towards him. I wanted to pet his feathers, but a certain fluffy minotaur held my romantic interests.

"We didn't mean to interrupt," I said politely, at the same time realizing what a unique opportunity this was to make a first contact with the Zelconians.

"It's fine, I'd already done the interrupting," he said, casting an amused look at his wife.

"Which you are welcomed to do whenever you please,"

Luana replied to him. "Rihanna, Wonjin, please meet my husband, Dakas Wakaro."

"It's a pleasure to meet you, Dakas," I said with sincerity.

"The pleasure is all mine, Rihanna," Dakas replied with a gentle smile before nodding at my companion. "Wonjin."

Socially challenged as always, Wonjin grunted in greeting. I repressed the urge to chuckle, but it didn't fool our hosts, who also seemed amused.

"To what do we owe the pleasure of your visit," Luana asked. "Do you need medical assistance? Are the spurs bothering Wonjin?"

"No," Wonjin replied before I could. "Our Clan Mistress has an inquiry. I merely wanted to thank you for the treatment." He brutally punched himself in the kidney, making Luana flinch while Dakas's feathery brows shot up. I cringed inwardly, while also finding him incredibly cute. "See? It is all good now."

"So good in fact that he royally spanked the dumbass who thought to exploit his former weakness," I said with excessive pride, as if I was talking about my own brother. "But that only happened three days later," I quickly added when Luana frowned, her displeasure evident.

She instantly relaxed and nodded. "Good. I'm glad I was able to help. Just don't brawl too much, and especially don't punch yourself like that. It's still early after what was a serious surgery, even though it looked simple."

"No worries," I replied reassuringly. "Frankly, there's been zero brawling in over a week in Mutarak—a record! Zatruk and Wonjin talked sense into the others. Right now, everyone is focusing on Zatruk's project. Which is actually what brought me here."

"Zero brawling? That's impressive," Luana said. "How can I help?"

"Would you guys happen to have a great engineer we could borrow to help us sort out an issue," I asked, carefully.

"An engineer?" Dakas asked, his interest piqued. "What for?"

I hesitated but then decided it was fine to share this part. "We're trying to build speeder bikes more or less like mine. But we're having performance issues with the engine. We're hoping a human engineer could help us identify the cause."

"You have the speeder here?" Dakas asked with an eagerness that took me aback.

"Not one of those we're building, but I came here riding the one I'd acquired off-world."

Dakas exchanged a look with Luana. By the way she nodded, I realized they were talking telepathically. Had she also gained telepathic powers on top of empathic ones from mating with a Zelconian?

"May I have a look at your speeder?" Dakas suddenly asked. "You have me quite curious. I happen to be an engineer."

CHAPTER 13
RIHANNA

My heart leapt in my chest, and my eyes nearly popped out of my head. To have a Zelconian engineer working with us would freaking rock. While I had no personal idea of the extent of their engineering skills, the Yurus claimed they were the most advanced species on Cibbos. If Dakas got onboard and gained enough pride and enthusiasm for the project, he would likely push to convince his people to let us use a Zelconian power crystal with it!

"Sure! I'd be more than happy to show you!" I said, failing miserably at hiding my excitement.

"I will ask our own human engineer, Lara, to join you outside," Luana said. "She's a new technology addict and will certainly be interested in what you are doing."

"Wonderful, thank you!"

Luana sat down and reached for her com system as we headed out. Despite my excitement, I forced myself to rein in my emotions. Dakas looked nice enough, but I hated that my emotions were an open book for him, that he could sense my hopes and fears. This project had become as important to me as it was to Zatruk and his entire people. However, years of working as a smuggler had taught me to never let the other party see your desperation. It was the best way to get screwed over or end up with a shitty deal.

Thankfully, Dakas appeared fascinated by my speeder. While he was busy examining it from every angle, an attractive Asian female in her mid-twenties came our way. Measuring about 5'8 and slender, she had shoulder-length dark-brown hair, almost the same color as her eyes, a nice pair of pouty lips, and a pointy chin. Something about her screamed a healthy level of sass and attitude.

"Hi," she said, coming to a stop near us. "My name is Lara."

"It's a pleasure to meet you," I said with a grin. "This is my friend, Wonjin."

To my shock, Wonjin stood transfixed in front of Lara, his lips parted, and his ears flicking. He seemed so mesmerized, he didn't even remember to do his usual greeting grunt.

"Hi," Lara responded, sparing him the briefest glance before focusing her attention on the speeder.

She almost shoved Dakas out of the way so that she could get a closer look. He chuckled, stepping away, although his attention shifted to Wonjin who was still gaping in awe at Lara. The Zelconian tilted his head to the side in a way eerily similar to how birds often did as he examined Wonjin's reaction. It appeared to fascinate him, and I would have given anything to know what he was perceiving from my companion.

No doubt sensing Dakas's stare on him, Wonjin abruptly turned his head towards the Zelconian. His brown skin darkened, and his ears flicked in that typical fashion I'd come to realize meant embarrassment or nervousness for the Yurus. He frowned and averted his eyes to have thus been caught drooling over a human.

I didn't know Lara, but it would be sweet to have another human living in Mutarak, if those two could hit it off. Sadly,

Lara was completely oblivious to the passion she stirred and only had eyes for the speeder.

"What seems to be the problem?" Lara asked.

"There's no problem with this one," I replied, approaching my bike. "We're building a few like these and are having performance issues with the engine. We were hoping a new pair of eyes could help our engineers sort it out. Our new ones fly the same as mine, but they can't achieve the same speed and responsiveness."

"Can you show us how this one performs?" Dakas asked.

"Sure!"

I always enjoyed giving a bit of a show with my baby. I straddled my bike and took it for a spin around the empty plaza. Gulkis and the others had led their freaky nyloths to the other side of the village where most of the farms and granaries were located. Still, considering the insane speeds my vehicle could reach, I had to rein it in to some extent to avoid crashing into a wall. However, once I flew it near its maximum height of twelve meters, I was able to cover a greater distance above the buildings at higher speed.

When I landed back down near the clinic, Lara looked on the verge of having an orgasm.

"This is so amazing!" she whispered, staring at the speeder as if it was the greatest wonder in the universe.

"It is quite impressive," Dakas concurred. However, something in his tone set all my senses on high alert. "Could you have gone higher than where you flew?"

I shook my head. "No, speeders aren't really meant to fly this high. They're designed to hover. Ten to twelve meters above ground is the maximum. But you don't want to remain at such heights for too long. It can get dangerous."

Dakas nodded with a neutral expression, but I didn't miss the way his shoulders slightly relaxed. Did he fear the Yurus could use these superfast vehicles to storm their sky city of Synsara?

"What are the Yurus building them for? For personal use?" Dakas asked, his tone still non-committal.

I shook my head again. "No."

"So, for off-worlders?" he asked.

"Yes."

He narrowed his eyes at my laconic responses. "To sell?" he insisted.

I shifted on my feet, unsettled by this less-than-subtle inquisition. "Look, I don't think it's my place to discuss Zatruk's plans in his stead. There's nothing fishy going on or that should warrant any concern for humans or Zelconians. But..."

To my relief, Dakas bowed his head in concession. "Fair enough. Would he talk to me, then?"

I recoiled, taken aback by the request and Dakas's obvious interest. I vaguely recalled Zatruk mentioning Dakas was part of the Zelconian Council. Was he on a fishing expedition?

"Probably, yes. I believe he would," I answered cautiously.

"Great. Would it be all right then for me to accompany you back to Mutarak?" Dakas asked.

"Sure. I will let him know you're coming," I replied, unsure as to how I felt about the Zelconian's insistence. This could either be a blessing or a disaster in the making.

"If it's okay, I'll tag along, too," Lara said with enthusiasm. "I'd like to take a gander at those other speeders and see if I can help, although I make no promises."

"Wonderful! You can ride on my speeder with me if you like," I offered.

Lara squealed with excitement.

I sent a message to Zatruk through my bracer. His simple "Very well" response made me wonder if he was upset. We said our goodbyes to Luana then set back for Mutarak, Wonjin on his krogi, Dakas flying overhead, and Lara behind me on my speeder.

We reached the village barely fifteen minutes later. Zatruk

was already waiting for us on the square, Jerdea by his side. Her excitement was palpable, but my husband couldn't have been more unreadable.

As soon as we stopped, a short distance from them, Wonjin jumped off his krogi and hurried to extend a hand to Lara in order to help her down from my speeder. She seemed as shocked as I felt by this unexpected act of chivalry. To my relief, she accepted his hand, letting go as soon as she was back on her feet.

I fought to keep the amused grin off my face that threatened to blossom as Wonjin's ears went into another bout of flicking up and down. With my stupid imagination, I could almost picture them turning into wings, making him fly away.

Dakas landed a couple of meters in front of Zatruk.

My husband struck his chest with his fist. "Greetings, Counselor Dakas."

Dakas bowed his head. "Greetings, Great Chieftain Zatruk."

"Seriously?" I asked, giving both males a disbelieving look. "We're going to be this formal? Should I start calling you Counselor Dakas?"

He laughed and shook his head. "No, Rihanna. Dakas is more than fine. I like things informal as well. Anyway, I'm not here as a Zelconian Counselor, but as an engineer."

"Then you may call me Zatruk," my husband said as I approached him.

"And you may call me Dakas."

Zatruk's face softened when I came to stand next to him. He gently caressed my cheek with the back of his hand. I smiled affectionately, then turned to introduce him to Lara, but not before catching the odd way Dakas was observing the tender interaction between Zatruk and me. In that instant, whatever doubt I still held that the Zelconian was here on a fishing expedition vanished. While I didn't doubt that the engineer in him was also quite interested in the speeder, the Counselor was here to assess any potential threat, my relationship with Zatruk, and the direction he was leading his people.

"Zatruk, Jerdea, please meet Lara, one of the engineers of Kastan. She agreed to come have a look at our speeders to see if she could help with the performance issues," I said. "Lara, this is my husband Zatruk and our Head Scientist, Jerdea."

"It's a delight to have you here," Jerdea said in a bubbly voice before turning to Dakas. "And you as well, Counse... Dakas."

"We are both eager to see what you have accomplished," Dakas replied.

"Yeah, definitely," Lara replied. "Thank you for welcoming us," she added, looking at Zatruk, appearing somewhat intimidated.

"Do not mention it," Zatruk said with a polite smile. He gestured at the large building framing the town square to the north. "If you would follow me, the development facility is right here."

"I will go park your speeder while I stable my krogi," Wonjin offered.

"Thank you. You're very kind," I said with genuine gratitude.

Holding my hand, Zatruk led the rest of us to the building. The ground floor resembled a ship hangar, with a large open space, workstations lining the walls, most of them facing large windows, and a few machines that served who knew what purpose.

While Zatruk made the introductions, I bit the inside of my cheeks not to burst out laughing. The Yurus females were falling all over themselves at the sight of Dakas. It dawned on me then that it was likely the first time one of them saw a Zelconian up close, even though Dakas was a hybrid. But the gentle and sweet way he interacted with them touched me. He almost seemed shy, embarrassed even by so much attention.

Wonjin returned just as his mother was beginning to show the speeders.

"These are the three we've built so far," Jerdea said, pointing at the two bikes in the center of the space, and then at the third one sitting on the testing device next to the main workstation.

Lara's eyes sparked with awe as she slowly circled around them, her fingertips caressing the sleek curves of the speeders. "These are absolutely stunning," she said in a wistful voice. "Especially that one. It's my favorite."

"Thank you," Wonjin said.

Lara's head jerked up, and she turned to look at him, wide-eyed. "You made this?"

Wonjin shifted on his hooves. "I smithed the chassis and frame."

"Smithed? As in you did this by hand?" she asked with an incredulous expression on her face.

"Yes. Deutenium isn't meant for machines. You have to listen to the metal and make it sing to bend it to your will," Wonjin said.

"Wow, you're really talented," Lara said, sounding impressed.

"My son is also very good with math and physics," Jerdea said proudly. "Wonjin does most of the calculations for our buildings, just for fun."

My jaw dropped at the same time as Zatruk's brows shot up. Clearly, he had also not known of Wonjin's side activities. But then, he had studied a long time as a youngling.

"It's just a hobby," Wonjin mumbled, looking mightily embarrassed while Lara looked at him with new eyes. "But once we've sorted the performance problems of the speeder, I can make one for you, if you wish."

"What?! Oh no! I can't accept that," Lara said, stunned.

Wonjin frowned, looking utterly confused. "You do not wish to own one?"

"Well… uhm… actually, yes. Who wouldn't? But I can't accept such an expensive gift."

"It is not expensive. It is only my time and skills," Wonjin said, even more baffled.

"Consider it compensation for helping us fix the performance issues," I interjected.

Lara opened and closed her mouth a few times before casting a helpless look at Dakas. He merely smiled, looking like a Mayan god, with his crest and large wings.

"I guess if I manage to help you guys, it would indeed be a fair trade," she conceded at last.

"Then I will make you one. It is settled," Wonjin said in a tone that brooked no argument, clearly not understanding the cause of her reluctance.

"Okay, then," Lara said, looking both thrilled and slightly overwhelmed.

Beaming, Jerdea proceeded to explain to both Dakas and Lara what the problems were. Most of it flew right over my head. I could patch minor problems in a ship or speeder, assuming I had the assistance of the onboard computer. But all this advanced stuff was above my pay grade.

However, another wave of pride filled my heart as both Zatruk and Wonjin answered a series of technical questions regarding the metal, assembly, the way the engine interacted with the chassis, heating and cooling, and a bunch of other shit that didn't mean squat to me. But the respect displayed by Dakas only confirmed they had impressed him beyond expectations.

"From what I can see, you do not have a construction problem, but a programming one," Dakas said at last, pointing at the monitor of the computer hooked to the speeder. "You have three systems sending conflicting commands to run their respective subroutines. In isolation, each system works perfectly, but see, this command to prevent overheating essentially also caps the engine's ability to reach higher speeds, as it's imposing the same heat restrictions."

"*Jaafan!*" Jerdea whispered, her eyes flicking between the two strings of code. "How did we not see this before?"

"Because it's not obvious," Dakas said in a gentle tone. "I only figured it out this quickly because I spent three months banging my head on the walls trying to fix a similar problem with one of our underground transport systems in Synsara before I finally realized what was happening."

"Ugh, then we are blessed the Goddess sent you our way. We cannot afford to waste three months on solving such a problem. Time is of the essence," Jerdea said.

Dakas tilted his head to the side. "Why is that? What do you intend to do with these speeders?"

Jerdea's eyes flicked towards Zatruk. Dakas turned to my husband. By the intensity of his gaze, I suspected he was also focusing on every emotion his empathic abilities could perceive from Zatruk.

"Would you mind telling me about your plans?" Dakas asked.

Zatruk eyed him silently for a brief moment before giving him a sharp nod. "Yes, but not here."

"Do you mind continuing without me for now?" Dakas asked Lara.

"No, we're good!" Lara said with enthusiasm. "We're probably going to have to do a lot of rewriting to work around these conflicts. We should be quite busy."

"Very well," Dakas said.

Zatruk gestured for the Zelconian to follow. He caressed my cheek again then left with Dakas.

CHAPTER 14
ZATRUK

I had not been certain of my feelings when Rihanna warned that Dakas was coming. I hated the Zelconians' ability to read my emotions. And the pretty hybrid unnerved me the most as he was neither a real human nor a pure Zelconian, making him harder to gauge and to anticipate. He had been the mastermind behind the defenses that had obliterated our forces during Vyrax's failed war. The record time in which he had gotten his people and the humans to erect them spoke volumes about his intelligence and efficiency.

I would not underestimate him.

But what were his intentions? He claimed not to be here in his capacity as Counselor, but we both knew that was a lie. When visiting a former enemy, one as prone to violence and warmongering as we were, you never fully shed your suspicions. You *always* looked for signs of brewing trouble.

"Thank you for helping identify the source of the problem," I said as we made our way to the house. "As Jerdea said, we are on a tight timeline."

"What deadline are you chasing?" Dakas asked.

"The one to begin the construction of our galactic gladiator arena," I said, matter-of-factly.

For the first time, the Zelconian's legendary control flagged as he recoiled in surprise before quickly regaining his composure. "A galactic gladiator arena?" he echoed, questioningly.

I nodded and gave him a quick breakdown of the project. I hated feeling so vulnerable and nervous. As much as I believed in this plan, I had not expected to make a sales pitch this early. And yet, this was a good rehearsal with what I wanted to believe was a sympathetic ear.

"It makes sense," Dakas said pensively as I gestured for him to enter my office. "This would provide a controlled environment for the Yurus to indulge in their passion for battle while creating wealth for your people. And the speeders would be the reward?"

I nodded, hating even more how relieved I felt that he seemed to approve. I'd never been the insecure type, quite the opposite. My strength and combat skills saved my ass countless times from the troubles my cocky arrogance had gotten me into.

"Currently, they are the main reward we're looking into, including weapons and armor," I confirmed.

"With sidinium power crystals? Not Zelconians?" Dakas asked with a strange expression.

I had known that question would be raised sooner than later. Sadly, Dakas's unreadable features and those wretched starry eyes that zealously kept their secrets, made it impossible for me to know what kind of answer he was looking for.

"First, we want to validate our ability to build desirable, quality rewards on our own," I replied in a non-committal fashion. "After that, we can start looking into partnerships that could further elevate our offerings."

Dakas slowly nodded in approval. "Very wise approach. You never want to be at the mercy of others to define your future. What are your biggest concerns with it?"

I carefully chose my words, wanting to give him enough to get him onboard, but not so much to leave us exposed and vulnerable.

"Logistics will probably be the biggest headache once we've ironed out the rewards issue," I confessed. "There will be a lot of visitors to handle simultaneously, and we'll need to cater to their needs."

"I'm glad to see you're already thinking of that," Dakas said.

I couldn't decide if I felt more flattered than offended that he should be so pleasantly surprised. Then again, I couldn't blame him for assuming most Yurus were complete idiots. My predecessors had not exactly distinguished themselves by their brilliance. And the truly smart Yurus were our females who never left the vicinity of the city.

"Once we're nearing the time to begin construction, I intend to invite the human and Zelconian leaders here to present the project to them," I said nonchalantly.

"To convince them to give you what you need?" Dakas challenged.

I shook my head. "No. To convince them to make this a Cibbos project. There will be a significant trickle-down effect that could benefit all three of our peoples. My mate and I are preparing the pitch while sorting out the matter of rewards. But that is merely a potential larger scale plan. The main plan we're focusing on is the one where the Yurus run this entirely on their own should the humans and Zelconians express little or no interest."

He stared at me for a few seconds, his face betraying none of his thoughts. "I see," he said at last, then suddenly turned towards the maquettes of the arenas I had aligned on a console by the wall. "Nice maquettes."

"Thank you," I said, watching him approach them, carefully studying each one in turn. Once more, I wanted to kick myself for worrying about how they would be received.

Dakas pointed at the more rectangular design of the three. "This shape holds the best potential for future expansion, should you so desire. These two will be more complex. May I?" he added, pointing at the rectangular arena.

"Wait," I said, picking it up and carrying it to the work table. I waved my hand over it, expanding a 3D hologram above it, allowing us to get a perfect view of each area of the model.

"Fancy. Jerdea designed this?" he asked, impressed.

I chuckled. "No. I acquired this through Vyrax's mercenaries prior to the war."

Once again, Dakas stared at me. I suddenly got the sense he wanted to query me about my thoughts on it but then appeared to change his mind.

"Your general design is great," he said, rotating the model. "But the seats are problematic. They're scaled for the Yurus, which is much too wide for most species."

"Isn't too wide better than too narrow?" I countered.

"Yes," he conceded, "but it's also uncomfortable as it doesn't provide enough support. People like having armrests, not floating in a large area. Furthermore, you're wasting a lot of space that could contain more seats. You do not want to turn away spectators because you do not have enough seats to accommodate them. You should scale down most of them to galactic standards. Then you can keep a section with wider seats, but make their width adjustable so armrests can be brought in at a more comfortable position."

I nodded slowly while reflecting on his suggestions, my mind already identifying the areas that could be modified. "This is a wise suggestion. I will take it into account."

Dakas smiled. "On a more selfish note, I would also suggest you consider lower backrests," he said, shifting his wings. "Synsara used to only have benches, as backrests get in the way of our wings. Since our rapprochement with the humans, we have modified our seats to have adjustable backrests so they can be lowered."

I pursed my lips, nodding once more while mentally berating myself for not thinking about that. "Right, there are other avian species out there. And then there are species who do not have legs and won't be comfortable navigating stairs. It appears I have quite a few adjustments to make."

"I coded the program and designed the system for adjustable backrests. I would be glad to share it with Jerdea, if she wants it," Dakas offered.

"Thank you for this... unexpected assistance," I said, still unsure what his angle was, or if he genuinely wanted to help.

The affable mask fell, and I immediately recognized the Zelconian Counselor coming back to the fore.

"You have honored the truce and trade agreements with the humans. And now, you are striving to sate your people's blood rage in a controlled environment, while maintaining the peace with your neighbors," Dakas said. "As long as your plans remain ethical, you will have my full support, including in terms of using our non-lethal crystals for your rewards."

My heart leapt in my chest. This was far more than I had hoped for.

"You are very kind."

Dakas snorted. "I'm not kind. I'm selfish. I want peace, and I want my mate to be happy. Luana is fond of your female and wants Rihanna to stay on Cibbos, happy. I can feel the strength of your love for her... and hers for you."

It was my turn to snort at that comment. Rihanna desired me and had some affection for me. But love?

Dakas tilted his head to the side in that bird fashion that I always found a little creepy. "Do not doubt her love for you, Zatruk. Kayog is never wrong."

Those words struck a nerve.

"He negotiated with you because he saw honor in you,"

Dakas continued. "He sent Rihanna to you because he knew she was your soulmate and that, together, you would achieve what others deemed impossible, like my Luana and I did. When you do your presentation to the humans and the Zelconians, make sure your mate is by your side. She's an off-worlder, and she knows the market you're trying to tap into. But more importantly, she believes in you and in your project. That will be your most powerful argument with my people."

"Your words have not fallen on deaf ears," I replied, moved more than I would ever show.

"Good! Now, I should get out of your way and go check on my mate."

"Ah yes, I understand congratulations are in order," I said, a surge of envy coursing through me, imagining my Rihanna pregnant with my child. And yet, the timing wasn't right. Under the circumstances, we had too much going on to also juggle the very first human-Yurus pregnancy.

"Thank you. We are very happy. Worry not, your turn will come sooner than you think."

With those mysterious words, the Zelconian bowed his head and left my dwelling.

The following days felt like sitting on a time bomb, praying it wouldn't go off before we finished. First, there was the situation with Doreg. After our healer had mended him, instead of challenging me to a public duel, he had fled Mutarak, no doubt in shame. A stupid decision. Here, we knew him. Despite the fury his threat on my mate had stirred within me, deep down, I had known he wouldn't have actually shot her, even under the influence of blood rage.

For all our savagery, Yurus males were viscerally incapable of physically harming a female. It was actually a source of concern for the future of the arena since Rihanna had mentioned that in some galactic species, the females were the warriors of their people, some as strong as a Yurus male and likely would wish to participate. I felt nauseous at the mere thought of raising a hand to a female, even in a consensual duel.

But that bone-deep protectiveness also made a male who threatened a female a total pariah. Here, we would have forgiven Doreg, elsewhere, not so much. The word of his nighttime attack spread far and wide, making him unwelcome everywhere he went. In desperation, after being turned away by four different clans, he challenged the Chieftain of Dhagarak for the right to stay. He had to have known he never stood a chance.

By all accounts, even after he lost, he refused to concede and kept fighting until he got himself killed. Another senseless loss to blood rage. Sadly, I believed he had sought such an end rather than live with his shame and his losing battle to his hormones. If nothing else, it further fueled my determination to solve this once and for all.

However, that deadly battle was only one of a few more fights, just slightly less bloody. With the steadily growing unrest, the females of every clan putting the males to work at their forges gave us a slight reprieve. The Yurus were social people. Keeping the warriors isolated and tiring themselves working reduced the opportunities for trouble and skirmishes.

And then two days ago, the great news I had been hoping for finally came. With a bit of help from Dakas, and a lot from Lara, Jerdea not only got our speeders to match the speed and performance of Rihanna's bike, but even to exceed it, thanks to the strength and stability of the deutenium chassis.

Now, the moment of truth was upon us. Any minute, the humans and Zelconians would arrive.

I wistfully observed my mate, focused on her tablet as she went over the last details of her presentation. My heart burst with love for my little sylphin. She had worked so hard over the past weeks. Never a complaint, always an optimistic and enthusiastic outlook on things.

I resented the lack of intimate moments with her, or even having the time to just have fun and get to know each other better. Granted, we spent most of our time side by side, physically together, but mentally focused on our respective tasks, except when we were brainstorming.

"You're staring," Rihanna said without looking away from her tablet.

"When am I not?" I grumbled.

"When I'm sitting on your lap. But I'm not moving from this chair."

"Why not?"

She gave me a teasing sideways glance. "Because I'm going to start fiddling with your beard, and braid your hair into flowers or bows. I don't think that's the look you want to sport when our guests arrive."

I frowned at her. "Then don't mess with my hair."

"You constantly say that. How many times have I listened?" My frown deepened, which only made her giggle. "It is genetically impossible for me not to play with your fluff, if it is within range. Therefore, the choice is yours. I can sit on your lap and give you pretty bow braids, or I can stay right where I am and keep my hands to myself."

Before I could respond, the town horn resounded outside. My stomach dropped, and I felt my blood drain from my face. I shouldn't be such a nervous wreck. We had a solid plan. We didn't need to form a partnership with our neighbors for our plan to move forward. And yet...

I rose to my feet at the same time Rihanna came to stand in front of me. I instinctively picked her up, needing the comforting feeling of her against me. She cupped my face between her delicate hands then kissed my forehead, each of my eyes in turn, and then the tip of my nose.

"You've got this, Zatruk," she said in a gentle, yet firm voice. "*We've* got this... with or without them. I believe in you and in this project. We're going to rock their socks... and bird feet. Let's go kick some ass."

She then gave me a long and passionate kiss, and the oddest sense of peace descended over me.

"My little sylphin," I whispered, brushing my lips against hers one last time before setting her back on her feet.

Then, hand in hand, we headed outside to greet our guests.

CHAPTER 15
RIHANNA

Tons of villagers gathered by the town square, their eyes turned up towards the sky. The three Zelconians flying above the two zeebises of the human delegation made for a majestic tableau.

Suddenly, it was my turn to feel nervous, not because I doubted our project, but because I wanted this so badly for Zatruk. I'd never seen anyone work so hard, so selflessly for people who didn't fully appreciate all the challenges he faced, most of them caused by themselves.

As all five of our guests landed, the appearance of the pure-blood Zelconians struck me by how much more bird-like they were. I'd grown too used to Dakas's human face and mostly human feet. As Dakas made the introductions, I stole furtive glances at Graith, the Zelconian Exarch—which was a fancy word for their leader—and his right hand, Skieth. Like Kayog, both had beaks and bird feet, with the kind of talons that could tear you to shreds with a single swipe.

I had heard how Graith had messed up Vyrax with his talons, claws, and beak. One look at him shouted for you to keep your head down and tail tucked between your legs, if you didn't want to get your eye pecked out. And yet, despite his obvious aura of don't-fuck-with-me, the Zelconian Exarch struck me as a rather charming male, with a hint of mischief.

"We meet at last, Rihanna Makeba," Graith said in a powerful voice. "I'd been curious about the mate Kayog had deemed the perfect match for the Great Chieftain."

"Let me guess, you didn't expect such a tiny little thing," I replied teasingly.

He snorted, echoed by Skieth, while a discreet smile stretched Dakas's and Mateo Torres's lips. Counselor Allan remained neutral.

"I confess that I did not," Graith conceded. "I had imagined a towering female warrior with a sharp tongue to handle him."

I shrugged. "According to Zatruk, both of my proportionally tiny hands combined aren't enough to handle him."

Skieth and Graith burst out laughing, while Dakas and Mateo repressed a chuckle. Although not as shocked this time, Counselor Allan seemed less than impressed. I didn't know why I enjoyed needling that man so much. Alienating him today wouldn't be a good idea either, but he wasn't my concern. Deep down, I knew he wouldn't be the deciding factor. I had an instinct about people, and I wanted to set a specific tone to this meeting from the start.

Zatruk frowned at me, although I could see the amusement behind his glare. "As you can see, Exarch, she certainly has a sharp tongue."

I batted my eyes innocently at him. "I merely quoted your own words."

"I like you, Rihanna Makeba," Graith said. "As humans say, good things come in small packages."

"They certainly do," I said with a curtsy.

Zatruk shook his head with an amused expression and gestured for our guests to head towards the house.

"Are these the famous speeders I keep hearing about?"

Graith asked, coming to a stop next to the six completed models we had lined up in front of the house.

"Yes," Zatruk said. "These are the first fully functional models, with performances that rival and even exceed galactic levels. Our engineers are still polishing them to make them even more responsive and have smoother speed transitions, among other things."

"Can we see one flying?" Mateo asked. "Those speeders are all Lara talks about these days."

"Sure! I'd be glad to demonstrate," I said with a smile.

After a short demonstration, somewhat similar to the one I'd given Dakas and Lara in Kastan, I landed back next to the other speeders. The same impressed expression could be read on every face.

"Remarkable," Skieth said pensively. The other guests nodded.

"Please, come in," Zatruk said. "I will explain to you how they—and potentially you, too—fit in our greater plan."

Zatruk led the way inside the great hall and then the dining room on the right, which truly served mostly as a meeting room. Graith's starry eyes widened when he noticed the presence of three chairs of familiar design. One sat at the head of the table next to a normal chair, and the other two were located on the left side. I didn't miss the discreet, approving glance Dakas cast Zatruk's way.

"Adjustable backrests? How unexpectedly considerate. I thought you'd have us standing under the sun through it all," Graith said, lowering the back of the chair at the head of the table before taking a seat.

Mateo settled in the regular chair next to him, Counselor Allan next to him on the right side of the table. Skieth and Dakas adjusted their own backrests, taking a seat on the left side, by Graith. Zatruk chuckled as he headed to the other end of the table with me in tow. I took a seat on the right side.

"It is indeed the way of the Yurus to negotiate standing up, preferably under the sun at its zenith," Zatruk conceded. "It forces people to negotiate quickly and efficiently. Too much comfort makes people complacent and things drag on forever. But this is not a negotiation. We're merely presenting an idea for you to consider maybe partaking in. Then you can go home and reflect on it. Should you be interested, that's when negotiations will start."

"Very well," Graith said. "We are listening."

"The speeders you saw are not to be sold but awarded to the winners of the intergalactic gladiator tournaments we intend to hold here on Cibbos," Zatruk said, going straight to the point. "This is the arena we will start building next week."

He launched a 3D hologram of the arena, waving his hand around it to show the different parts and sections, zooming in on specific areas as he described them, answering questions as they arose.

"It should take approximately four months to build, and the first competitions would begin in the following one to three months, depending on what logistical hurdles we may need to iron out first," Zatruk continued. "We will hold all the similar combat modes available in other galactic competitions, and also introduce new ones."

"That's certainly an interesting plan, but also a very elaborate and complex one," Counselor Allan interjected. "Why not just sell the speeders?"

Zatruk waved a dismissive hand. "We do not need credits, but we do have a genetic and physiological need to fight. I'm sure you will concur with me that it would be better for us to do so in a controlled environment with consenting opponents than through raids."

Chastised, Counselor Allan swallowed hard and gave my husband a stiff nod.

"Our plan comes in two versions; Yurus only or all of

Cibbos, involving both of your peoples," Zatruk said. "Considering the logistics involved in such a project, having the participation of all of our peoples would be ideal."

"How so?" Skieth asked.

"The competition is only the first part. But outside of the events, visitors will need medical care, food, lodging, transportation, entertainment," Zatruk explained. "Currently, we trade food with Kastan, but we would want to significantly increase those quantities to meet the demand our guests will create. We'll need an improved and more secure spaceport to handle the greater traffic, shuttles to bring the visitors here from the port. We will build at least one hotel near the arena, but there will be demand for tourism."

Now that caught everyone's attention, especially Mateo and Allan, who exchanged a look. I couldn't tell if they had already considered that possibility or if this had taken them aback. Graith folded his hands on the table, leaning forward, his starry eyes even more intense.

"We can already anticipate that some guests will request to stay in Kastan or Synsara, eat in your restaurants, and buy your local goods. They will want to attend your entertainment events, fly zeebises, and sail the Shaheya River, to name a few," Zatruk continued. "We need to know if that is something that your people will be able or even willing to cater to."

"That sounds like a heavy burden for each of our people to shoulder in order to help you with your plan," Counselor Allan challenged.

"It's only a burden if you wish for Kastan to stagnate instead of prosper and evolve," I interjected, rising from my chair.

All heads turned my way, and Zatruk gestured for me to come stand in front in his stead. I smiled at him as I did so.

"I've seen Kastan, and I've learned about the creation of the colony, wanting a fresh start, and again embracing values that have gone to the wayside in today's modern Earth," I said, choosing my words carefully. "But I also see the desire for your younger generation to evolve while juggling that balance."

"You are correct," Mateo said, his poker face impenetrable.

"But your population is small, bordering on inbreeding. There are no real innovative career prospects for your youth or creative people," I continued, my voice taking on a passionate edge. "This arena will bring new blood to Kastan and Cibbos in general, new trade opportunities, more clients for your zeebises and the wool they produce."

I turned back on the holographic projector and displayed the hotel maquette Zatruk had worked on.

"This is the hotel we intend to build. It will need to be furnished, decorated, and maintained. We will need a lot of staff to man it, from the concierge, to the cooks, to the entertainers, including the souvenir store," I explained. "All of this means an influx of galactic credits that will allow you to acquire things you currently can't."

Mateo frowned. "As you said, we have a relatively small population, and all of this will demand a lot of staff. Simply providing you with the increased quantity of food will require a lot of our own people joining the farming and product transformation workforce, many of whom would not be interested. Even if we agreed to participate, Kastan wouldn't be able to cater to your staffing needs. Frankly, I can already think of many who would rather start their own touristic venture in Kastan."

I grinned broadly as he made my arguments for me.

"You are correct. But there are a lot of people who would be more than happy to come settle on Cibbos, with the promise of a stable job and safe living conditions. Many of them are human, which would mean new blood for Kastan as they would more than likely gravitate towards your colony for a place of residence."

I turned to Graith who seemed as unreadable as Mateo.

"The same applies to Synsara and the other Zelconian cities.

You have unique sports and events that people will want to see, goods they'll want to buy. AND, should we reach an agreement for the use of some of your crystals to enhance our rewards, it will strengthen your position with the UPO."

"Strengthen our position?" Graith asked. "What makes you think we need it?"

I smiled, recognizing a bluff from all of my smuggling years. "Because they're panting after your crystals, and you keep dangling that carrot without giving in. That means you're not satisfied with the deal they're offering you. Knowing them, they're offering you useless technology in exchange for it, and you're waiting to be in a stronger position to negotiate in terms that will suit you. Am I right, or am I right?"

Graith smiled but didn't answer, the same amused and impressed expression reflected on the faces of his companion.

"This is all around massive free marketing for both your peoples, and you set the terms you want. Instead of being limited to the customers the UPO has 'allowed' you to connect to through their network, you will be able to meet potential business partners face-to-face. Once up against real competition, the UPO will have to play ball."

Graith shifted his wings while nodding pensively. "You make compelling arguments. But what happens if we choose not to partake in this venture?"

"Then we will go with the Yurus only version," Zatruk said. "It will merely add two to three months to the timeline."

"How are you going to handle it?" Mateo asked.

"We will build the arena in the Toukma Valley, southwest of here, with its own spaceport and hotel," Zatruk explained. "Our males have already crafted a large quantity of weapons, shields, and armor pieces, some with smart functions, such as heating blades and cooling armor. So, even without Zelconian crystal enhancements, my Rihanna had secured many buyers for our deutenium weapons. Those funds will go towards buying the goods we need and hiring the staff necessary, especially farmers."

"Farmers?" Mateo asked with a frown.

"We needed to plan for the probability that Kastan wouldn't be able to supply our food needs beyond the current trades," I replied. "We intend to hire the daughters of Meterion."

"Which daughters?" Graith asked.

"Daughters of Meterion," I replied smugly. "I was looking for farmers seeking to relocate when I stumbled on a program set up by the Prime Mating Agency for the third daughters of Meterion. Meterion is one of the biggest farming colonies in the galaxy. It's a matriarchy where the first daughter inherits the lands, the second daughter becomes her right hand, but any additional daughter becomes a burden that is cast out at the age of twenty-five. She usually ends up as a servant or doing mind-numbing work in factories in the city."

"Sounds rather unappealing," Dakas said.

I nodded. "Extremely. One such daughter escaped that fate through a marriage arranged by Kayog with a reptilian species on Xecania. Since then, Kayog has been offering such women the opportunity to relocate to planets deemed primitive to help with food production."

Mateo and Counselor Allan once more exchanged a look. I bit the inside of my cheeks to repress a triumphant grin.

"With or without your participation, we intended to suggest you reach out to Kayog for these women to help expand and perfect your farming capacity," I added. "Meterion males also have little prospects. Their good fortune depends on how good a marriage they manage to secure. Many will gladly come here as guides, security personnel, spaceport agents, hotel and arena staff, you name it."

"This is an extremely interesting program, well-worth looking into," Mateo said. "Thank you for bringing it to our attention."

I nodded then shifted my attention to Graith. "As for the Zelconian crystals for enhancing our weapons and speeders, we have found alternatives. Granted, none rival yours, but they will do a good enough job. Either way, we will auction off one of our speeders to create a starting fund."

"What's the interest like?" Dakas asked.

"Extremely high," I said, honestly.

By the way the three Zelconians slightly narrowed their eyes at me, I could guess they were gauging my emotions to know if it was a bullshit boast or the truth. I let my feelings freely flow out. We were genuinely getting crazy interest in the speeders.

"As you can see, we can do it alone," Zatruk said. "And we will, if we must, with strict rules for our visitors so they do not interfere with your lives. But I believe it is the wrong choice for all of us."

"What makes you say that?" Graith asked.

"We all want peace. The best way to achieve it is for each of our people to grow and prosper in parallel, not isolated. How comfortable will you be in a few years when the Yurus are wealthier and far more advanced technologically than either of your species, thanks to all the off-worlder engineers and scientists the proceeds from our ventures and interactions with the greater world will have granted us?"

The same unease flitted over every face, Counselor Allan shifting in his seat.

"It is your decision, but decide quickly."

"Why the rush?" Graith asked.

Zatruk heaved a sigh. "The Yurus are entering blood rage. We are days, at best weeks away from another Great War erupting. If that comes to pass, there is a possibility that the next time the head of our peoples meet, you'll be dealing with a different Chieftain than me."

I shuddered at the thought. I'd been trying to deny that possibility, but the reality was that once they all went insane, regardless of his combat skills, Zatruk could be killed during a free-for-all by a treacherous backstab.

"If you are only days away from a war, how do you expect to complete the construction of your arena that will take months?" Mateo challenged.

"By keeping our males busy and too exhausted for it to trigger," Zatruk said, calmly.

"Fair enough, but it will still take you four months to build the arena. Why rush us into giving an answer?" Counselor Allan insisted.

"Because your decision will determine the location of the arena that we want to start building next week," Zatruk explained. "If we're doing it alone, the Toukma Valley is isolated enough not to bother either of your peoples. But for a joint project, I would choose a more central location to build, such as the Harwa Valley northeast from here."

"You have given us much to consider, Great Chieftain Zatruk," Graith said in a solemn voice, thus marking the end of the meeting. "We will get back to you with our decision in a timely fashion."

CHAPTER 16
ZATRUK

Two days after that meeting, we finalized the sale of our weapons with Rihanna's trading partners. That created another headache for us with the need for setting up a galactic bank account to receive the credits. All the security steps we had to go through, all the approval processes from the various providers connected to the galactic network had made me want to crack some skulls. In the next couple of months, we would have to set up a service point in Mutarak, at the arena and hotel.

Fingers flying over the keyboard, Rihanna brought up the page of our online account, showing the large deposit sitting in it. Like the rest of my people, I didn't care about wealth or credits. The Yurus possessed a currency that was mostly used to bet on fights. But those credits brought a smile to my face. They were the key to overcoming the last hurdles to my plan.

Once more, guilt surged through me looking at my little sylphin. She'd been working like a beast with relentless energy.

She shifted sideways on my lap, and I slipped my left arm behind Rihanna to support her back as she leaned backward. As was her wont, her dainty fingers went straight for my beard, undoing my braid.

"You're hopeless," I said, affectionately.

"Hopelessly adorable," she deadpanned, moving on to make her usual weird braid patterns and shapes with my beard.

"Can't you just stay still for once?" I asked, even as I slightly bent my head to give her better access.

She shook her head. "Nope. I'm too restless. Plus, this is my reward for a job well done."

My chest constricted some more with guilt. There had been no accusation in her voice, but I felt like a terrible mate for all the burden I'd unloaded on her shoulders.

"It is truly a job well done," I conceded. "I couldn't have done half of what we've accomplished without you."

Rihanna's fingers stilled, and her eyes flicked up to lock with mine. "Yeah, you would have. Between you, Jerdea, and Wonjin, you would have figured it out. You already had trades going with the humans."

I shook my head. "We still wouldn't be where we are now, with true hope of success," I argued. "I'm sorry I shoved you into all of this almost from the day of your arrival. You deserve to be treated like a proper new bride."

Rihanna stared at me as if a second pair of horns had suddenly grown on top of my head. "Are you kidding me? You didn't 'shove' me into anything. I *love* this shit! Hustle is my middle name. I'm a smuggler and bounty hunter. Finding the impossible stuff people need, hooking up unlikely partners, making deals, that's me."

"But this is a massive undertaking. Certainly a bigger headache than you've faced before," I countered.

"You better believe it! The biggest challenge and for the greatest cause. I'm having a blast with this. So, don't you dare apologize to me. Without you, I'd be in hell on Molvi, getting maimed or God knows what else by the other inmates. Instead, I'm here doing this. For the first time, I feel important, valued, like I'm making a real difference and for the greater good."

I gently caressed her face. "Because you are, my mate. You are making a huge difference on every front. My little sylphin."

"My fluffy giant," she replied, lifting her face towards mine.

I leaned down and captured her lips in a tender kiss. Despite the passion that burned between us at night, right now, I just wanted to express the love growing in my heart for her. By the way she responded, I could tell similar feelings were blossoming in her heart for me.

When our lips parted, I rested my forehead on hers, enjoying a brief moment of tenderness with my mate.

"I will do whatever it takes to make Cibbos safe for my people, for *you*, and for our future offspring," I whispered in a pledge.

Rihanna smiled, pulling away to look at my face and caress my cheek. But her wistfulness suddenly faltered, a troubled expression quickly repressed flitting over her features.

"What? What thought just crossed your mind?"

My mate lowered her eyes, looking uncomfortable. She began fiddling with my beard again, this time more as a nervous tick while seeming to choose her words.

"The other day, after Doreg's attack, you mentioned your mother leaving for another clan," she said cautiously, before casting a worried look at me.

"Yes. What troubles you about it?" I asked in a gentle voice.

"Is... is your father's killer still here in Mutarak?"

I gave her a sad smile. "No. Gorax is no longer here."

"Did you...?"

"Kill him?" I asked with a chuckle. "No. In fact, Gorax raised me after Mother left."

Her eyes widened in shock. "Really?!"

I nodded. "Mother couldn't stay here. Aside from being haunted by the happy memories she'd shared here with my father, Mother couldn't bear to see her brother anymore. But I couldn't follow her to the other clans. Because so many of those other males had killed the adults that had been my friends and mentors growing up. Even though we all understand there had been no malice in their actions, there is always generational resentment."

"I never thought of that. It must have been awful," Rihanna said, her eyes filled with sympathy.

I shrugged, slightly turning my head so she could abuse a different section of my beard.

"We got over it, but Gorax didn't. Guilt aged him before his time. Less than a year ago, ten months to be exact, he left for another clan. But first, he made me promise that I would do everything in my power to prevent another Great War... no matter the cost." I heaved a sigh as the memories flooded my mind. "I asked him if he was sure this was what he wanted. And he insisted that I should do whatever was required."

"There's more to this isn't it?" Rihanna asked.

I nodded. "Mmhmm. He knew what the cost would be, as did I. His last words to me before leaving was to apologize for his weakness. But he didn't have the strength to do what our females have been doing for generations."

"What? Start over?" she asked.

"No. Watch his son die because he lost his head to blood rage. And die, he did three months later."

"His son? What...?" Rihanna's voice trailed off, her eyes flicking from side to side as she worked it out. "No! Vyrax?! His son was Vyrax? He was your cousin?"

I nodded slowly, the old anger and resentment surging again deep inside. "Yes, he was. Gorax left the minute his son called for the war on humans. In truth, I had expected the humans to cower and submit to his will, and then for half of our people to get slaughtered by the Zelconians. Even if we appropriated all of the humans' trained zeebises, we could never win an aerial battle against the birds."

"But Kastan's energy wall spared the clan that horrible fate," she said.

"Yes, although I wouldn't have allowed it to go that far. I would have stopped him before then. Even with the technology Vyrax had been acquiring from traders under unrealistic promises of giving them Zelconian crystals, we couldn't have won against the birds. Despite the game they are playing with the United Planets Organization, they have far more powerful technology than they let on. They could rain death down upon us without breaking a sweat."

"Really?" Rihanna asked, shocked.

"Really. I have seen the effects of some of the laser beams from their damage crystals. They could level this dwelling, turn it into ashes and cinders in seconds. The birds are not to be underestimated. The Yurus are lucky they are not a belligerent species. Those eyes full of stars you find so pretty can hypnotize you and plant in your mind the most horrible nightmare that will make you want to take your own life."

"Wowzer! But they look so sweet!"

I chuckled, yielding to my mate as she turned my face again, now that she'd made a total mess of my beard, so that she could move on to my hair.

"Appearances are often deceiving," I said teasingly. "Don't get me wrong. They are not bad people, they're just not as inoffensive as they let on. But even without their technology, they shouldn't be underestimated. Graith destroyed Vyrax in a fair duel. Frankly, that duel had been the greatest gift the Exarch could have given me."

Rihanna recoiled. "What? Why?"

"Because he'd spared me the burden of spilling my own cousin's blood by turning him into a vegetable. But Luana had to come to his aid. I had so hoped not to have to perpetuate the cycle of kin killing kin." My face twisted in anger. "I resented Vyrax for putting me in that position."

My mate gently rubbed my chest in a soothing gesture. "Were you close, growing up?"

I snorted. "With that waste of air? Certainly not. He was an idiot who enjoyed reminding me that his father killed mine."

"Jeez! What a charming guy," Rihanna said, her voice filled with outrage.

"Indeed. He was a *jaafing hoodah*, but a great fighter who grew too cocky. There is no question I would have defeated him in a duel, but not without taking some serious damage."

"I'm sure—"

A ping on my armband startled the both of us, interrupting her. My heart leapt at the sight of the message. "A Zelconian is approaching!"

"They must be bringing their answer," Rihanna said, the same excitement and worry I felt reflected on her face, before giving way to horror. "Shit, your beard…"

An endless string of curses and swear words spilled out of my mouth when I ran my hand over my beard. It felt like a *jaafing* obstacle course left by a tornado after it leveled a city.

Between bouts of laughter and half-hearted apologies, Rihanna worked frantically to undo some of the damage she had done while I did the same with the other half. I nearly ripped clumps of hair doing so.

"You wretched female… You are never touching my beard again," I grumbled.

By the mischievous look she gave me, she clearly intended to do it again at the first opportunity.

"There, you're good," she said at last. "Let's go!"

I combed my beard with my fingers, grumbling the whole way. Although I didn't feel any knots, it wasn't neatly braided as I usually had it, especially when in the presence of a foreign official.

To my shame, I marched towards the square to find Dakas already standing there.

"Apologies for making you wait," I said as a greeting.

Dakas waved a dismissive hand, although the amused smile tugging at his lips hinted he could feel my flustered emotions and was no doubt speculating about what his impromptu arrival had interrupted.

"No need to apologize. I should have warned you of my impending visit. As you are on a tight schedule, I figured you would want to hear as soon as possible."

My stomach knotted, but I succeeded in keeping a neutral voice and expression. "So, you have made a decision?"

Dakas nodded. "Yes. I am here on behalf of both the humans and the Zelconians. Both of our peoples accept your offer to join you in this endeavor."

I barely repressed a victorious roar, although my fake stoicism didn't fool him. "That is great news. But?"

Dakas grinned. "There is indeed a but. These two holocards contain our respective terms for your review. We can meet after to discuss the details. Also, we would like to request a different location than the Harwa Valley to build the arena. The humans want to keep it for farming as the soil is rich in that area."

"What location do you have in mind?"

"We would like to suggest the Kenthea Plateau instead. It is centrally located, has enough space for a large hotel next to the arena, and offers a stunning view of the valley below as well as the river. It will make for breathtaking views of the awakening nights. It is also a short distance from the existing spaceport. It should be easier to expand it than to build another from scratch."

"Fair points. That request is acceptable," I said.

"Excellent! Then we shall wait to hear back from you regarding our other terms. Be well, Great Chieftain," Dakas said, before nodding at my mate. "Rihanna."

She nodded back, and we watched him take flight. He no sooner departed than every Yurus eye of those gathered on the square turned to stare at me inquisitively.

"The humans and Zelconians have chosen to join our battle arena project, but have a few terms outlined. I will go review them, and then I shall share them with you," I shouted.

Despite some disappointed and displeased expressions at this additional uncertainty, excitement and hope dominated. I had made no secret of how much work making all of this a reality would be. But now, not only were we no longer alone in this endeavor, the humans and Zelconians joining us meant they, too, believed in the merit of this plan. Their validation made it no longer just the fevered dream of a Chieftain addled by praxilla petals.

I returned to my office with Rihanna, who was almost bursting with excitement. I couldn't decide what emotion dominated within me between thrill and apprehension. I wanted to believe their demands would be reasonable, not only so that we could proceed with a partnership, but mostly because outrageous ones could trigger the Yurus males, already on edge.

Heart pounding, I inserted a card in my reader, displaying its content on my monitor.

"These are the humans' demands," I said, my voice tense. "I figure their terms will be the least problematic."

"They better be, or I'll kick their asses," Rihanna mumbled, making me smile.

I kissed her temple before starting to read. "Number one, all visitors to Kastan will have to observe Kastan rules, which will have to be enforced by Yurus patrols."

"No problem there. I can already think of a few Yurus males who love nothing more than throwing their weight around," Rihanna said with a mischievous grin.

I chuckled. "Many more than you know, my mate. Two, all patrolling agents must first be vetted by a Zelconian empath." I rolled my eyes. "I wouldn't assign one of the troublemakers to such roles. But fine, if that reassures them, they can waste the birds' time. Three, all human staff must first settle in Kastan for three months after which time they are free to move where they please."

"Not very subtle, but I expected no less," Rihanna said.

"That would be ideal. Kastan already caters to every human need. It will be great for us not to have to worry about that for a few months."

"Agreed. Frankly, I suspect most of them will want to remain in Kastan, and I doubt the Zelconians will significantly open their city to permanent off-worlder residents, unless they mate with one of theirs."

"I concur. What next? Four, the price for the food, goods, and furniture humans will provide for the arena and hotel is to be negotiated separately from the current Yurus trade. Fair," I said, to which Rihanna nodded. "Five, proceeds from any sales and business concluded in venues in Kastan, including tourism-related, will go entirely to the owner of said venue or business."

"That's a no-brainer, but a wise stipulation to include," my mate said.

"Six, Kastan humans working for the Yurus in the arena, hotel, or other venues will be fairly compensated. Also self-evident, but then wages are something we will need to determine not only for them, but for the off-worlders we will hire."

"That is going to be a bit of a headache. Wages should be based on the local cost of living. But luring off-worlders might be tricky if the wages do not compete with other galactic openings. We can deal with that one later. Next?"

"Nothing that raises any concerns for me," I said, relief flooding through me. "They want a medical clinic inside the arena, which is a given. They also want things like a Cibbos tax fund to be levied on all three species to cover the spaceport expansion, its staff, maintenance, the shuttles, and everything related to it."

"Well, that wasn't so bad," Rihanna said, shifting restlessly on my lap while I switched the cards.

"I didn't really expect anything different than that. It's the Zelconians I'm worried about."

"For some reason, I'm not worried about them either. We had the humans at the daughters of Meterion. We had the Zelconians at negotiating power with the UPO, but also with maintaining the peace."

"Let's see if you're right," I said, bracing for it.

The first few demands revolved around Zelconians empathically vetting all off-worlder employees before they were allowed to work on Cibbos, be it in the arena, Kastan, or in Synsara. Every visitor would also have to submit to an evaluation, including the gladiators. Although that wouldn't prevent the latter from competing, those deemed overly dangerous would have their movement on the planet restricted.

"It makes sense for violent gladiators. Nobody wants a potential serial killer hanging out with a family sightseeing between bouts," Rihanna said. "But I hope they have a way of quickly assessing people. Nobody wants to face a ten-minute interrogation after a long intergalactic flight, when all they can think about is getting to their hotel."

"Agreed, we will have to make sure it is non-distressing to the visitors."

The next point was about the joint development of the shuttles to and from the spaceport. The concept would be equally owned by the humans, Zelconians, and Yurus. That made me smile.

Rihanna snorted. "See, you hit a nerve with that last comment about neither of their species wanting to see the Yurus steer way ahead, technologically speaking."

"Especially since I know for a fact that the Zelconians are trying to achieve space travel. Unlike Vyrax, I have no such ambitions. I am happy with Cibbos. But if the speeders are any indication, the joint efforts of our engineers should yield phenomenal results for the shuttles in record time."

"And you know both Dakas and Lara will be all over it. They take pride in their work. They will want them to be the finest shuttles this side of the galaxy."

As expected, visitors to Synsara would be subjected to strict rules established by the Zelconians. But the following points were the ones that truly held my interest. Non-lethal Zelconian crystals would be provided under specific rules to be negotiated. Any potentially lethal reward that used their crystals would have to be vetted by a Zelconian, who would also be in charge of the coding. However, further rewards or merchandising combining deutenium and crystals could be jointly developed.

"They do not want us to use their crystals to secretly develop weapons that we could eventually turn against them," I said, amused and not in the least surprised. "But I will want Jerdea involved with the coding. It would otherwise give them too big of an edge over us. In the end, nothing prevents us from acquiring different crystals elsewhere if it ever came to that."

"I totally agree. Anyway, if they want to develop joint technology using deutenium and crystals, they can't simply lock you out of the process once they have the metal. It will be joint all the way or not at all."

"Like with the humans and their food, we will have to discuss the compensation costs for their crystals. That's going to be so much fun."

Rihanna chuckled with sympathy.

I quickly read through the rest of the requests, none of which made me cringe. One, in fact, I really liked. It stated that at least one Zelconian empath should be present during any battle to sense if anything was about to get out of hand, whether between the gladiators or the crowd itself.

I could have wept with relief when I pulled the card out from the reader.

"You did it," Rihanna whispered. "You fucking did it!"

CHAPTER 17
ZATRUK

Despite the many issues left to sort out with our new partners, construction of both the arena and the hotel on the Kenthea Plateau began three days later. Yurus males from every clan came to do their share. They trickled in over a few days, setting up temporary camps where they would reside during the construction.

But not all of them came here. The best smiths stayed home to build more weapons, shields, and armor to sell for now. Soon, they would shift to making the frame and chassis of our future shuttles once our engineers completed the design.

In the meantime, Rihanna's traders had countless requests pouring in, some with specific enhancements. Following my mate's suggestion, we raised our prices and only agreed to two more shipments to help fund our project. We would then hold off offering anything else to create further demand.

We were making insane progress, construction proceeding much faster than I had anticipated. My brothers were working themselves into the ground. Granted, the large testosterone and serotonin influx all that hard work gave them played a significant part in it. It kept them in a semi-state of euphoria they wanted to maintain, which also significantly reduced the instances of fights or brawls.

However, a great deal of determination and hope also drove them. Seeing things falling into place, our arena and hotel taking shape, and the galactic buzz our project was generating finally made it all real.

Riding my krogi through the woods with Rihanna leaning against my chest, I couldn't wait to see how far progress had gone in the past forty-eight hours. Digging, building the foundations, and the underground beast holding cells had seemed to drag on forever. But now that the outer walls had gone up and that we'd started making the divisions, things suddenly appeared to move at an exponential rate.

Just as we were entering the last stretch of the trail to the plateau, a flash of light swooped past us.

"What was that?" Rihanna asked.

"I don't—"

I didn't finish my sentence as the flash returned, swirling over our heads before hovering in front of Rihanna's face.

"The sylphin!" my mate exclaimed.

We hadn't seen the little fairy since that first night in the woods, nearly two months ago. Seeing one once was extremely rare, but twice, and especially during daylight, was almost unheard of. My heart filled with gratitude when she once more bumped her face over Rihanna's nose, cheek, and forehead, bestowing yet another blessing on us.

She then flew to me, hanging on to my right tusk with one of her three-fingered hands and used the other to pull at my upper lip.

Rihanna chuckled, staring at us over her shoulder. "That's so stinking cute. I wish I could take a picture of you two."

I playfully glared at my female while the sylphin bumped her face on my lip. She then flew to similarly 'kiss' the tip of my nose and my eyes before wrapping her arms around my braid and letting herself slide down, once again as if it were some kind of playground.

"She really likes you," Rihanna said wistfully.

"No, she just really enjoys messing with my hair, like you do," I grumbled.

"You did call me your little sylphin before we even met this one," she said without the slightest remorse. "Therefore, either you knew this was normal behavior for a sylphin, or you jinxed yourself."

I mumbled something in response as we cleared the tree line onto the plateau. When the sylphin took flight, I assumed she would flee back to the safety of the forest. Instead, she wrapped herself around the tip of my horn and closed her eyes. Her inner glow faded, making her look suspiciously like a mere flower.

Seeing the worksite erased any thought of the sylphin. The imposing structures of both the arena and the hotel screamed power and strength. The dark stones and metal gave it an extra air of mystery and danger. Rihanna called it modern gothic. I just called it Yurus pride.

I approached the arena, finding most of the males sitting on stone blocks or improvised seats while eating the meal Relven and her team were cooking on site every day. I liked coming during meal time for an inspection, so as not to get in their way while they worked.

I stopped Okous a short distance from the arena's main entrance and hopped down before helping my mate dismount. But even as I did so, my gaze remained locked on the building. They'd already begun working on some of the external ornaments and the pathway connecting the two venues.

A loud, mocking laugh pulled my attention away from that masterpiece. Sitting on a stone block, eating from a large bowl, Vradrak Clan's Chieftain Bogram was staring at me with a disdainful expression.

"It looks like our Great Chieftain has eaten so much of that *jaafing* praxilla he tries to shove down all of our throats that flowers now grow on him!" he shouted, loudly enough for everyone in range to hear.

His clanmates and those of a few other clans joined in his laughter. This kind of taunting didn't surprise me. Every Yurus male wanted to become Chieftain, and every Chieftain wanted to become Great Chieftain. While none had so far worked up the courage to directly challenge me in a duel, they never missed an opportunity to take a jab.

While shocked to indeed see a 'flower' on my horn, my clanmates put down their food, many taking menacing stances towards those laughing. Whatever their views on praxilla, disrespect to their Chieftain was disrespect to them personally.

I smiled and slowly advanced towards Bogram. All laughter faded, tension settling on every face. As I closed in on the Chieftain, he put down his bowl, rising warily to his feet, not wanting to be in a vulnerable position if I lunged at him. I stopped directly in front of him, the silence and tension around us thick enough to slice with a blade.

Bogram lifted his chin defiantly but didn't say a word. For all his cockiness, he didn't want to fight me. He knew he couldn't win. Worse still, his loss would result in his leadership being challenged, with each of his clanmates seeking to depose him for his shame.

A slow, menacing smile stretched my lips as I savored watching him fight the urge to squirm. However, as much as I enjoyed this little show of dominance, I couldn't allow the tension to build further. We'd been doing wonderful at avoiding fights and brawls. I wouldn't be the cause of one.

I suddenly leaned left, startling him into taking a step back and falling into a defensive stance. My almost malicious smile broadened as I reached instead for a berry in the plates of greens and fruits that always accompanied our cooked meals. My gaze never straying from his, I straightened and brought the berry up to the tip of my right horn. The 'flower' regained her glow as the sylphin opened and stretched out her little arms to accept my offering.

Gasps, *jaafans*, and other shocked sounds erupted all around us. Bogram's yellow eyes appeared on the verge of popping out of his head while his mouth gaped in disbelief. Words such as sylphin, blessed, and Chosen One were repeated in awed whispers.

The sylphin made quick work of devouring the berry, much bigger than her own head, then greedily licked her three-digit fingers, sucking on their rounded tips with a popping sound. Once done, she flew down from my horn to bump her face on my cheek before resuming her perch, and fading to a flower appearance.

I continued staring at Bogram who slightly bowed his head.

"Chosen One," he said in concession.

I smirked, then turned around without another word. To my shock, Tarmek slapped his fist to his chest before throwing it in the air.

"This site is blessed! Hail the Chosen One!"

My throat tightened, and it took all of my willpower to keep a neutral expression on my face as every male, including our females, echoed "Hail the Chosen One." I made my way to my Rihanna, who still stood by Okous, her face glowing with pride as she watched me approach. I took her hand and led her inside the arena.

~

After what felt like far too short a tour, Rihanna and I headed to Kastan. My mate had a meeting with the human crafters for the hotel and the arena. I hadn't fully appreciated the scope of all the things we had to do.

Our seamstresses had partnered with theirs since the hotel

would need a ridiculous amount of bedding, linens, curtains, towels, uniforms for the human staff, and sashes for species that didn't require clothing. Then the crafters had also partnered to mass produce soaps, furniture for every room, and signage, in addition to maps. Even the website for information, registration, and reservations represented its own set of headaches.

My little sylphin spearheaded a lot of those things, including a properly filled bar and wine cave with both local and imported bottles. It was all foreign to me. The Yurus enjoyed their mead. I couldn't pronounce half of the names of the wines and liquors Rihanna deemed essential.

Once more, my heart soared when we entered Kastan. The human colony, too, had turned into a construction site. Brand new inns and hotels were going up, larger restaurant terraces were being built, new crops were being planted, and a whole lot of female stuff I gladly took no part in was happening. Even the medical clinic was being transformed to accommodate more patients at once, with multiple examination rooms and a large patient ward.

Before Rihanna would go to her meeting, and I to my own with Kastan's head of security to discuss Yurus patrol in the colony, we first stopped by Mateo Torres's dwelling. Last night, Luana had given birth to a son named Darius. She'd chosen to deliver here in Kastan because of the high-tech medical pods Kayog had given them as wedding presents in case of complications. Naturally, she hadn't wanted to make the flight to Synsara right after. I also imagined her father had wanted his grandson nearby.

It still felt odd to enter Kastan as a welcomed guest instead of a dreaded enemy. Three months ago, who would have thought that I would be entering the personal dwelling of the human colony's leader to be introduced to his grandson?

Dakas greeted us at the door, his eyes widening at the sight of the colorful box in my hands. I gave it to him.

"It's a gift for the baby," Rihanna said with a grin.

Dakas recoiled, looking both surprised and completely confused.

"It is wrapped," I explained, feeling awkward. "It is apparently a human thing to hide a present first in a container, and then in colorful paper with ribbons to make it harder to access."

Rihanna elbowed me. "It's not to make it harder to access. It's to make it pretty!"

"You say people rip off the paper and cut the ribbon. How is that not merely making it harder to access?" I challenged.

My mate rolled her eyes, as if I was a hopeless case. "Men, they never get this stuff."

Dakas chuckled, appearing to share part of my confusion and invited us inside. It was a surprisingly humble residence, functional, with minimal furniture, and little adornments, not the stately mansion one would expect for the leader of one's people. But then, the humans of the Kastan colony had originally illegally settled here in order to flee the extravagant ways of their homeworld and return to simpler values.

It felt odd entering Luana's old bedroom when she lived with her father. That room, too, was humble, with a bed so small it would be barely deemed suitable for a child, by Yurus standards. And yet, based on some of the bed sizes Rihanna had been requesting for the hotel, it would match the common double-beds in the galactic standards. Half of my legs would be hanging off the edge of such a tiny bed.

However, it was Luana that retained my attention. Lying in the middle of the bed, her curly hair splayed over the pillows piled up behind her, she was looking with infinite love at the youngling in her arms. She'd lowered the left shoulder of her bed dress to bare her breast while feeding the little one.

Once again, a powerful longing struck me with an unexpected violence. But instead of Luana, it was my little sylphin lying in that bed, feeding a little human-Yurus hybrid with either brown skin and fur after his mother's complexion, or coal skin and black fur, like my father's, which I probably would have inherited if not for my albinism.

My gaze shifted to my mate. Judging by the powerful emotion on her face as she watched that lovely tableau, I couldn't help but wonder if she, too, was imagining herself with our offspring. Her hand blindly reached for mine. I took, squeezing it gently.

"Hey guys," Luana said with a sweet smile, looking a little tired. "I'm sorry to be receiving you like this, but little Darius here is a bottomless pit. I'd thought he'd be done feeding by now."

"No need to apologize," Rihanna said, sounding emotional. "A healthy appetite is a good sign. How are you feeling?"

"As well as you can imagine after delivering a ten-pound, twenty-five-inch baby with wings," Luana said, scrunching her face.

Rihanna grimaced in sympathy. "Ouch. I'm assuming you went with a C-Section?"

"Hell yes! Darius was not coming out any other way. He would have split me in half!"

I scratched the back of my right ear, feeling a little awkward hearing such a conversation. Dakas seemed as uncomfortable as I felt.

"Yeah, I can't deny I wondered about that," Rihanna said pensively. "I imagine horns and hooves might prove just as problematic."

"Are you kidding? Judging by the size the Yurus grow to, I suspect their babies are even more massive at birth," Luana said with a shudder. "And let's not talk about the back pain from both the baby's weight and your breasts overflowing. Frankly, it's a good thing this little one is always so hungry to relieve some of the pressure."

The most vicious warrior threatening me with bodily harm

didn't distress me, but two females discussing childbirth and breast milk had me squirming. Dakas cleared his throat with a slight frown towards his mate. By the overly innocent and wide-eyed look she gave him, it finally dawned on me she'd been deliberately trying to make me uncomfortable.

My head jerked towards my mate, and I narrowed my eyes at the little traitor. The way she bit her bottom lip, failing miserably to hide her grin, confirmed she'd been in on it.

"If you're done abusing our guests, they have brought a present for our son," Dakas said, amused.

He showed the box to Luana, and her eyes lit up. "Oooh! It's so pretty. What a lovely wrapping! You didn't have to bring a gift. But that's a very thoughtful gesture. Open it, sweetie."

Even as she spoke those words, Darius seemed to finally be sated. She covered herself, placed a towel on her shoulder before placing her son on top and gently rubbed his back between his small wings, the same midnight blue color as his father's.

Just like I would have done, Dakas started carefully unknotting the ribbon forming a bow.

"No, honey. Just cut it," Luana said.

He gave her an 'are-you-sure?' look. After she nodded, he took on an air of resignation. He sliced it clean with the claw that came out of his index finger. He then proceeded once more with care to try and unwrap the colorful paper before my mate intervened this time.

"No, Dakas. You're supposed to tear that shit up. It's part of the fun."

"But you went through what appears to be great care to wrap it so beautifully," he argued.

"And your point is? Have you ever seen a really fancy cake that took over ten hours to decorate only to get cut and devoured within minutes?" Rihanna countered. "The wrapping has served its purpose. Tear it up!"

Luana chuckled while nodding. Dakas and I exchanged

another look. I shrugged, and he proceeded to tear the papers to shred.

"Oh wow!" Luana said at the sight of the beautiful metal box embossed with ancient Yurus symbols representing strength, health, wisdom, and happiness. "This is gorgeous."

"Exquisite work," Dakas concurred.

"The box was crafted by Wonjin," I said. "You will find several people contributed to this present."

"That was so sweet of him," Luana said, looking touched.

Dakas opened the box and this time looked stunned. He cast a baffled look our way before turning back to the box and carefully removing the baby mobile from it. I had never seen such a thing before Rihanna suggested it.

"Zatruk crafted each of the pieces," Rihanna said with a nervous laugh. "They are sylphins holding Zelconian crystals. Graith gave them to us. He said that combination should provide peace, focus, and health for the little one."

"It will," Dakas said, sounding moved as he held it up, the eight little sylphins dangling at varying heights on strings.

"Wave your hand under it," I said.

Dakas complied, and the sylphins started moving to a Zelconian lullaby. Dakas gasped, a powerful emotion fleeting over his features.

"Your brother Renok gave us a list of Zelconian lullabies, especially your favorites," Rihanna explained. "I've included a number of human ones as well. They will play in random order, but you can also trigger them by a vocal command. Jerdea coded that."

"And my mate sweet talked each of us into doing our part," I said, gently caressing her hair.

She scrunched her face, looking embarrassed, and shrugged. "I'm a hustler. It's what I do."

"That's an extremely thoughtful gift," Luana said, looking as touched as her husband. "It's absolutely beautiful."

"We're glad you like it!" I grumbled, uncomfortable with sweet moments like this.

No doubt sensing my discomfort, Luana's grin broadened. She cast a look at her son's face after he'd made a couple of resounding burps, then looked at my mate. "Would you like to hold him?"

"Yes! Absolutely," Rihanna said with surprising enthusiasm. "I thought you'd never offer!"

Luana chuckled. "Well, I didn't want to make you uncomfortable. Some people hate when parents unload their kids on them."

Rihanna picked up the little one with a world of care, giving me my first good look at him. Aside from the rather bulky diaper on him, Darius was completely naked. Some very fluffy-looking down feathers covered his little chest, shoulders, and wings. He had a stunning face, the perfect mix of his parents, with the blue skin and midnight blue eyes filled with stars of his father, and his mother's nose, lips, and high cheekbones. But where Dakas's crest was a golden orange, Darius's was blood red. With his human mouth and legs, he would grow into a hybrid similar to his sire.

He looked at my mate with an almost awed fascination, holding his head up on his own with the same type of strength Yurus newborns did. He delicately touched my mate's face while she showered him with praises about what a good and pretty little boy he was.

The same violent sense of longing struck me. I couldn't tell if Darius had felt it, having no clue when the Zelconian's empathic abilities first manifested. But he suddenly turned to look at me. He stared at me for a few seconds before extending a hand towards me.

"Looks like someone wants to meet Uncle Zatruk," Rihanna said teasingly.

The wave of panic that coursed through me shamed me. And

yet, I cast a look towards Dakas, hoping he would feel extremely uncomfortable having his firstborn at the mercy of a Yurus. Instead, a fiendish grin settled on his lips.

"Surely, the Great Chieftain of the Yurus isn't intimidated by a suckling babe?" Dakas asked in a taunting tone that had both our females chuckling.

I glared at him and swallowed my discomfort as I took Darius from my mate. I had held younglings before, but this was the firstborn of a Zelconian Counselor. What if I dropped him or inadvertently hurt him? It would destroy months of hard work and peace.

But my gaze no sooner locked with the little one than my worries evaporated. By the tingling sensation at the back of my head, I knew for a fact the baby had used his mesmerizing powers on me. His little hand reached for my right tusk. He fiddled with it at first before starting to pull, as if he wanted to rip it out.

"It is attached to my face," I mumbled, to the others' amusement.

That didn't seem to deter Darius who continued to methodically try to pull it out. When that failed, he turned his attention to my other tusk, with the same result.

"It's also attached to me," I said.

This time he stopped and stared at me in a way that almost made me believe he had understood me, even though I knew it wasn't the case. He suddenly switched his attention to my left ear where the large golden ring that identified me as the Great Chieftain dangled. He then started batting my ear with his little hand, which had the other three wretches bursting out laughing.

"I told you that you have cute ears. Even a newborn baby can't resist," Rihanna teased.

"It's undoubtedly the human side of him. You are all insufferable," I growled.

Darius flipped my ear one last time before looking at me.

Time appeared to stand still for a moment, even though he wasn't using the hypnotic powers of his eyes on me. He lifted his small hand, caressed my cheek and my beard, then buried his face in my neck with a tight hug. Even his small wings, too short to cover my chest, attempted to wrap around me.

My heart melted, and I gently caressed his back and wings.

"My son loves you," Dakas said in a gentle voice. I looked up at him in disbelief, and he nodded with a soft smile. "You make him feel safe... protected."

"Then his survival instincts are skewed," I grumbled.

Dakas snorted. "I doubt it. But it's okay. We won't tell your clanmates what a good babysitter you make."

I bared my fangs at him, which only made him laugh further.

"On a more serious note, you will be happy to hear that we're making great progress on the spaceport," Dakas said. "We've almost completed the expansion. All the construction is done. There are only the security features left to implement and test."

"That's very good to hear," I said, still caressing Darius's back. "I've also seen a lot of work happening in Synsara. From down here, it looks like a whole new plateau and dwellings on a new peak."

He nodded. "We will have a small, expandable hotel as a trial. Then we'll take it from there."

"I've been here for months and still haven't visited Synsara," Rihanna said with a frown.

"We will have to remedy that," Dakas conceded. "As soon as Luana has recovered enough for us to go back to Synsara, we'll have the both of you over for dinner... I'll cook."

"He'll make you eat fake maggots," Luana mumbled.

"What?!" I exclaimed.

Dakas burst out laughing and gave his mate an amused look. "Don't mind her. She's still not over a stunt I played on her when she first visited our city. On a side note, you need to give us back Lara."

Rihanna snorted. "That's not up to us. You need to take that up with her... *and* Wonjin."

I chuckled and nodded. Lara had become a semi-permanent fixture in Mutarak. She was spending most of her time with Jerdea and Wonjin. His infatuation with her had been undeniable from day one. While she'd been initially oblivious—or uninterested—she now appeared to have mellowed to him. It turned out that Wonjin had studied a great deal of engineering under his mother. Aside from building Lara a speeder in his spare time, he was building the frame of the first shuttle that would be operating from our new spaceport.

"Speaking of which, we must get going," I said in an apologetic tone. "I must meet with the human head of security."

"And I have linen and beddings to discuss with your seamstresses," Rihanna said.

With surprising reluctance, I handed the youngling back to his mother. He gave me a wide, toothless grin that turned me upside down.

"Congratulations again to the both of you," I said to Dakas and Luana before leading my mate out of the house.

CHAPTER 18
RIHANNA

Standing on the terrace of one of the penthouses of the Mugrak Hotel, named after the Yurusian God of War, Zatruk and I watched the night forest, valley, and Shaheya River awaken under the moonlight. Despite the breathtaking view of this enchanting moment, I could feel the tension knotting Zatruk's muscles as my back rested against his chest.

Tomorrow, we would celebrate the grand opening of the first Yurusian Gladiator Tournament. For nearly a week now, a swarm of visitors had either been trickling in, or arriving in large clusters that put us to the test.

Obviously, we faced a few hiccups, some slightly more problematic than others such as scanners malfunctioning, counterfeit registrations, and hacking attempts. Thankfully, I'd convinced Zatruk to invest in hiring a badass programmer that spanked would-be hackers into oblivion.

As a shameless smuggler myself, I'd informed the Zelconians and security personnel manning the spaceport of all the tricks I'd used to fool security. Sure enough, we'd caught plenty of people trying to sneak in illegal drugs, weapons, contraband goods, pets, live plants, roots, or vegetables that could represent a serious threat to Cibbos' ecosystem, just because they wanted to enjoy their favorite treats during their short stay here.

I turned to face Zatruk, not in the least fooled by his attempt at looking relaxed. "Stop worrying so much, you big fluff. Everything is going to be fine. We've properly trained our staff, rehearsed everything until we turned blue in the face, and tested everything a billion times over."

"Many things went wrong this week," he countered, his mask of stoicism faltering.

I shrugged. "And we fixed them in a timely fashion. Shit was bound to happen and will continue to happen, even ten years from now when we have this down to a science. It's the way of life and a law established by some asshole named Murphy."

"Bring that Murphy to me. He and I shall have a talk," Zatruk grumbled before picking me up.

I smiled as I wrapped my legs around his waist, my hands settling on the silky fur of his shoulders. "A lot of people tried to get their hands on him. He was smart enough to keel over centuries ago."

"I still can't help but wonder if there is something else we have omitted," Zatruk confessed.

"If we did, we'll deal with it. The only thing that matters is that tomorrow, your dream, the dream of an entire race and its future, will come true. You did it, Zatruk. You kept your people from going into a bloody war and gave them a hope of prosperity."

"It's really happening, isn't it?" he asked with an air of wonder and disbelief.

I nodded. "It is. And now, I need you to relax and enjoy the moment. And I know just how to do it, too."

"Do you, now, my mate?" he asked, his arms tightening around me as his voice dropped an octave.

"Mmhmm. I figured since we're going to baptize the hotel's presidential suite, we should go all out."

"What do you have in mind?" he asked, his gaze darkening as I caressed a path down his muscular chest before my index finger started circling around the areola of his right nipple.

"Well, when you couldn't find me for an hour earlier today, I may have dropped by Kastan in order to get rid of a certain implant," I said, suddenly feeling nervous.

Zatruk froze, all playfulness vanishing from his features as he stared at me intently, his red eyes flicking between mine. "You have removed your contraceptive implant?"

I nodded, my throat suddenly feeling too constricted to speak.

"You still have four months to decide whether you want to stay with me on Cibbos or leave at the end of the one-year trial period Kayog imposed upon you," Zatruk said, his voice tense. "If we conceive before then, no offspring of mine will leave this planet."

"I know," I whispered. "You made that abundantly clear. And it's a good thing, too, because I have no intention of leaving. I knew more than three months ago that I wouldn't leave. I may have fallen in love with a fluffy, cuddly, mountain of muscles," I added with a nervous laugh.

"My mate... my sylphin... I love you, too, Rihanna," Zatruk said in a voice filled with emotion that had shivers running down my spine. "But... if you knew three months ago, why now?"

"Because we had too much work to do for me to be swelling in every limb and waddling around with the mammoth baby I'm sure you're going to give me," I said, teasingly. "But now that we've got everything up and running, I'll still have enough time to help iron out any issues before I become a help-less tubby."

"You will not be a helpless tubby, whatever that means," Zatruk whispered in a rumbling voice. "You will be the most beautiful and most cherished expecting mother in the galaxy."

"Well then, let's get to work."

"Your will, my mate," Zatruk said, capturing my lips as he carried me to the bedroom.

Zatruk was a phenomenal kisser. I'd been initially worried about both his tusks and fangs, but they didn't interfere in any way. To the contrary, the fangs had a wonderful way of gently scraping against my tongue that added an element of thrill and danger that I loved.

Everything about my man screamed danger, from his size, his strength, his body, his face, even his voice. And yet, he handled me like the most precious treasure in the world and melted like so much snow under a burning sun beneath my touch.

I kicked off my slippers right before he laid me down on the gigantic bed of the presidential suite. Kneeling at my feet, Zatruk kissed his way up my legs, his beard and long hair tickling my skin. His hands slipped under the sheer, white negligee I'd donned after our joint shower earlier, lifting it as he pursued his upward path.

My stomach quivered when his breath fanned over my sex. But my wretched husband didn't linger there, kissing and nipping the skin right above it and around my pelvic area. He chuckled at my frustrated groan, then licked my belly button in a teasing fashion before rubbing his face on my stomach.

He resumed his journey, barely pausing on my breasts, that he usually loved fondling, lifting my nightgown only enough for the fabric to clear my mouth and my nose. With my arms up over my head, tangled in the fabric, and the upper half of my face still covered with it, I made to rid myself of the garment, but Zatruk stopped me with a single word.

"Stay!" he ordered in a menacing tone, the gravelly sound of his deep voice making my toes instantly curl and my inner walls contract.

Leaving me effectively blind and loosely 'bound,' Zatruk claimed my mouth in a passionate kiss while his hands explored my body. His lips moved down to my neck, where he grazed his fangs on my skin, gently biting, not enough to break it, but enough to make me throb with need. He spent the following minutes worshiping my body, licking and sucking on my breasts with the typical eagerness I'd come to expect from him.

Before Zatruk, I'd never realized just how responsive my nipples were to being masterfully cajoled. By the time his mouth finally ventured between my legs, I was already soaking wet and aching to be filled. My husband knew how to pleasure a woman. The raspy feel of his long tongue on my clit sent electric tendrils coursing through me. His thick fingers sinking inside of me, stretching me while stroking my sweet spot with almost supernatural accuracy, had me cresting in no time.

Every time my husband made me climax, it felt like an atomic bomb went off inside of me, flattening me, burning me from the inside out, and turning me into ashes. Even as I floated in a blissful void, he continued to pleasure me until I finally came back to reality. Only then did he free me from my negligee that still covered my eyes and 'restrained' my arms.

Not touching him when he demanded submission was always a challenge. I loved the softness of his skin and fur under my palms, in direct contrast to the hardness of his muscles beneath.

My stomach did a backflip when Zatruk kneeled between my legs, slowly removing his loincloth that tented before him from his massive erection. He looked like an ancient vengeful god under the moonlight seeping in through the huge windows, giving his alabaster skin a dreamy glow. His red eyes locked on my face burned with an intensity that made his lustful expression take an almost savage edge.

He tossed his loincloth to the floor. His thick cock, standing proudly, immediately made my mouth water. I didn't let Zatruk lie on top of me. I sat up instead and pushed him onto his back. Despite his frown at me thwarting his plans, he yielded to me. I fucking loved that about my husband. However dominant he naturally was, my fluffy beast always allowed me to have my way as well, as an equal partner.

Like he had done to me, I took my sweet time to lick, kiss, and caress every centimeter of his massive body. Every curve, every groove, and bulging vein received its due attention. The way he shivered beneath my touch, his rumbling moans and hisses of pleasures made me feel like a freaking sex goddess.

When I wrapped my 'proportionally tiny hand' around his length, his breathing immediately accelerated. He hadn't been kidding saying he doubted both my hands would suffice to handle him. Zatruk's cock was massive, and beautiful. It resembled an ivory sculpture between my fingers. Generally smooth, his shaft possessed five ring-shaped ridges equally distanced in the lower half. You'd almost think he had implants there, but they were merely natural pleasure enhancers, aside from the second ring from the bottom.

That one was a little wider than the others and would swell to form the knot, locking Zatruk and I together to increase our chances of conceiving once he spilled his seed inside of me. My inner walls constricted in anticipation. Bluish veins ran up his length to the pinkish head of his cock, which was fairly human in appearance.

While my hand gently stroked him, I kissed and licked his *vylus*, located right above the base of his shaft. At rest, it was the cutest thing, like a small outie navel. Zatruk extruded it in response as I accelerated the movement of my hand on him. The thumb-like appendage had a rounded head and was covered in tiny bumps for extra feels. Remembering how it felt, flicking from side to side on my clit, had moisture pooling between my thighs.

I sucked on it for a few moments before shifting my attention to his smooth testicles, laving them with my tongue as my second hand joined my first one in stroking him. Zatruk's moans and his increasingly loud breathing testified to how much he enjoyed what I was doing to him. When I finally brushed my lips against his shaft, tracing each ring, each vein with my tongue, my husband emitted a growling moan that would have sounded menacing under different circumstances.

As soon as I felt his hand in my hair, I knew it was only a matter of time before he climaxed. I took him in my mouth, stroking him frantically in counterpoint to the movement of my head bobbing over him. He hissed, made another growling sound, then said my name with such a deep rumbling in his voice that I barely recognized it.

Just when I thought he would fall apart for me, Zatruk yanked my head away from him. I yelped in surprise, and the room spun. Before I could figure out what had happened, I was on my back with my husband pushing himself inside of me.

"You will not waste my seed," he growled before crushing my lips in a brutal kiss.

Despite how active we'd been the past few months, and how insanely wet he'd already gotten me, Zatruk's cock still burned going in, insanely stretching me. I fucking loved how full, vulnerable, and fragile I felt beneath my man as he thrust into me. He wasted no time, picking up the pace as he moved in and out of me, his *vylus* going wild on my clit.

An inferno raged inside me, too many sensations sending me tumbling down a whirlwind of pleasure. His mouth devoured mine as the head of his cock pummeled my sweet spot, making me see stars. Even as I surfed the waves of ecstasy, Zatruk pulled out of me, flipping me onto my stomach, then ramming himself back in from behind. I cried out with pleasure-pain as the searing heat of his muscular body settled on my back.

He wrapped his massive hand around my neck, tilting my head back to get better access to my neck. Once more his fangs grazed and stung my skin while he pounded into me. I never saw the next orgasm come. It slammed into me with such violence, it felt as if my soul left my body.

Zatruk seemed possessed in the unbridled way in which he unleashed his passion on me. He wrested one orgasm after the other from me with unrelenting stamina. My world had narrowed down to his hands and mouth on me, the sounds of our moans of ecstasy, of our flesh meeting in a frenzy, of his taste on my tongue, of his voice growling words of love and passion in a language I didn't understand, and of pleasure... endless pleasure that threatened to fracture my mind.

Lying on his back with me riding on top of him, Zatruk was pumping into me, his face constricted in an almost feral expression. When his *vylus* sent me flying again, my mate finally joined his voice to mine in an ear-bending roar. His seed shot into me in powerful spurts as I collapsed on top of him. Holding me with bruising force, he continued thrusting into me a short while longer until the last of his seed was spent, filling me to the brim.

Even as I rested my head on his chest, listening to his thundering heartbeat, his knot swelled inside of me, locking us together. I tightened my embrace around my beast while he gently caressed my trembling body.

"My love, my little sylphin. You are mine," Zatruk whispered.

I smiled.

∾

Sitting in the VIP box overlooking the battle arena, I felt overwhelmed by the reality of it all. Around me, Graith, Skieth, Dakas, Luana, Mateo, Counselor Allan, Jerdea, Wonjin, and Lara, looked just as mesmerized as I felt.

Although we hadn't sold out the entire arena—not surprising for a first event—the bleachers were nonetheless packed. And the crowd buzzed with excitement. Giant screens all around allowed people further back to get a good view of what was happening inside the arena. But the battle hadn't started yet.

We launched the first tournament in a similar fashion to the Olympics back on Earth, with an opening ceremony featuring highly choreographed dances and stunning visual effects, the haunting singing of the Zelconians, and breathtaking aerial displays and acrobatics involving the zeebises, their human riders, and the Zelconians.

As soon as the last performance ended, the gladiators paraded inside the arena, some grouped by species or teams—mainly those who intended to participate in the brawls—and others individually or in loosely formed clusters. The audience greeted the gladiators with shouts, chants, and even songs, some waving holographic flags and sigils representing their federation, planet, city, or species.

Once the warriors were all in position inside the arena, Zatruk appeared on a balcony overlooking the arena, followed by the Chieftains of the six other Yurus clans.

Instead of an Olympic flame marking the official start of the competition, each Chieftain brought down his massive hammer onto his respective bull-horned anvil. It triggered the animation of giant pieces of molded deutenium overhead. They spun and pivoted, moving around each other to eventually form an immense mask of Mugrak, the God of War. As soon as the shape was completed, its red eyes, made of Zelconian damage crystals, lit up.

The crowd erupted in a powerful cheer that made me fear the walls would crumble. Their voices only faded when they saw Zatruk advance to the front of the balcony that also served as stage.

"Greetings, gladiators and visitors," Zatruk said in a powerful voice. "I am Zatruk Abbas, Great Chieftain of the Yurus clans of Cibbos, and your host for this great tournament.

On behalf of all the Yurus, the Zelconians, and the humans of the Kastan colony, I bid you welcome to Cibbos."

The crowd shouted its excitement in response, quieting down when he raised his hand.

"This arena was built in the honor of Mugrak, the Yurus God of War, to feature the greatest warriors and gladiators of the galaxy. Many signed up, but only the finest were chosen, for your strength, skill, and savagery."

Another approving roar rose from the crowd, while a vicious grin tugged at Zatruk's lips, giving a glimpse of his fangs. In that instant, he looked beautifully terrifying.

"The rules are few, but will be strictly enforced. Break them, and we will gladly teach you the error of your ways. Fight fiercely and with the pride of your ancestors. Win with honor. Lose with grace. Stand toe-to-toe with the finest, and make history."

More cheers greeted his words as he walked off the stage, followed by the other six Chieftains. Simultaneously, as per the instructions that were given to them, two-thirds of the gladiators exited the arena, while two dozen Yurus entered. Heart pounding, I stared in wonder at the sixty males that would participate in the very first weaponless "Last man standing" battle of the tournament.

Two Zelconians flew down to the balcony overlooking the arena where they would both monitor evil intent from the fighters, and play referee, if needed. Meanwhile, the gladiators took their preferred position, some distancing themselves from those who seemed a little too eager to stand closer to them.

Moments later, Zatruk entered the VIP box and made a beeline for me. Standing side by side, we looked down into the arena where both the gladiators and the crowd appeared to be holding their breaths, waiting for the signal. Zatruk gave me a sideways glance. I smiled, and he responded in kind before tapping the interface of his armband.

The blaring of a horn resounded throughout the arena. The crowd jumped out of its seats, shouting as the gladiators rushed each other with savage war cries. But I no longer saw them. Zatruk picked me up, our lips meeting at the same time the first bodies clashed below.

EPILOGUE
RIHANNA

The two weeks of the tournament were a constant whirlwind of excitement, drama, near disaster, joy, and fear. Once again, we met a few hiccups along the way.

While the gladiators mostly behaved, the crowd proved to be quite the handful, some getting overly heated when their favorite lost or a most unexpected underdog rose to prominence. It didn't help that increasingly outrageous amounts of credits were being bet as we drew closer to the finale of each competition.

We made mad bank from all the betting, as they had to be handled through our bookies. We also couldn't complain about all the fines we collected on those who tried to secretly hold their own private betting circles. The Zelconians took their job very seriously. You couldn't fool them. And those dumb enough to try to throw their weight around quickly learned not to fuck with them.

After a massive, seven-foot tall Zamorian, with the bulging muscles of his four arms, and his terrifying orcish face with four eyes pissed himself and was reduced to a crying puddle by a single mesmerizing stare of a Zelconian, nobody else tried their luck. Once you got caught cheating, you quietly paid up. I didn't know what the hell kind of nightmare they could conjure up in their target's mind. However, that it could make one of the top gladiators of the tournament fall apart to this extent said it all.

Although the Yurus participated in most of the qualifying combat modes, and despite many of them reaching the highest tiers, they all bowed out of the finals. They didn't want the titles or rewards. They just wanted to fight. And did they ever.

At first, I worried they wouldn't be able to get enough to sate their blood rage. While we had both armed and unarmed combat modes, some species possessed natural offensive and defensive abilities that made it impossible to have a fair fight. It was especially true when it came down to species with flight ability, psionic powers that could kill or paralyze with a thought, lethal venoms, darts, stingers, you name it.

Therefore, like boxing had weight divisions, we had lethality and class divisions, with venomous species agreeing to either get their venom sacs drained or take a neutralizing injection before battle. Thankfully, other galactic tournaments had provided us with basic templates to follow. But that didn't stop some contestants trying to press their luck, thinking we were too green to account for all of this.

Still, the free-for-all provided the opportunity for any class and species to battle each other by compensating with the use of a limited selection of defensive and offensive equipment. To my relief, Zatruk didn't participate in that one.

It was a tough balancing act for him to sate his own blood rage while remaining a proper host, and especially an undefeated one. He found plenty of opportunities to kick ass. Not so much during the tournaments but instead in the fight rooms below the arena. There, duels could be agreed upon and bet on by anyone, warriors and visitors alike. These provided the Yurus the true release they sought as classes didn't matter, as long as both participants were willing to battle each other under agreed upon rules for that specific fight.

Saying I enjoyed seeing all that violence would be a lie. Truth be told, I attended few of the actual battles. But I didn't need to like it. My new people were getting what they needed to thrive. And did they ever...

The atmosphere in Mutarak changed. I hadn't realized before the extent of the constant state of tension that reigned in the village. The Yurus females were literally glowing with happiness. The males were no longer so easily triggered, or so aggressive. In the weeks and months that followed the first tournament, many of them took on new, more intellectual hobbies or even studies, their abated blood rage allowing them to focus again.

Despite the success of this first tournament, we didn't hold another one for four months in order for all of us to do a proper post-mortem, assess what we did right, what we did wrong, and make improvements. But everyone agreed we should pursue and expand this.

In the six months that followed Kastan partnering with us, their human population increased by a couple of hundred people, and new applications kept flowing in. This new blood also brought with it new technologies, new knowledge, new fashion, and new ideas that had the colony on the right path to a healthy evolution within the constraints that they had set for themselves.

These newcomers also helped me understand why Kayog had imposed a one-year trial period on me instead of six months. Surely, his empathic senses had told him that I didn't need longer than any of the previous candidates to fall in love with my match. Then I realized it had never been about giving Zatruk enough time to convince me to stay. It was all about Kayog giving *himself* the time he needed to help us to the extent he wanted to.

In accordance with their rules, the Prime Mating Agency could provide whatever support necessary to the people they matched throughout the trial period, including access to a discretionary supplemental budget if needed. Kayog had known of

Zatruk's plan and correctly guessed we couldn't finish every-thing within six months. As a matter of fact, we didn't hold the first tournament before the seventh month.

In the five months following that grand opening, Kayog had us benefiting from more assistance. He flew in highly qualified workers at the PMA's expense not only from Meterion, but also from other colonies, including refugee ones, where the people living there had few prospects for a better life. When I announced my pregnancy, six weeks before the end of our trial period, on top of sending us five top-notch medical pods—as if I needed that many just for me—someone conveniently left a series of blueprints for powerful speeder, shuttle, jetpack, and hovercraft engines within one of the pods.

Although the Zelconians remained somewhat elusive in their mountain city, they did expand their hotel and relaxed some of their rules for the second tournament. During the first tourna-ment, visitors witnessing their national sport, Lazgar, raved so much about it, it eventually became a parallel competition people started flying to Cibbos to participate in.

Apparently, young Zelconians between the ages of five and six reached their fastest flying speed. Intoxicated by the adren-alin rush it gave them, they would constantly get chased by their parents seeking to avoid them getting hurt by crashing into walls. This gave birth to the sport named after Lazgar, the most noto-rious such fledgling. The sport consisted in trying to catch a drone flying through a special arena with looping obstacles that shifted over time. Groups of twelve to twenty individuals would compete with each other to catch it before time ran out.

The jetpack engine blueprint Kayog sent us came in quite handy as countless wingless contestants used jetpacks to partici-pate in the Zelconian events.

All in all, the battle arena met its purpose and exceeded it. Who would have thought more fighting would have brought peace to Cibbos and a tightening of the relationship between its local populations? And yet, there we were.

ZATRUK

I returned home to find my mate lounging on the sofa, reading on her tablet while caressing a swollen belly. In a few more weeks, our daughter would be born.

Sitting on the large fur in front of the fireplace, our four-year-old son Turvak was submitting himself to Ristia's abuse of his hair. Dakas's and Luana's three-year-old daughter was a menace. The spitting image of her mother, with a light brown skin and golden-brown feathers, she was far too cute for her own good. The brat had no qualms using her mesmerizing abilities to entice us to her, when she didn't simply bat her eyelashes and give us that irresistible smile to make us melt.

Like my mate, Ristia had an obsession with braiding hair. She was pulling quite the number on my son's silver-white mane, identical to mine. When he noticed my presence, Turvak lifted his almost perfectly human face devoid of tusks to look at me. His red eyes sparked with mischief, and he smiled, baring his small fangs in amusement at my frown. He always laughed at me for complaining about his mother messing with my beard, claiming he couldn't wait to have one of his own for Ristia to braid for him, too.

On the breakfast table in the corner, Wonjin's hybrid son Zurox was trying to assemble some complex 3D puzzle with Darius. While Turvak had inherited my face, horns, hooves, tail, and albinism, Wonjin's son had taken after his mother Lara from the human legs to his face, aside from his father's brown fur, tusks, tail, ears, and horns.

"Hi, Uncle Zatruk," the two boys said in almost perfect sync.

I grunted in response.

"Uncle Zat'uk!" Ristia exclaimed with her baby voice, noticing me at last. "Your hair is next!"

"I think not!" I grumbled, glaring at her.

She beamed at me, not in the least intimidated. "I think yes!"

Rihanna chuckled at my disgruntled expression.

"This is your doing, setting a terrible example," I said, coming to sit next to her before pulling her onto my lap.

"I'm setting the perfect example," she said, unfazed. "Consider this practice for when our daughter comes. Remember, you wanted one."

"That was before I knew you intended to corrupt her, too."

"Stop being grumpy and properly kiss your wife," she ordered.

I captured her lips in a tender kiss while gently caressing her swollen stomach. "How are you doing?"

"Not too bad. She's taken a break from kicking me. Darius's singing calms her down."

I turned to Dakas's oldest and nodded as a thank you. He smiled smugly, looking more than ever like his father.

"When I have my singing voice, I will also sing for her," Ristia said to me with her high-pitched voice. She then turned back to look at Turvak. "And for you, too, Tu'vak."

Turvak's floppy ears flicked, and he smiled at her while scratching the back of his right horn in the typical way that marked his embarrassment.

She leaned forward and kissed his cheek. "All done! Now I'm ready for you, Uncle Zat'uk."

I groaned inwardly as Ristia flapped her wings to ease her climbing onto the couch next to me. She proceeded to 'braid' my hair, although the mess she actually did hardly qualified as such.

"Want to help me, Aunt Wihanna?" Ristia asked.

"With pleasure, sweetheart," Rihanna replied.

My mate leaned forward, nipped my ear, and whispered, "I love you."

"I heard that!" Turvak exclaimed.

"Mind your business," I growled, making him laugh as he started untangling the disaster Ristia had made of his hair.

Turning to my mate I smiled, as she got to work on my beard, my heart filling with love for my greatest blessing, my little sylphin.

THE END

ZATRUK

ZEEBIS

KROGI

NYLOTH

SYLPHIN

ALSO BY REGINE ABEL

THE VEREDIAN CHRONICLES
Escaping Fate
Blind Fate
Raising Amalia
Twist of Fate
Hands of Fate
Defying Fate

BRAXIANS
Anton's Grace
Ravik's Mercy
Krygor's Hope

XIAN WARRIORS
Doom
Legion
Raven
Bane
Chaos
Varnog
Reaper
Wrath
Xenon

PRIME MATING AGENCY
I Married A Lizardman
I Married A Naga
I Married A Birdman
I Married A Merman
I Married A Minotaur

THE MIST
The Mistwalker
The Nightmare

BLOOD MAIDENS OF KARTHIA
Claiming Thalia

VALOS OF SONHADRA
Unfrozen
Iced

EMPATHS OF LYRIA
An Alien For Christmas

THE SHADOW REALMS
Dark Swan

OTHER
True As Steel
Bluebeard's Curse
Alien Awakening
Heart of Stone
The Hunchback

ABOUT REGINE

USA Today bestselling author Regine Abel is a fantasy, paranormal and sci-fi junky. Anything with a bit of magic, a touch of the unusual, and a lot of romance will have her jumping for joy. She loves creating hot alien warriors and no-nonsense, kick-ass heroines that evolve in fantastic new worlds while embarking on action-packed adventures filled with mystery and the twists you never saw coming.

Before devoting herself as a full-time writer, Regine had surrendered to her other passions: music and video games! After a decade working as a Sound Engineer in movie dubbing and live concerts, Regine became a professional Game Designer and Creative Director, a career that has led her from her home in Canada to the US and various countries in Europe and Asia.

Facebook
https://www.facebook.com/regine.abel.author/

Website
https://regineabel.com

Regine's Rebels Reader Group
https://www.facebook.com/groups/ReginesRebels/

Newsletter
http://smarturl.it/RA_Newsletter

Goodreads
http://smarturl.it/RA_Goodreads

Bookbub
https://www.bookbub.com/profile/regine-abel

Amazon
http://smarturl.it/AuthorAMS

Printed in Great Britain
by Amazon

78994173R00149